Till Death do us Tart

OXFORD TEAROOM MYSTERIES

BOOK FOUR

H.Y. HANNA

Books in the Oxford Tearoom Mysteries:
A Scone To Die For (Book 1)
Tea with Milk and Murder (Book 2)
Two Down, Bun To Go (Book 3)
Till Death Do Us Tart (Book 4)
Muffins and Mourning Tea (Book 5)
All-Butter ShortDead (Prequel)
~ *more coming soon!*

DEDICATION

For my mother, who is as inspiring,
lovable—and exasperating!—as Gemma's
mother... and I wouldn't want her any
other way.

CONTENTS

CHAPTER ONE 1
CHAPTER TWO 14
CHAPTER THREE 28
CHAPTER FOUR 35
CHAPTER FIVE 51
CHAPTER SIX 60
CHAPTER SEVEN 74
CHAPTER EIGHT 86
CHAPTER NINE..95
CHAPTER TEN 106
CHAPTER ELEVEN 114
CHAPTER TWELVE 125
CHAPTER THIRTEEN 136
CHAPTER FOURTEEN.......................................147
CHAPTER FIFTEEN..154
CHAPTER SIXTEEN 166
CHAPTER SEVENTEEN 177
CHAPTER EIGHTEEN..191
CHAPTER NINETEEN 203
CHAPTER TWENTY 215
CHAPTER TWENTY-ONE 224
CHAPTER TWENTY-TWO....................................236
CHAPTER TWENTY-THREE..............................249
CHAPTER TWENTY-FOUR...............................256
CHAPTER TWENTY-FIVE 270
CHAPTER TWENTY-SIX.....................................282
CHAPTER TWENTY-SEVEN 289
CHAPTER TWENTY-EIGHT.................................300
CHAPTER TWENTY-NINE 312
CHAPTER THIRTY..320
CHAPTER THIRTY-ONE.....................................330
EPILOGUE...344
GLOSSARY OF BRITISH TERMS.......................358
VICTORIA SPONGE CAKE RECIPE 366
ABOUT THE AUTHOR 371
ACKNOWLEDGMENTS 372

CHAPTER ONE

If there was one person who could go to an English village fête and end up stumbling on a murder, it would be me.

To be honest, murder was already on my mind even before I started for the village fair—the murder of my mother, that is. I stood in my parents' front hallway, weighed down with litter tray, food bowl, water bowl, blankets, salmon treats, vaccination certificate, toy mice, and baby wipes... and wondered how I'd got myself into this mess. I had been looking forward to a rare weekend off—the first holiday I'd had since opening my little tearoom in the nearby Cotswolds village of Meadowford-on-Smythe over six months ago—and, in particular, to spending some time with my long-lost, recently-found-again boyfriend, Devlin O'Connor.

Devlin was in the Oxfordshire CID and, like most detectives, worked all the hours that God sent—and then some. And I wasn't exactly a 9-to-5 office girl either. The Little Stables Tearoom was my pride and joy, but it was also a black hole that ate up all my free time and energy. With the coming of the warmer spring weather and tourists flooding into Oxford and the surrounding Cotswolds countryside, business had boomed and I could barely keep up. Aside from the usual serving hours at the tearoom, there were now catering orders which kept me busy well after closing time. Oh, it was wonderful that business was growing like this—it was what I had dreamed of when I'd left my high-flying corporate job to sink all my savings into the tearoom—but it did mean that I barely had a moment to catch my breath, never mind think about a romantic assignation with my boyfriend.

So what with Devlin's long work hours and mine, we'd hardly spent much time together since we'd "found each other again" (long story!) and you can imagine how delighted I was when he told me a few weeks ago that he had put in for special leave to take this weekend off. *Ooh!* I'd instantly started daydreaming of romantic escapes together—a weekend in Paris, maybe? Or a visit to Tuscany? Or wasn't Copenhagen meant to be really nice this time of the year? Honestly, even just two days ensconced in a cottage somewhere here in the Cotswolds would have been heavenly!

And then came the blow. Earlier this week, Devlin had rung me and, even before he had said anything, I could tell from the tone of his voice that it was going to be bad news. He had been asked to do an extra shift this weekend and we had to cancel our plans.

"But why can't you just tell them to sod off?" I asked, my temper getting the better of me. "You put in for that leave ages ago and it was all approved and everything! They have no right to ask you to do this now!"

"Gemma…" Devlin's deep voice was regretful. "I *could* have said no but I decided it was better to accept."

"What? Why?"

"The Detective Superintendent specifically asked for me. You see, there's been an increase in 'agri-crime' lately. It's something that's been getting worse in the past few years and we seem to be having an epidemic of it in Oxfordshire in particular."

"Agri-crime? What's that?"

"Agricultural crime. Thefts from farms and rural properties. Livestock, equipment, fuel, tools… it's quite a serious problem. Costs the country tens of millions of pounds each year."

"What does that have to do with you?" I demanded. "You're CID! You don't deal with petty crime like theft!"

"No, we don't normally, but in this instance, one

3

of the recent victims was Julian Greco."

The name stirred a memory. "Julian Greco? The actor?"

"The multi-billionaire top Hollywood actor. He's also a personal friend of the Superintendent and he decided that he wasn't happy with just Uniform branch dealing with it. He wanted the best man in the CID to be put on the case and he'd heard about me after the recent murder investigations, especially that stabbing of Professor Barrow in Wadsworth College. That was a pretty high profile case." Devlin paused, then added, his voice dry, "And you know, when rich, famous people want something, they usually get it."

"I still think it's stupid and unfair," I grumbled.

"Well, sometimes in life, you have to remember which side your bread is buttered on. This could be a huge point in my favour when it comes time for my promotion to Chief Inspector. In any case, it's an honour to be selected as 'the best man in the CID'—and it's a matter of 'face' for my Superintendent. I can't let him down, Gemma."

"So you decided you could let *me* down?" I said sharply.

Devlin sighed. "You know I've been looking forward to this weekend as much as you. I'm just as disappointed as you are. But there will be other weekends, sweetheart. In fact, I've already spoken to the Super and he's promised me a weekend at the end of next month. It's only a few weeks more and the weather will be even better in May."

He was right, I knew, and I was probably being childish and unreasonable, but I couldn't help the feeling of bitter disappointment. I had been looking forward to this weekend so much and now it was being snatched away from me at the last minute.

Wait... *at the last minute...*

Suddenly I thought of something else. "I've given everyone this weekend off," I said. "So now I can't even open the tearoom—"

Devlin groaned. "Can't you ring Cassie and Dora and asked them to swap around to a weekend next month?"

"Cassie might but Dora can't. She's gone off to visit her sister in Bournemouth. I can't ask her to change her plans now and we can't do without our baking chef because we haven't got any supplies for this weekend. In fact, I asked her to bake less this week so we wouldn't have too much leftover food. Oh, and actually, Cassie is going to be busy too. There's the annual village fête in Meadowford this weekend. When Cassie heard that I was closing the tearoom, she decided to get a stall there to sell her paintings."

Devlin groaned again. "I'm sorry, Gemma. I really am. I wouldn't be doing this if it wasn't important."

I heard the genuine contrition in his voice and my heart softened. It wasn't as if Devlin didn't want to spend time with me. I knew the importance of a promotion at this stage in his career. Wasn't I being selfish not to support him?

"How about if we go out to dinner on Sunday night?" said Devlin. "I should be free by six. I know it's not the same... but I promise I'll make it up to you, Gemma. We'll go somewhere nice next month— make it a really special weekend."

I softened even further. "All right," I said at last. "I'll see you on Sunday then."

I hung up, still feeling a bit peeved, and my mood was not improved when I told my mother the change in plans.

"But that's wonderful, darling!" she said. "You can come to the village fête with me and Muesli!"

I looked at her in surprise. "What are you and Muesli going to do there?"

"Don't you remember? I told you—Audrey Simmons from the village fête committee has been telling me all about the Show."

"The Show?"

"The Cotswolds Cat Fancy Club Show, darling! It's held every year at the Meadowford village fête. There's a marvellous cash prize donated by English Country Pets, that big pet food manufacturer, and it's such an honour to be picked as 'Best in Show'. Anyway, I've entered Muesli."

I gaped at her. "You've what? But, Mother, cat shows are for pure breeds. Muesli is a moggie and—"

My mother waved a hand dismissively. "I'm sure they'll never know, darling. Muesli is so pretty, the judges are bound to fall in love with her."

"But they'll be looking to see what kind of breed she is—"

"Oh, I'm sure Muesli can lay claim to all sorts of breeds in her heritage. In fact, Audrey was telling me about some of the cat breeds and I'm sure I can see all the traits she was describing! Muesli is remarkably clever and loves to explore, just like an Abyssinian... she has the white 'gloves' on her front paws, just like a Birman... she loves talking back to you, just like a Siamese ... and her lovely stripes and spots are *just* like a Bengal's..." My mother indicated my little tabby cat who was sleeping on her lap. "And there's even a bit of curl to her coat, just like a Cornish Rex! Don't you think?"

What I thought was that my mother was completely delusional. Muesli looked like nothing more than a common farmhouse moggie. A very pretty farmhouse moggie but a moggie all the same. Still, my mother was not to be dissuaded. Once she got an idea into her head, it set like cement.

"And now that you're free this weekend, darling, it's ideal! You can come and help me at the show."

So that was how I found myself being dragged out of bed early this morning to help my mother wash, groom, and primp Muesli in readiness for her big day. After the bath and blow dry—which left me more traumatised than my cat—my mother brushed Muesli's short, plush coat until it gleamed and even I had to admit that the little cat had never looked so good. Her dove-grey fur looked almost silver and her beautiful dark stripes spiralled out in perfect symmetry on either side of her spine.

"*Meorrw...!*" said Muesli, regarding herself with smug satisfaction in the mirror of my mother's bathroom.

"Now, I will just have time to get dressed and do my hair..." My mother looked at me with disapproval. "You're not going to wear *that* to the village fête, are you?"

I looked down at my comfy old chenille sweater and faded jeans. "Yeah, why not?"

My mother tutted. "Girls are so slapdash these days, with no sense of feminine pride. Presentation is everything! One must always make the effort to look one's best at all times."

"I think I look fine."

"Nonsense! You look like something even a cat wouldn't want to drag in. Why don't you wear that nice wool dress I bought you, darling—such a lovely style and suits your colouring so admirably."

"Mother—"

"What will the judge think if he sees you looking like that? Such a lack of proper respect for the occasion. We must do everything to improve Muesli's chances."

The only thing that would have improved Muesli's chances at this point were genetic mutation and total body transformation but I kept my mouth shut and took myself off to my room to change. With mothers, sometimes it was easier to give in than to argue. Besides, I had already written the day off in service of "making my mother happy" so why not humour her all the way?

But now as I stood waiting for her in the hallway, pulling at the scratchy collar of my "nice wool dress", I was feeling irritable and peeved. I should have been strolling hand-in-hand with Devlin through some gorgeous European city. Instead, I was going to be staggering hand-in-hand with my mother and sixteen kilos of cat paraphernalia through some smelly community hall.

Then my mother's elegant figure appeared at the top of the stairs and she came down slowly, carrying Muesli in her cage. I had to grudgingly admit that they made a very smart pair. Okay, I admit—I might have also begun to feel a pleasant anticipation for the show. In fact, as we drove out into the countryside and approached the quaint, picturesque village of Meadowford-on-Smythe, I found it hard to stay in a grumpy mood any longer.

It had been years since I'd been to a proper village fête, although I remembered them vividly from childhood: the egg-and-spoon races and tug-o-war games, the Home-made Cake and Jam stall where I stuffed my face, the coconut shy, where I could never hit the coconuts on the poles, no matter how hard I tried, the shaggy Shetland ponies offering rides around the village green... I smiled to myself as the memories came rushing back: how excited I'd been, running from stall to stall, eagerly trying everything!

As we stepped out of the car, I breathed deeply of the fresh country air and felt my smile widen. Yes, this weekend might not have turned out the way I'd planned, but maybe coming to a traditional English village fête wasn't such a bad substitute after all.

***

"Oh good, there's our spot," my mother said as she led the way across the pavilion.

Contrary to my bad-tempered musings earlier, the cat show was not being held in some faded community hall but in a large medieval-style pavilion erected in one corner of the village green. I looked around with interest as I followed my mother between the long tables, all draped in white cloth and holding rows upon rows of cat cages, containing every conceivable type of cat. Big cats, small cats, fluffy cats, sleek cats, spotted cats, striped cats, cats with eyes like huge sapphires, and cats with faces like squashed teddy bears... I never realised cats came in so many shapes, colours, and sizes!

My mother stopped in front of an empty cage at the end of a row and began unpacking our things. I transferred Muesli from her carrier to the show cage and the little tabby peered eagerly around, her whiskers quivering with excitement. The cage to her right seemed to be empty except for a large, fluffy white cushion, but in the cage to her left, two biscuit-coloured Siamese cats untangled themselves from their bed and came over to stare at her insolently.

"*Meorrw?*" said Muesli, giving them an inquisitive sniff through the bars.

The larger Siamese narrowed his blue eyes and gave a hiss. "*Maaa-ooowww!*" he snarled.

I didn't need to speak Cat to know that it was something very rude. Muesli stiffened, then flattened her ears and puffed up.

"Meeeeorrw!" she said indignantly.

The Siamese gave a contemptuous twitch of his tail and let out an even louder: "*MAAAA-OOOWWW!*"

Not to be outdone, Muesli puffed herself up even bigger and thrust her little nose in his face.

"*MEEOOO*—" she started to say but I cut in hastily.

"Er... *NICE* kitties! Nice kitties... come on, now... let's be friends..." I raised my hand towards the Siamese's cage and made a cooing noise.

"*What are you doing to my cats?*" a voice snapped behind me.

I jumped and turned around. A thin, middle-aged woman, with a pinched face and wispy brown hair escaping from a dishevelled bun, stood in front of me, glaring.

"Nothing," I said in surprise. "Nothing... I was just saying hello."

She gave me a suspicious look. "I saw you put your hand in their cage. Were you adding something to their water?"

"What? No—why would I do that?"

She narrowed her eyes. "Don't think you'll get away with it."

"Get away with what?" I said, exasperated.

"Poisoning my cats," she snapped. "Oh, yes, I know what you're all trying to do—all the tricks used to sabotage me. Everyone knows my cats are the best in the show and people will stop at nothing to prevent me from winning."

I stared at her. Okay, this was a crazy cat lady in person.

She wagged her finger at me. She had a weird pale lavender nail polish which made the skin on her hands look sallow and sickly. "A young woman like you, resorting to such disgusting, devious methods—you ought to be ashamed of yourself!"

"Now, look here..." I said, starting to get annoyed. Then I stopped. Her hands were clenched tightly together and her face was pale, and I realised that there was genuine fear in her eyes. I felt a wave of compassion. Whatever her reasons, she was not being unpleasant on purpose. This woman was terrified.

I softened my voice. "I promise you, I'm not

trying to do anything to harm you. I'm just here to show my cat... look, this is her. Her name's Muesli." I pointed to Muesli in her cage.

The woman hesitated, then relaxed slightly, although her eyes still darted anxiously around. She sidled closer and inclined her head towards mine.

"You have to help me," she said urgently. "Nobody seems to believe me but it's true."

"What's true?" I said, completely confused now.

She dropped her voice to a whisper. "There have been attempts to kill me. Somebody wants me dead."

CHAPTER TWO

I stared at the woman in front of me. Was she serious? Or was she completely off her trolley?

"Er... um... are you sure?" I said at last.

She jerked back and glared at me. "Of course I'm sure! Do you think I would joke about a thing like that?"

"Well, it's just... why would anyone want to kill you?" I asked helplessly. "It seems a bit incredible—"

"So you don't believe me either!" She drew herself up to her full height, quivering with indignation. "Fine! But just you wait... one of these days, my body will turn up horribly murdered and then you'll be sorry you doubted me!"

She gave me another glare then turned her back on me and began talking to the Siamese cats in a baby voice, to which they responded with ear-splitting yowls and cries.

I stared at her for a moment longer. *Bloody weirdo.* Then I heaved a sigh and turned back to my own table. Audrey Simmons from the village fête committee had arrived while I was distracted by the Siamese cats and was now chatting to my mother. I'd met Audrey once or twice before: a pleasant, mousy woman who seemed to be perpetually volunteering for things and running around being a general dogsbody for everyone. She was the Vicar's sister and lived with him at the Vicarage; in fact, it was at the Vicar's recent wedding that I'd met her for the first time. The Vicar was in his forties and everyone had expected him to remain an eternal bachelor. His engagement had come as a complete surprise and had provided the senior residents of Meadowford with weeks—months—of pleasurable gossip.

My mother gestured to me as I joined them. "...and of course you must know my daughter, Gemma."

Audrey smiled at me vaguely. "Yes, of course—you own the Little Stables Tearoom. I haven't had a chance to pop in yet but I hear so many people talk about it. Your scones are some of the best in Oxfordshire, I hear!"

I flushed with pleasure. "Thank you. You can try the scones here at the fête actually—I've donated several batches to the Cream Tea Stall."

"Oh, yes, that's right," said Audrey. "Mabel Cooke and her friends are manning that stall. They were doing brisk business, I can tell you! I hope there will still be some left when I go back later." She glanced at the table next to us with the Siamese cats, then lowered her voice. "By the way, Gemma, I saw you talking to Theresa Bell. Don't worry if she... er... makes some accusations. She can have quite a... uh... vivid imagination."

I grinned. "Thanks. I wasn't quite sure... She did seem very... uh... 'worried'. So is there no basis for her fears?"

"Well, there was quite a fuss at the last show— she claimed that someone was trying to poison her cats' water—"

A contemptuous snort came from the table on our right. I realised that there was now a large, middle-aged woman standing next to the empty cage with the white cushion. She had obviously been listening to our conversation.

Audrey gave an exclamation. "Oh, how remiss of me! I haven't introduced you to my very dear friend, Clare Eccleston." She gave a little laugh. "Or I should really say, Dame Clare Eccleston."

"Dame Clare?" said my mother. "Not the Dame Clare who is the Tutor for Admissions at St Cecilia's College in Oxford? I've heard my husband mention her."

The large woman turned around to face us. "Yes, I am she."

She had a deep, almost manly voice, a long, aristocratic nose, and piercing dark eyes. Her hair was steel grey and also drawn up in a bun, although nothing like Theresa Bell's wispy mess. No, this was a sophisticated coiffure, piled atop her head and held in place by a tortoiseshell comb. She was dressed in a silk blouse, with a high ruffled collar and a cameo brooch at her throat, and looked as if she belonged in some severe Victorian portrait.

As she came forwards, I realised that she was a very large woman—not just in terms of weight but also in terms of presence. A very grand dame indeed. I could just imagine dogs, no matter how big and ferocious, instantly dropping on their bums if she said "SIT" (and probably quite a few humans too!). Next to her domineering presence, Audrey Simmons faded like an insipid watercolour. She was speaking in a faint voice now, saying something about Dame Clare's champion show cats.

"Oh, where are they?" I said, trying to show friendly interest. I peered into the cage next to us. "Are they underneath that big cushion?"

Dame Clare gave me an icy look. "That *cushion*, as you call it, is my prize Persian, Champion Camilla Diamonds Are Forever."

Oops.

"Oh! Sorry..." I stammered. "It wasn't moving so I thought..."

She reached into the cage and lifted out a fluffy white cat with a snub nose and a sweet, placid

17

expression. She turned and glared at me. "Persians are renowned for their serene, dignified demeanours. They do not make fools of themselves, running around and climbing everywhere or caterwauling constantly, unlike *some* cat breeds I could name." She glanced with disdain over at the Siamese cats in their cage, raising her voice slightly so as to be sure to be overheard.

"How dare you!" cried Theresa. "I'll have you know that the Siamese are descended from the royal felines who acted as sacred guardians in the ancient Thai temples. They are also the most loyal, affectionate, and intelligent of cat breeds—whereas everyone knows that Persians are the stupidest cats in the world!"

"Now, now, ladies..." said Audrey hastily, stepping between them. "I'm sure every breed is wonderful in its own way. That is why we're here today—to celebrate the marvellous diversity in the cat world."

Dame Clare sniffed, then turned her attention to our cage. She peered down her long nose at Muesli.

"And what—may I ask—is *that*?" She drew back in disgust. "Audrey, I cannot believe the committee is letting common riff-raff into the show!"

My mother bristled. "Muesli is not riff-raff! She is a... a rare prized tabby!"

"Rare prized tabby, my foot!" Dame Clare laughed, a high-pitched sound like a horse neighing. "That cat is a common garden variety moggie! Absolutely no breeding or quality whatsoever!"

My mother got very red in the face and snapped, "Perhaps *you* are not qualified to recognise real quality when you see it but I'm sure the judge will have no such problems!"

Audrey gave a nervous laugh and said quickly, "Ahh... Clare, have you got anything to donate to the Cake & Jam Stall?" She held up a wicker basket that was slung over one arm. There were various pots of jam and preserves, as well as a few plates of cakes and buns nestled at the bottom. "I'm just collecting things to take over."

"Oh, yes! We do," came a small voice.

I realised with surprise that there was a plump young woman standing behind Dame Clare. She had been so quiet that I hadn't noticed her until now. From the strong physical resemblance, I guessed that this must be a daughter and I was proven right a moment later when the girl said softly:

"I've baked Mummy's favourite Victoria sponge and some jam tarts for the stall. Here, let me get them for you..."

She bent over a picnic hamper and lifted out the ultimate classic British cake: a beautiful round of double-layered golden sponge cake, with home-made strawberry jam and snowy white whipped cream sandwiched between the top and bottom layers, all finished off with sliced fresh strawberries to garnish and a dainty dusting of icing sugar on top. The jam tarts that followed looked equally delicious, their scalloped pastry edges surrounding a rich centre of dark red jam filled with plump fruit pieces. The heavenly smell of buttery baking wafted over.

"My... those look fabulous, Mary," said Audrey, eyeing them appreciatively. "I'm sure they'll be snapped up immediately at the stall!" She lifted the wicker basket closer. "Do you think you could balance the cake on top of these jars?"

"There are two actually," said Mary, lifting out a second Victoria sponge cake. "I might be able to squeeze them both in next to each other—"

"One," Dame Clare spoke up. "We are only donating one."

Her daughter looked at her in dismay. "Oh, but Mummy—"

"Are you stupid, girl? I told you before we left the house—the second cake is for ourselves. There is no other cake here to match the quality of ours and I am *certainly not* going to the stall to buy a slice of my own cake for tea."

"But Mummy—are you sure you should be having any?" Mary said anxiously. "I mean, remember... your heart... Dr Foster did say that you shouldn't eat so much rich, creamy—"

"Poppycock!" said Dame Clare. "What does that old fossil know? I shall eat what I like and enjoy doing it."

"Clare... Mary is right," said Audrey feebly. "It's really not advisable. In fact, Dr Foster was saying that it would be a good idea perhaps if you lost some weight..." She faltered as her friend gave her a withering glare.

"I beg your pardon?" Dame Clare drew herself up to her full height and said in a booming voice, "The women in my family have always been large. There is no shame in that! And Mary is continuing the tradition—she always requires the largest size available, at least an Extra-Large. In fact, sometimes they don't make the trousers big enough for her hips!" She gave a whoop of laughter. Glancing at her daughter, she barked, "Isn't that right?"

Mary flushed red to the roots of her hair as several people at the tables around us turned to stare at her. "I... I... I think so, Mummy," she whispered, looking like she wanted to die.

My heart went out to her. No girl wants to have her dress size discussed in public, especially a larger, curvy girl like Mary. I couldn't believe her mother's insensitivity.

"In fact..." Dame Clare indicated one of the Victoria sponge cakes, obviously deciding to make a point. "I've decided that I don't want to wait until afternoon tea to have the cake. Cut me a piece now," she commanded.

Mary Eccleston bit her lip and something flashed in her dark eyes. For a split second, the submissive

21

girl was replaced by an angry young woman, her face filled with bitterness and resentment, then she blinked and the impression was gone. In fact, I wondered if I had imagined it.

She lowered her head submissively. "Yes, Mummy." She shot Audrey an embarrassed glance. "I'm sorry," she added in an undertone.

"That's quite all right," Audrey reassured the girl. "One cake for the stall is already a generous donation. I quite understand your mother wanting to keep one for herself."

"Would you like a piece too?" Mary asked her. "You always come and have tea with us in the afternoon anyway, Aunt Audrey..."

"Oh, all right." Audrey gave a guilty smile. "I shouldn't really, but yes, I'd love a small slice now. I didn't have time for breakfast this morning and I'm ravenous!"

Mary carefully placed one of the Victoria sponge cakes into Audrey's basket, then turned back to the other one on the table. She nearly collided with Theresa Bell who had drifted over from her own table and was now eyeing the Victoria sponge cake greedily.

"Oh! I'm sorry..." Mary hesitated, then said, "Would you like some cake too, Theresa?"

The older woman sniffed and hunched a shoulder. "No, thank you. I had better not."

"Probably worried there's poison in it!" guffawed Dame Clare.

Theresa glared at her. "It is no laughing matter! I am being victimised in the most dreadful manner."

"What a lot of nonsense!" said Dame Clare scornfully.

"It is not nonsense!" cried Theresa, trembling with anger and indignation. "I know that someone is after me! I know someone tried to poison my poor Moo-Goo and Yum-Yum! And... I know it had to be you!" she hissed suddenly, narrowing her eyes at the other woman. "*You* were the only person close enough to me at the last show. I know you'd do anything to stop my cats from winning!"

Audrey looked around desperately for some way to distract them. I felt sorry for her and stepped in.

"That Victoria sponge looks absolutely delicious," I said to Mary Eccleston. "We have it on the menu at my tearoom and it's always very popular, although I must say, yours looks a lot lighter than ours. Do you follow a particular recipe?"

The girl looked grateful for my interruption. "Yes, it's one that's been in my family for generations. Would... would you like a slice? And your mother too?"

I looked at her in pleasant surprise. "Oh, thanks—that's really kind of you. Yeah, I'd love a taste."

Things calmed down a bit and peace was restored as Mary cut the slices and passed them around. Audrey sat down on one of the canvas chairs next to Dame Clare and invited my mother to sit down next to her. I leaned against the table and took a large mouthful of the cake. It was as delicious as it looked: the vanilla sponge was moist and fluffy, the strawberries and jam filling sweet and luscious, and the fresh whipped cream bursting out of the sides of the cake sandwich.

Over Mary's shoulder, I could see Theresa Bell pretending to fuss over her cat cage, all the while eyeing us enviously. I felt slightly sorry for the woman—she was obviously desperate to have a taste of the cake but was too stubborn to back down from her ridiculous claims of persecution.

"This is absolutely delicious, Mary," I said, licking the jam and cream off my fork appreciatively. "I might have to beg you for a recipe."

The girl flushed with pleasure. "Oh, of course..."

"The home-made strawberry jam makes all the difference, doesn't it?" said Audrey, beaming. "I know you can grow strawberries in greenhouses, but really, I don't know how you manage—"

"You need Joseph," Dame Clare said. "I have told you time and time again, Audrey—you need to get Joseph to come and redo the Vicarage gardens."

"Oh, I'm not sure they need that much work," Audrey protested gently. "I was thinking maybe just a bit of re-bedding in the borders—"

"The gardens need to be redone. Completely," declared Dame Clare. "Ring Joseph on Monday and organise for him to go to the Vicarage. And tell him I

24

want the borders redone like ours at Eccleston House."

"I—" Audrey started to protest again, then sighed and acquiesced. "I suppose you know best, Clare." Hastily, she stood up and put down her empty plate. "Now, I'd better get going and take these things to the Cake Stall."

"I'll come with you," I said impulsively, licking the last bits of cream from my fork. "I want to pop out and get a drink."

Leaving my mother finishing off her cake next to Dame Clare and hoping that they could remain civil to each other, I followed Audrey out of the pavilion tent. It had been hot and stuffy in there and I took a grateful breath of the cooler, fresh air outside. I let Audrey hurry off whilst I took a slower route to the refreshment tent, enjoying the sights and sounds of the fête.

It felt almost like stepping back in time—there was still the bouncy castle full of screaming children, the hoopla games and apple bobbing; there was the Hand-knitted Crafts Stall and antique knick-knacks, the Largest Vegetable competition and the lucky hamper raffle, the shaggy Shetland ponies giving rides around the green, the garlands of British flags—miniature Union Jacks—strung across the stalls and fluttering in the breeze... and most of all, there was still that wonderful sense of camaraderie, the sense of a local community coming together to have fun and raise funds for the village. (This year, they were hoping to raise enough to renovate the school library.) Everywhere I looked, I could see neighbours enjoying a good gossip and tourists avidly photographing this slice of English country life.

As I turned a corner, I saw my best friend standing behind a stall displaying several of her paintings. Cassie was a brilliant artist but unfortunately, like most artists, found that talent alone didn't quite pay the bills—so she worked at my tearoom most of the time and painted on the side. Still, it was really nice to see her in her element, sharing her work with the public. She was beaming now as she wrapped up a canvas for a young couple with a pram; I caught her eye and waved but didn't stop.

A bit beyond her was the Cream Tea Stall—the stalwart of a traditional village fête—selling cups of hot tea and freshly baked scones, accompanied by lashings of jam and clotted cream. Four little old ladies stood behind the table there, busily taking orders and serving a long queue of people. They were (secretly) called the "Old Biddies" by Cassie and me, and were exactly the sort of bossy, meddling, nosy old aunts that everyone dreaded having... except that I had to admit that they'd grown on me. In fact, I thought of Mabel Cooke and her friends, Glenda, Florence, and Ethel, more often now with affection than irritation.

Still, the Old Biddies were best taken in small

doses and I gave their stall a wide berth as I passed. I was just approaching a second-hand books stall and wondering if I had time to stop and have a quick look when a strong arm snaked around my waist and hauled me close to a hard male body.

I gave a squeal of surprise, then laughed as a deep baritone said in my ear, "I think I might have to arrest you, Miss Rose, on grounds of suspicious behaviour."

I whirled around. "Devlin!"

CHAPTER THREE

I looked up at Devlin O'Connor and felt my heart give a little flip-flop, like it always did whenever I saw him. He was looking very different from his usual detective persona—instead of a classic tailored suit, he was wearing faded jeans and a pale grey Henley T-shirt which moulded itself to the muscular contours of his chest and shoulders. His black hair was slightly ruffled by the breeze and there was a shadow of dark stubble along his jaw. He looked handsome, relaxed, and incredibly sexy.

"What are you doing here?" I said.

"We've had a tip-off. We think there's a gang behind the recent 'agri-crime' thefts and it sounds like they might chance their luck at the fête." He jerked his head towards the other side of the village green. "There's a display of quad bikes, tractors, and other farm equipment over there, next to the pony rides. They would be a likely target, so I'm here to keep an eye on things. I've got a team here too, mingling in plainclothes, so that if the gang do strike, we'll be ready. If this is an organised crime job, then breaking into the ring would be a big coup."

I glanced at the crowd milling around us. "So any sign of potential thieves so far?"

Devlin made a rueful face. "Not even a sniff of a pickpocket. But that's all good," he added quickly. "This is exactly how a village fête should be: happy, safe, and peaceful." He smiled. "And it gives me a chance to sneak some time with my girlfriend."

He pulled me to him and pressed a kiss to my lips.

"Devlin!" I cried, looking quickly around and stifling a giggle. "Stop! Everyone will see!"

"So what? It's not as if we aren't already the talk of the village. I'm sure everybody is gossiping about us all the time anyway. Did you know that Susan Bromley asked me the other day whether we would name our son after your father or mine?"

"She didn't!" I gasped.

"She did," said Devlin, his blue eyes alight with laughter. "And Mrs Sutton at the post office asked when we were planning to move in together."

I made a sound of exasperation. "That's really none of their business! Why is everybody so nosy in the village?"

"So why don't we give them something to *really* talk about?" said Devlin with a wicked grin as he pulled me close again.

I shook my head and pushed him gently away. "Sorry, I need to get back to the cat show. The judging is about to start any minute. I only came out to grab a drink."

He looked bemused. "Cat show?"

I rolled my eyes. "Don't ask. I'll tell you later." I reached up on tiptoe to give him a peck on the cheek. "I'll come find you when we're done."

Hurrying back to the pavilion several minutes later, carefully carrying two full cups of home-made lemonade, I hoped desperately that the judging hadn't started. The queue for the lemonade had been horrendous and I'd been away much longer than I'd planned. As I was ducking in the pavilion entrance, I nearly crashed into a tall, thin man coming out.

"Oomph!" I stumbled backwards and overturned one cup of lemonade, nearly spilling it down my dress. I managed to save the other one, although not without losing a large portion of it.

"I beg your pardon..." the man said, in an irate tone that completely belied his apology.

He shuffled left and right, just as I did the same, each blocking the other.

"Excuse me!"

"Sorry!"

He made another sound of irritation, caught hold

of my arm to hold me in place and stepped around me, hurrying off without a backward glance. I gave his departing back a dirty look. Okay, so he might have been in a hurry but he didn't have to manhandle me like that!

Heaving an irritable sigh, I hurried into the pavilion, back down the rows towards our table. I was relieved to note that the judging didn't seem to have started yet, although the excitement had reached fever pitch and everywhere I looked was a hive of activity as people dashed around brushing coats, fluffing tails, sprinkling powders...

My goodness, they really take this seriously, I thought, as I walked past cages where owners were practising holding their cats up for the judge to examine. The tension in the air was palpable. When I got back to our table, I could see that even the great Dame Clare was affected. Her beloved Victoria sponge cake was all forgotten now, a half-eaten plate sitting next to the cat cage, as she manically gave Camilla one final brush and her daughter hovered anxiously around her.

My mother, however, looked serene and confident as she stood next to our table. I marvelled at her calm complacency and thought uneasily again of Muesli's ineligibility to be in a show like this. There was no way that was going to escape notice when the judge arrived. I hoped he wouldn't be too harsh. No matter how exasperating I found her, I hated the thought of my mother being humiliated in front of everyone.

The judging began and I joined everybody else in anxiously watching the judge's progress as he made his way slowly down each row of tables. The pavilion seemed even hotter and more airless now, and I felt myself sweating in my wool dress.

"He's coming this way!"

"He's here!"

"He's coming!"

The murmurs rolled across the pavilion and I straightened hurriedly as I saw a small bald man begin to make his way down our row. Owners watched tensely as he paused by each table to examine the cat, lift it up, look into its face to gauge its expression. His hands moved deftly over each cat's body, feeling the shoulders, spine, haunches, gliding over the length of the tail, checking the line of the jaw. Nothing escaped his expert eye and I swallowed nervously as I thought of his critical gaze on Muesli, with her slightly over-long tail and her mismatched white paws. Her shortcomings would be even more glaring after he had seen all these fine specimens of beautiful purebreds.

He was coming closer—he was only a couple of cages away now—and I felt my heart pounding in my chest. *This is ridiculous*, I told myself. *I didn't get this nervous when I was taking my final exams at Oxford!* It was only a stupid cat show—who cared what one little man thought? It didn't mean that Muesli was a lesser cat or less beautiful than any of the other felines here just because she wasn't awarded a blue ribbon.

Still, it was hard to control my nerves. And looking around, I could see that I wasn't the only one. In fact, even Dame Clare, a veteran of cat shows, looked flushed and uneasy, beads of sweat standing out on her forehead. She tugged at the high collar of her Victorian blouse and I could see her breathing with effort. I glanced at my mother and marvelled again at her serene demeanour. She looked supremely unconcerned, her hands gently holding Muesli, her head tilted back gracefully and an expectant smile on her lips. If you could get marks for poise and elegance, my mother would have won the show already.

The judge stopped at the table just before the Siamese, where a large Ragdoll cat sat placidly, waiting to be examined. But as he moved forward to pick up the cat, the air was suddenly rent by a shriek of distress.

"It's gone! It's gone! Someone's snatched it!"

Theresa Bell reeled back from her own cage, clutching her neck frantically. She stumbled sideways past our table and tripped, crashing into Dame Clare behind us.

"Aaaaaaah!" she screamed, as both women fell to the ground.

Everyone turned to stare and several people started forwards to help the two women. The judge was the quickest and he bent down gallantly to help

Theresa to her feet. But as he leaned down again to Dame Clare, he stiffened suddenly and froze.

There was a gasp. "Mummy?" cried Mary, dropping down by the inert form of her mother. "Mummy? Are you all right?"

More people rushed forwards and a crowd surrounded the fallen woman. Shouts and cries of panic filled the air. People were yelling for a doctor, an ambulance, for someone to start CPR... and through it all, you could hear Mary's breathless voice crying:

"Mummy? Mummy! Speak to me!"

Then suddenly, in the middle of mayhem, came a deep voice I recognised. It was Devlin. He was there in the pavilion, his calm, authoritative voice quelling the panic, asking the crowd to move back, commanding someone to call an ambulance. Then he knelt down besides Dame Clare. I saw him put a hand to her neck to feel for a pulse. There was a pause, then he sat back on his heels and looked up at us.

Silence filled the pavilion. He didn't need to say it. We all knew. She was dead.

CHAPTER FOUR

"No..." said Mary faintly. She seemed unable to move.

In fact, we were all paralysed. Somehow, I couldn't believe it. It seemed wrong... Death... here in the midst of a happy village fête, with people laughing and stuffing their faces and children playing on bouncy castles and riding miniature ponies...

Dead?

Everyone gradually drifted back to their tables in a stunned silence. A hush fell over the pavilion. There was no question of the cat show continuing now. The shrill wail of a siren came faintly from the distance and, a few minutes later, the ambulance arrived. People clustered together and pointed and whispered as the paramedics hurried in, carrying a stretcher, followed by Dr Foster, the village GP, who had been hunted down and brought in to see his long-time patient.

"Dear me... Dear me..." the old doctor tutted, standing aside and shaking his head as the paramedics transferred Dame Clare's limp form to the stretcher. His wrinkled, sad face looked like an old hound dog's. "I did warn her about the risks of a sudden heart attack."

"So are you citing that as the cause of death, Doctor?" asked Devlin, standing next to him.

The doctor nodded and made a tutting sound again. "Very sad, you know, but as I always tell my patients: the body cannot hold out forever. And in her case, with her heart condition—and her diet and the excess weight she carried..." He shook his head again.

"Was she on any medication for her heart trouble?" asked Devlin.

"Yes, Mummy was taking some pills for her angina..." came a quavering voice next to us.

I turned to look. It was Mary Eccleston, leaning against the table, a blanket around her shoulders. She looked white and shaken, although she was not crying. Next to her, Audrey Simmons was rubbing her arm and making comforting noises.

The girl gulped back a sob. "We... we always carried some. Dr Foster said to take them when Mummy felt the pain coming on..."

Devlin glanced towards the doctor for

confirmation and the old GP nodded.

"Yes, that's right—glyceryl trinitrate sublingual tablets—I prescribed them to her only a few weeks ago. She had been complaining of tightness in her chest and pain radiating down her arms from time to time—classic angina symptoms, you know. Very common, particularly in times of stress. The tablets help to relieve the symptoms very quickly, though of course, they wouldn't cure her heart condition. She really needed to tackle her weight and diet. I did give her stern advice, in particular with regards to avoiding rich, sugary, buttery baking and desserts..." He sighed and said to Mary, "I'm very sorry, my dear. I know this must be a horrible shock for you."

Mary looked distressed. "Mummy had some Victoria sponge cake... I know you said not to let her have any sweets, Doctor, but Mummy liked her cakes very much and I... I couldn't stop her..." Her eyes widened with sudden horror. "Oh, do you think it was the cake that caused her heart attack?"

"No, no, my dear, don't worry yourself on that account," the old doctor said quickly, reaching over to pat her hand. "It was the culmination of several things—her high cholesterol, her weight, her sedentary lifestyle and rich, sugary diet... these are all risk factors for a heart attack."

The girl seemed comforted. Audrey put a gentle hand on her arm and led her back to the table, where a cup of hot, sweet tea was waiting.

Devlin turned back to the GP and said, "And you are sure, Doctor, that a heart attack *is* the cause of death? We would normally need a post-mortem to certify death from natural causes, unless the person's own doctor—"

Dr Foster bristled. "Are you doubting my diagnosis, young man? Naturally, I'd be happy to sign the death certificate! Yes, Dame Clare died from a heart attack—she had all the classic risk factors and symptoms. And in fact, you can see that the poor lady must have been feeling ill and had been about to take some medication..." He indicated the woman's outstretched hand which flopped down limply at the side of the stretcher.

Devlin stepped forwards and carefully uncurled the dead woman's fingers. Clutched in her right hand was a small white pill. In spite of my previous dislike for her, I felt a stab of pity for Clare Eccleston. Perhaps if she had only got to her angina tablets in time, she might have prevented the heart attack. Devlin must have read my mind because he asked the doctor the same question.

"Perhaps," said Dr Foster with a shrug. "Heart attacks can be unpredictable things. It is not an attack, per se, you understand—that is just a lay term used by the general public. It is either a cardiac arrest caused by a sudden arrhythmia or a myocardial infarction caused by a clot in the coronary artery. The end result is the same—the heart suddenly stops beating."

"Was it brought on by anything in particular, do you think?" asked Devlin.

"Stress is a very likely trigger," Dr Foster said. "The stress of the show... and there was also the shock of a sudden physical trauma in this case, I believe?"

I saw Devlin's eyes flick to Theresa Bell, who was being questioned by a constable a few feet away. "Yes, unfortunately there was a... an accident of sorts and another competitor collided with the victim and knocked her to the ground. The other lady thought someone had stolen her necklace—when actually the clasp had broken and the necklace had simply fallen to the ground."

"Yes, hmm..." The old doctor's moustache quivered thoughtfully. "Well, that is just the kind of sudden shock that might be too much for a weakened heart to take. Of course, if Dame Clare had listened to my advice regarding her weight and diet, her heart might not have been so vulner—"

"Ahh... yes, Doctor, thank you very much for your help," said Devlin quickly. He indicated the young man next to him who had been scribbling notes onto a pad. "If you could go with my constable here and attend to the death certificate..."

The old doctor was led away and Devlin heaved a sigh, then glanced around. His face brightened as our eyes met and he took a step towards me, but before he could speak, we were interrupted by a yell from the pavilion entrance. A constable ran in, his chest heaving.

"Inspector! Come quick!"

"What is it?" said Devlin, hurrying over to him.

"The quad bikes! They've been nicked! Two of our boys have gone after them, though, and we might still be able to head them off if we circle round the other side of the village."

Devlin swore under his breath and took off racing after the constable as they both disappeared in pursuit. A great hubbub rose in the pavilion after they'd left, as people excitedly discussed the new drama. I saw the members of the committee huddling together, their faces filled with dismay. Their thoughts were plainly written on their faces: as if a tragic death from a heart attack wasn't bad enough, now there was the possibility of a full-scale police chase after an organised crime gang! The village fête was falling into a shambles.

"I cannot believe the way the police have completely ignored me and my troubles!" cried an aggrieved voice next to me.

I turned to find Theresa Bell at my elbow.

"I could have been the victim of a horrible theft! The police should be focusing on that instead of asking questions about Dame Clare. That woman always hogs all the attention! For goodness' sake, she had a heart attack! What's the big deal? People have heart attacks every day! It's not as if—"

"Oh shush!" I said quickly, glancing across at Mary Eccleston who was leaning against the table next to us, her arms wrapped around herself as if she was cold. She was alone—Audrey Simmons must have gone to join the rest of the village fête committee—and the poor girl was looking completely lost. Leaving Theresa Bell still spluttering behind me, I went over to Mary and touched her gently on the arm. She gave a violent start and turned to me, her eyes wide and scared.

"Are you all right?" I asked gently.

"I... uh... yes..." She looked miserably towards the paramedics. "Should I be going with Mummy...?"

"I don't think you need to—they'll just be taking her to the hospital morgue. I'm sure you could... um... visit later."

"I'd like to go home," she said in a small voice. She glanced at the white Persian in the cage. "I'm sure Camilla would like to go home too."

"Yes, of course," I said soothingly. "Have you got a friend or family member you could call? Is your father—?"

"Daddy passed away several years ago."

"Oh, well then... what about any other relatives?"

"There's Aunt Audrey... She's not really my aunt but I call her that. She used to be at school with Mummy." She glanced hesitantly across the pavilion. "But she looks busy at the moment."

Busy was an understatement. As a member of the village fête committee and particularly the one in charge of the cat show, Audrey had her hands full dealing with the aftermath of what had happened. I glimpsed her hurrying between tables, trying to soothe everyone and respond to all the people clamouring for her attention.

"Is there anyone else?" I asked.

Mary shook her head slowly. "Not really... I'm an only child and Mummy didn't like most of our relatives, so we weren't on friendly terms with them... I... I suppose Professor Ashton from the college might come over... She's the Principal and I know her quite well. I work in the college offices, you see..." She faltered. "But it's the weekend and I'm not quite sure..."

"Look, would you like me to drive you home? I'd be very happy to do that." I gave her a smile.

She looked at me gratefully. "Thank you. That's... that's really kind of you."

I let my mother know what I was doing and left the pavilion a few minutes later with Mary. She showed me to her car and I helped her load Camilla and the accompanying show paraphernalia into the back, then I took the wheel. A man came running up just as we were about to set off.

"Mary! Mary! I just heard what happened..." He paused, panting, next to the car.

Mary lowered the passenger window and, as he bent down and looked in, I realised suddenly that I had seen him before. This was the tall, stoop-shouldered man I had almost crashed into earlier when I was carrying the lemonade and returning to the pavilion.

"Oh Edwin... Mummy had a heart attack!" said Mary tremulously.

"Yes, I heard, my dear. I'm so sorry," he said. He made an awkward gesture as if about to reach out to clasp her hand, then he stopped himself. "You should have come to me immediately, Mary. You know I would have taken care of you. I'll drive you back to Eccleston House now, shall I? I can stay with you as well."

"Oh, I..." Mary seemed confused and uncertain. "I... I don't know... Gemma is taking me home." She looked helplessly at me, as if hoping I would answer for her. Her eyes were slightly glazed over and I could see that it was all becoming too much for her.

I hesitated, not sure if I should interfere. From the man's familiar tone and manner, I took him to be a family friend—probably of Clare Eccleston or Mary's late father, given his age. Perhaps he saw himself in the role of Mary's uncle? On the other hand, I didn't like his peremptory manner...

I made a decision. "I think Mary needs a bit of time alone now," I said firmly. "Perhaps you can give her a ring later tonight or tomorrow morning?"

The man compressed his lips and looked slightly annoyed. "Well, if you're sure, Mary..."

"Yes, thank you, Edwin... Gemma's right... I... I just want to go home now and rest for a bit..."

We left him standing on the edge of the village green, watching us as we drove away. Mary sat in a daze for most of the drive, only speaking up to give directions, and I didn't press her for more conversation. I had a feeling that the shock of everything was starting to hit her now and she was struggling to hold herself together. I glanced across at her hands, clenched so tightly in her lap that the knuckles showed white, and noted that her face was pale and strained as she sat staring ahead at the windscreen.

It would probably have helped if she could have burst into tears and had a good cry but I was sure that Mary would have been brought up with the old-fashioned English ideal of "always keep a stiff upper lip": to never show your emotions, no matter how upset you are. Oh, it wasn't the official line anymore; modern Englishmen (and women) were encouraged to cry and rage in public as much as they liked—and frequently did with shameless abandon if reality TV was any guide—but I was sure that for a traditionalist like Dame Clare, to indulge in such excesses of emotion would have still been seen as weak and "vulgar" and her daughter would have been raised with such standards in mind.

We swung at last into the wide curving driveway of a large country manor—an imposing Georgian residence set in its own formal gardens. I looked around with quiet admiration as I got out and helped Mary unload the car, and my admiration increased as we went through the front door and into a large foyer with a black and white chequered marble floor. A sweeping staircase curved down one side of the foyer and an elegant chandelier hung suspended from the high ceiling.

Three Persian cats came running to meet us and milled around our legs, purring softly.

"Hello Tabitha, Chloe, Lancelot..." said Mary absently. She opened the cat carrier and let Camilla re-join her friends. Then she led me into an anteroom to the right of the foyer.

"Mummy likes—" Mary broke off, then swallowed and continued, "I mean, she liked to keep all the cat show things in here."

I looked around the large utility room filled with feline supplies and equipment. Rows upon rows of "Best in Show" and "Best of Breed" ribbons and rosettes hung on the walls, together with framed pictures of Persian cats in various colours.

"Is there a particular place you'd like me to leave the things?"

"Um..." Mary looked vaguely around the room. "The... the blankets should go over there, unless they are to be washed, of course, and the grooming brushes on that shelf... and the bowls—if they're clean—go in that cupboard, but if they're dirty, we leave them on that wooden bench by the door... and then I take them to the kitchen later... oh, this is where they were..." She looked blankly at the end of the bench where a bunch of picnic forks lay. "I was looking for these at the show. I must have forgotten to pack them this morning... I was in such a hurry,

I knew I would forget something and Mummy said to tell Joseph to help, except that he wasn't really much help... and oh, the litter trays—I need to give them a wash too... Mummy always said we could just scoop out the soiled litter and top it up with more but I think it's better if we give things a thorough wash; one never knows with litter trays—I always feel like they're so *dirty*, you know, even though I know they're not really and I do always wash my hands after handling them—"

"Hey, hey..." I said gently, catching Mary's arm. Her eyes were slightly wild and she was gesticulating frantically. I spoke slowly and softly, as if calming a frightened horse, "It's all right, Mary. It's going to be all right."

She stopped and took a deep shuddering breath. "We... we have to put everything back properly... that's how Mummy liked it," she insisted anxiously.

"Okay," I said soothingly. "We'll do that. You just tell me where to put things and we'll do it together, okay?"

I helped her unpack and return most of the items to their proper places. By the time we'd finished, I thought Mary looked better—the activity seemed to have done her good. Her eyes had lost that wild look and she seemed to have regained her composure.

"You will have to contact the family solicitor," I reminded her gently as we left the anteroom and stepped back into the front foyer. "Although tomorrow is Sunday—so perhaps on Monday morning?"

Mary looked slightly uncertain. "I've never gone to see the solicitor without Mummy before."

"What about Audrey? Could she go with you?"

"Yes, yes, you're right," Mary looked at me with relief. "Yes, Aunt Audrey said she would help me with anything I needed. She's coming over later tonight, I think..." She licked her lips. "Um... would you like some tea?"

"No, thank you. I'm sure you'd like some time to yourself now," I said, thinking that the last thing the girl would want was to have to sit down and make polite conversation. However, to my surprise, instead of looking relieved, Mary's face crumpled and her eyes filled with panic.

"What is it, Mary?" I asked. "Is something wrong?"

"I... I don't know what to do!" she burst out suddenly.

"What do you mean?" I said in surprise.

She made a helpless gesture. "I don't know what to do with myself now."

"What do you normally do when you come back from a show?"

"Well, I would usually get Mummy's slippers for her and massage her feet—because they get very sore, you know—and then I'd make tea. Mummy likes—liked—to have tea in the front parlour. And then I might have to see about supper. Riza does most of the cooking but I help her and I can make the simple dishes. Anyway, usually after we come back from shows, Mummy likes to have cold meats, with bread and cheeses, for supper. And then... and then I run her bath and turn down her bed and make sure she has her hot water bottles prepared..." She looked around a bit forlornly. "But now... but now Mummy's not here... I don't know what to do!"

I glanced around the room and spied the TV set in the corner. Turning back to Mary, I patted her hand gently. "Look, try not to worry about things too much tonight, okay? You've had a shock and it's natural to feel unsettled—but things will be clearer in the morning. I think you should just take it easy—maybe have a little something to eat, watch some TV to take your mind off things—"

"Mummy always decided what we watched on the television."

"O...kay, well, tonight maybe you can decide yourself, hmm?" I saw the look of terror on her face and changed tack. "On second thoughts, forget the TV. Why don't you just have a hot bath and then an early night?"

"Y-yes, you're right. That's what I'll do," said Mary, looking immensely grateful to be given specific instructions. She gave me a shy smile. "Thank you, Gemma."

I returned the smile, struck suddenly by how young and childlike Mary seemed. She must have been in her mid-twenties—no more than a few years younger than me—and yet we were worlds apart. Then I thought of Dame Clare's domineering personality. Maybe it wasn't so surprising after all that Mary had remained so immature and dependent, particularly if she was too quiet and shy to make friends on her own.

The sound of wheels crunching on the gravel outside alerted me to the fact that my mother had arrived to pick me up. As we walked to the front door together, I looked hesitantly at Mary again. I didn't really like leaving her alone.

"Do you have a housekeeper?" I asked.

"We have a maid, Riza, but she normally has the weekends off. She's gone to London to see a friend and won't be back until late. Joseph had to help us load the car this morning."

"Joseph?"

"He's our gardener. I mean, not ours, really. He's the St Cecilia's College gardener but he comes and does extra work here when Mummy asks him to."

"Is he still here?"

Mary looked uncertain. "He might still be around, outside in the gardens somewhere..."

"I don't like the thought of leaving you alone," I said.

Mary gave me a small smile. She bent down and scooped up one of the Persians in her arms, cuddling it close. "I'm not alone. I have the cats. And I know what I should do this evening now." She gave me another grateful look. "I'll... I'll be okay, Gemma. Thank you."

"Well... if you need anything, give me a call." I gave her my mobile number. Then with a final smile and wave, I left the house and went out to my mother's car.

CHAPTER FIVE

"What a dreadful business," my mother said at breakfast the next morning as she lifted the local newspaper from the pile of mail and stared at the headline on the front page: "*Tragic Death at Village Fête!*"

I saw that, underneath that, there was a slightly smaller sub-heading and a piece about the theft of two valuable quad bikes from the fête. I winced for Devlin. From a police PR point of view, the fête had been an absolute disaster. I had only had a terse text from Devlin last night and I knew that he would be wrapped up most of today dealing with the aftermath, but I was pleased that his message confirmed that we were still on for dinner tonight.

"It was pretty rotten luck," I said as I sat down next to my mother with two slices of toast and reached for the jar of home-made marmalade she had picked up at the village fête. It was a nice treat to be sitting here in my parents' sunny kitchen, enjoying a lazy breakfast on a Sunday morning—normally, I'd have been up early and at work already, as weekends were usually our busiest times at the tearoom.

I spread some of the beautiful thick-cut marmalade onto the toast and took a bite, then said, chewing, "Dame Clare was a bit of an obnoxious woman but you can't help feeling sorry for her. If she had managed to get to her pills in time, she might not have died. Such bad timing."

"Don't speak with your mouth full, Gemma," my mother admonished. "And what do you mean—bad timing?"

"Well, she had obviously been trying to take her heart tablets when she collapsed. In fact, I remember noticing that she looked very flushed and queasy as we were waiting for the judge to arrive. I thought at the time that it was just show nerves—but now I wonder if it wasn't the onset of her heart attack. She must have been feeling ill and started to take some pills—and then that silly woman, Theresa Bell, crashed into her—"

"She can't have been taking her pills, darling," said my mother absently as she turned the pages of the newspaper.

"What do you mean?"

My mother looked up. "Her heart pills weren't

TILL DEATH DO US TART

touched."

"How do you know that?"

"I saw her pillbox—a lovely little guilloche enamel silver affair just like the one Eliza Whitfield has. Only Eliza's has a nightingale on it; Dame Clare's had a picture of a cat. At least, I think it was a cat... I wasn't really close enough to see... it could have been a rabbit, I suppose. Or a guinea pig? Although really, why anyone would want to have a likeness of one of those ugly little things... but I suppose there's no accounting for taste and—"

"Mother, what has all this got to do with Dame Clare's heart pills not being touched?" I interrupted impatiently.

She paused and looked at me in surprise. "Oh. Didn't I say? Well, I overheard Mary telling Dame Clare that she was putting the pillbox with their other things in a corner of their table. They had some tissues and cotton wool and show pamphlets and other bits and pieces. The pillbox was tucked under the pet first aid kit, near the bottom of the pile."

I looked at her blankly. "So? I still don't understand, Mother."

"Well, after the ambulance people had left and everything had calmed down a bit, I happened to glance over at their table and I noticed that the pillbox was still exactly where it had been."

"So what?"

"Well obviously, darling, if she had removed

some pills from the box, it wouldn't be in the same place, would it? She would have replaced it at the top of the pile."

"Oh Mother, perhaps you remembered wrong. Your memory is a bit unreliable sometimes."

"Nonsense, my memory is excellent."

Not when it comes to computer passwords, I thought sourly. I had only been asked about her Apple ID password eight times this week. "Are you sure? I mean, it was pretty chaotic yesterday and you could have easily got things mixed up. They definitely found Dame Clare holding a pill in her hand—"

"No." My mother was firm. "I did not get anything mixed up. That pillbox had not been touched— which means that whatever Dame Clare was holding, she didn't get it from her own pillbox."

An uneasy thought flashed through my mind. *If she hadn't got that pill from her own pillbox, where had Dame Clare got the pill that she had been clutching when she died?* I pushed it hurriedly away.

"You must be wrong, Mother."

My mother drew herself up to her full height. "I am never wrong."

Ooooh! I was itching to argue that but restrained myself. "Well... maybe Dame Clare had a second pillbox—or some pills in her pocket," I suggested.

"I think that is very unlikely. The whole affair is very odd. Very odd indeed." She gave me a meaningful look.

I stared at her. "What are you saying, Mother?"

"Well, darling, I think there is something suspicious about Dame Clare's death," my mother said excitedly. "And what's more, Mabel Cooke and her friends agree with me. We were having a talk at the fête yesterday just before I left. They think it might have been..." She leaned towards me and lowered her voice to a dramatic whisper. "*Murder.*"

I groaned. "Mother, you can't listen to them! They think everything is murder!"

"Darling, they might be right in this instance. I wouldn't be surprised if there are any number of people who wanted to murder that unpleasant woman. How dared she call Muesli 'riff-raff'!" My mother gave an indignant sniff.

I glanced across at Muesli who was sitting on the kitchen windowsill, watching sparrows in our backyard. The little tabby's tail was twitching back and forth and she was "chattering" excitedly, her whiskers quivering. She couldn't care less what she had been called.

I turned back to my mother. "Mother, you know how people get in these shows. It's all stupid snobbery anyway."

"Perhaps. But that wasn't all. Look at the way she treated her own daughter! Really, the woman had the most cavalier attitude. I wouldn't be surprised at all if she had many enemies—and one of them decided that they had had enough!"

"Dr Foster was there. He was her GP and he confirmed that she had died of a heart attack."

My mother gave a dismissive wave. "Oh, Dr Foster is an old fuddy-duddy! Everyone knows he should have retired long ago! Mabel says that he diagnosed her with meningitis when all she had was arthritis in the neck. I wouldn't be surprised if he had got it completely wrong... Ah!"

Her face brightened as she found an advertising supplement tucked into the pages of the local paper. "Oh, how marvellous. That new garden centre is having a sale. I must go and stock up on some new begonias," my mother added, for all the world as if she hadn't just been discussing a possible murder. She picked up the supplement and flipped through it quickly. "Hmm... they've got a very good deal on some late blooming primroses as well. Perhaps I'll pop in later today... ugh, really, things just aren't what they used to be. Look at the dreadful quality of this paper—and the ink too! Stains your fingers horribly and gets paper dust everywhere. I have half a mind to write to the company to complain. The way they cut corners these days is absolutely shameful..."

I tuned out as she droned on about the deteriorating quality of newspapers in general and how crosswords were impossible to find nowadays, buried amongst the adverts and cartoons... I thought longingly of a time when I would be able to sit and eat my breakfast in the peace and quiet of my own apartment. *Well, that day might not be far off,* I thought cheerfully. With the tearoom doing so well lately, I had finally decided that I could afford my own flat. In fact, I was going to check out a few apartments with Cassie later this afternoon.

I felt a thrill of happy anticipation at the thought of a place of my own. I couldn't wait. Not that I didn't love my parents or wasn't grateful that they'd given me a place to stay, rent-free, when I came back to England. But when you're heading into your thirties, living with your parents is just bad for your blood pressure. Actually, my father's all right—in fact, most of the time you barely noticed that he was there. He was a semi-retired Oxford professor who spent most of his time with his nose buried in his textbooks, when he wasn't spending it watching his beloved cricket on TV.

My mother, though, was a whole different kettle of fish. When she wasn't meddling in my love life or buying me hideous things I didn't want to wear from online shopping sites, she was usually doing something else to humiliate me or drag me into activities I didn't want anything to do with. As if right on cue, I came back to the present to hear my mother saying:

"...with Dorothy back from holiday this week, we're finally having a book club meeting and I thought you could join us tonight as the—"

"I can't tonight," I said quickly. "I'm going out to dinner with Devlin."

My mother looked like she had tasted a sour lemon. "Oh. Gemma, you're not *really* thinking of taking up with him again?"

I felt a flicker of irritation. "Yes, I *am* 'taking up with' Devlin, as you call it. Why shouldn't I?"

"Oh darling—really! When you could have the pick of all the nice men in Oxford and you have to choose the... the village bobby!"

"He's not the village bobby, Mother," I said through gritted teeth. "He's a top detective in the Oxfordshire CID."

"Yes, but he mixes with... *criminals!*" My mother shuddered delicately. "Murderers and rapists and other ghastly types. Who knows what kinds of horrible perversions he might be picking up?"

I rolled my eyes. "Mother, criminal behaviour isn't like germs. You can't get infected by contact with it."

"Oh, but darling—I'm sure it must affect you. In fact, I've read that detectives are good at their jobs *because* they could almost be criminals themselves! Their minds are arranged the same way or something... which means they could easily slip and go over to the other side! What if you find out that Devlin is actually a serial killer?"

"*Mother!*" I said, holding onto my temper with effort. "Devlin is *not* a serial killer! He's a detective because he cares deeply about justice, and he's noble and compassionate and dedicated to his work..." I stopped and took a deep breath, then let it out slowly. Why did I always let my mother get to me?

My mother pursed her lips, then she brightened. "Oh, well, if you *must* see him, at least you should get something out of it. Find out if the police are doing anything to investigate Dame Clare's death, and if they're not, then *make* him!"

I sighed. "All right, all right, I'll mention it to Devlin tonight."

CHAPTER SIX

"Maybe it looks better on the inside," Cassie suggested hopefully as we stood across the road from an ugly brown brick building which looked like a relic from a 60s nuclear factory.

I sighed, not sharing her optimism. This was the third property we'd seen so far and if the first two were anything to go by, what you saw on the outside was often what you got on the inside. Still, I reminded myself that you couldn't judge a book by its cover—so maybe you couldn't judge a property by its vomit-coloured outer façade either. Besides, I was living *inside* the building, wasn't I? So what if it looked hideous from the street? As long as it was airy and comfortable inside...

A few minutes later, however, my hopes were cruelly dashed as I stood looking in dismay at a dingy, cramped sitting room-cum-kitchen-cum-dining room-cum-laundry, with a bit of linen cupboard thrown in for good measure. The walls had peeling paint and there was black mould visible in the corners of the ceiling.

The agent—a young man with oily hair and even oilier manners—stood by the door and reeled off a practiced speech about the flat's attractions:

"... and as you can see, it's a very cosy set-up. Everything at your fingertips, so to speak—ha—ha. And if you come to the window over here..." He led the way across to the dust-streaked pane of glass along the far wall. "You can get a lovely view of the 'dreaming spires of Oxford', to the east over there—"

"If you have a telescope and use a lot of imagination," muttered Cassie.

I grinned and turned back to the agent. "How much did you say the rent was again?" I asked.

He named a figure which made my eyes water slightly.

"What? I can't believe they have the cheek to charge that for this pigsty!" Cassie cried.

The agent flushed and said stiffly, "That price is very competitive for this area of the city. You are well aware that Oxford is one of the most desirable locations to live in, in England, and the property prices reflect that. This flat in particular is very well situated to take advantage of the rail and motorway links down to London, as well as being so close to the countryside, not to mention all the history and culture that Oxford has to offer. Really, you're lucky to be getting such a great location for this price."

"Lucky—!" Cassie spluttered.

I put a restraining hand on her arm and said politely to the agent, "Thank you for showing us the place. I'll let you know if I'm interested."

"Well, I wouldn't advise you to leave it too long," he said haughtily. "I have many other people interested in this flat, you know."

"Huh! Good luck to them," said Cassie when we'd come back out onto the street again. "The place is disgusting. Seth could probably set up a biological weapons lab from the stuff growing in that apartment."

I laughed in spite of myself. Seth Browning, my other best friend from college days, had stayed on in Oxford after graduation and climbed the academic instead of the corporate ladder. He was now a Senior Research Fellow and tutor at one of the colleges, specialising in Organic Chemistry, and would probably have loved this apartment, though for all the wrong reasons!

As we got back into my mother's car and looked despondently at the dwindling number of properties on my list, I felt my heart sink again.

"Cass, I'm never going to find a place," I said in despair.

"Hey, we haven't finished looking at them all," said Cassie. "You never know—one of these last two might be perfect." She shook her head. "Bloody hell,

I didn't realise how lucky I had it with my place."

Cassie had a studio flat in Jericho, one of the trendiest suburbs in Oxford. It was a large airy space—really just one huge room—with dormer windows and sloping ceilings, tucked up in the attic area of a three-storey terraced house near the canal. Cassie had her bed in one corner and a second-hand couch and beanbag in another, but most of the area was filled with easels and canvases, and looked more like an artist's working studio than a flat.

"You were really lucky," I agreed. "How did you find the place?"

"It belongs to a lady who came to one of my dance classes at the studio," said Cassie. "She was a regular and we got friendly. She heard that I was looking for a place and she told me that she had been wanting to sublet the attic space in her house but she was worried about renting it out to any old stranger—she's a single mum, you see, and she's got a young son. Anyway, it worked out really well. I get a discount on the rent because it's not really a proper apartment—the bathroom's very primitive and the plumbing's a bit dodgy. And it's pretty draughty in winter. But I can live with that. You just can't beat the location."

I sighed. "I wish I could find something like that."

"We just need to keep looking," said Cassie encouragingly. "Come on, we're going to be late for the next appointment if we don't get a move on."

As I started the car, Cassie's phone beeped and she glanced down at it, then made an exclamation of annoyance.

"What?" I said, looking at her.

"The little blighter!" fumed Cassie. "It's my younger brother, Liam. Mum and Dad got him a new camera for his sixteenth birthday and he's been going around taking pictures of everyone since. Building a portfolio, he says..." She rolled her eyes.

"Does he want to be a photographer?"

"Yeah. Fancies himself as the next David Bailey."

"I'll bet he takes some great pictures," I said, thinking that anyone in Cassie's family probably had more artistic talent in their little finger than the rest of Oxfordshire's population combined.

"He's not bad," said Cassie grudgingly.

"Then why did you make that sound?"

"Because he always takes such horrible pictures of *me*!" said Cassie irritably. "Honestly, I don't know how he always gets me in those poses! Look at this picture he's just sent me—he took that at the village fête on Saturday. I look like I have a triple chin," she grumbled.

I leaned over to look. Okay, it was definitely not Cassie's best angle. She had been snapped while she was in the middle of a conversation with someone and her mouth was pulled open in the most unattractive way, with her chin tucked down and disappearing into the folds of skin around her neck.

I chuckled. "You look a bit like Jabba the Hutt's prettier cousin."

"Don't laugh! You wouldn't find it funny if it were you!"

"Did he take one of me?" I asked in alarm.

"Dunno—I haven't seen the whole set from the fête yet. I think they're still on his camera. It's one of those fancy ones which can connect to the internet and he's just picking the ugly shots of me to send. He always does stuff like that to wind me up."

I grinned. "That's younger brothers for you. Anyway, just think—when he's all grown up and famous, you'll have a few Liam Jenkins originals which you can sell for a lot of money."

Cassie shuddered. "No way! I'd rather pay someone a lot of money to delete all those pictures of me from existence!" She texted him back. "Hang on—let me ask him if he's got one of you…"

Her phone beeped again a few seconds later and I leaned over apprehensively to look.

"No fair!" cried Cassie, pouting. "You look gorgeous in the one he took of you!"

I had to admit—with great relief—that she was right. Liam had caught me at my best angle, with my head slightly in profile, my eyes large and shining, and a hint of a smile on my lips. It had been taken in the cat show pavilion and I was standing by our table, looking down at Muesli in front of me, with my mother next to me, half out of the frame. Behind me was the mayhem of the cat show—the rows of tables filled with cat cages, the other competitors and their cats—but Liam's skill with the lens had brought me and Muesli sharply into the foreground as the focus of the shot. Muesli was sitting in that perfect cat silhouette with her back arched, her ears small and dainty, and her tail curled around her paws.

"Oh, can you send a copy to my phone?" I asked. "It's a beautiful shot—I think it's one of the nicest shots I've got with Muesli. And I love it because it's so natural—neither of us is looking at the camera. It's like a moment captured in time."

"Yeah, sure," said Cassie, slightly dourly.

"Cheer up," I said, laughing as I released the handbrake and eased the car out onto the street. "You haven't seen the rest of the photos. There might be a gorgeous one of you in there."

The next property was closer in to the centre of Oxford. I was feeling hopeful until we pulled up outside the address. It was right next to a busy road junction, with commuter traffic and buses going past regularly.

"I can't live here—not with Muesli!" I said in dismay as we sat in the car looking at the block of flats. "Even if I never intend to let her out the front door, she might dart out when I'm not watching. You know how naughty she is and how good she is at escaping. And then she could get run over so easily."

Nevertheless, Cassie persuaded me to go in to have a look, which only made me feel worse because the flat wasn't that bad. It was compact but clean and had large windows which let in a lot of light. But the proximity to the road was a deal-breaker for me. I couldn't put Muesli in danger.

We left regretfully and fifteen minutes later found ourselves at the last property on my list. I parked the car and looked at it eagerly. It looked wonderful. Part of a converted Victorian terraced house, the last in a row down a quiet side street, and with its own attractive gardens. Cassie and I exchanged a smile, then we hurried in to meet the agent. The flat was on the ground floor and, inside, we found a lovely bright U-shaped sitting room, with a kitchenette tucked at the end of one arm of the "U" and a small area that could be used as a study at the other. The bedroom was simple but spacious and the bathroom looked relatively modern.

"This is great!" I whispered to Cassie.

She nodded excitedly and said, "D'you know what they're asking for the rent?"

"I think so—it was mentioned on the real estate agency website—but I'll just check again…"

The agent confirmed the price and my heart leapt with excitement. It all seemed too good to be true.

"So the property is available straightaway?" I asked eagerly "Do I just put in an application—"

"Yes, if you just fill out the form and drop it in to our office with the accompanying documents, we'll process it right away and let you know within a day or two if the landlord accepts. He was hoping to get the carpets cleaned so there may be a slight delay—"

"Oh, that's no problem at all," I said happily. "It will take me a few days to get my stuff sorted anyway, and my cat—"

"I'm sorry, you have a cat?" The agent frowned at me. "I didn't realise you were planning to keep a cat here."

"Yes, I am. When I looked on your website, it said this property was pet-friendly."

"Oh, that must have been a mistake, because the property definitely isn't available to pet owners."

I stared at him, not wanting to accept what he was saying. "Well... it's not like I'm going to keep a big dog—"

"The landlord doesn't want any kind of pet. He's had bad experiences in the past with damage to the property and odours."

"No, wait, you don't understand," I said. "Muesli is a really small cat—you'll hardly even notice her. She's incredibly clean. She doesn't smell at all. And she's very quiet and sleeps all day and never makes any trouble."

Okay, the last part was a blatant lie but desperate times call for desperate measures.

He shook his head firmly. "I'm sorry. The

landlord expressly said no pets. No exceptions."

Chagrined, I left, with Cassie trailing after me. I was feeling deeply depressed as we got back in the car. Even my best friend seemed to have run out of optimistic things to say.

"Well... we'll just have to keep looking," she said at last. "I'm sure something will turn up. There'll be new listings next weekend."

I sighed but didn't reply. We drove for a few moments in a despondent silence, then I realised suddenly that we were very close to Eccleston House. For a moment, my own house-hunting troubles were forgotten as I thought of Mary. I wondered how she was.

I turned to Cassie as the car paused at a crossroads and said, "Hey, Cass—are you in a rush to get back?"

"No, why?"

"Do you mind if we stop off somewhere really quickly? I'd like to pop in to see Mary Eccleston."

"The daughter of the woman who died at the fête yesterday?"

"Yeah, I drove her home. She seemed a bit... lost. I'd just like to check that she's doing okay."

"Sure."

The Ecclestons' maid, Riza, met us at the front door and told us that Mary was in the gardens at the rear of the house. We wandered around for a while but could see no sign of her. Finally, we returned to the house, and this time Riza apologised and showed us into a utility room at the back of the house, where we found Mary grooming one of the Persians. She looked up distractedly as we entered.

"Oh, hello. I'm sorry, I'm not really dressed for company..." She gestured down at herself. She was wearing leggings and a faded smock-type top, which was liberally covered in white hairs.

"That's okay." I smiled at her. "I didn't realise you had to do so much grooming still. I would have thought that you can relax now until the next show."

"Oh no, with Persians, you really need to groom them every day—otherwise they're prone to tangles and mats because of their long, thick fur. Mummy also..." Her voice quavered and she swallowed. "Mummy also liked to bathe them regularly, with a shampoo and conditioner, sometimes with a degreaser and even a colour enhancer treatment. And then we would blow dry their fur... Ours are show cats, you see, so we have to keep them in top condition. So even if we're not taking them to a show, they still each need about an hour every day."

Bloody hell. I thought guiltily of my once-a-month hasty brush of Muesli and felt like a neglectful owner. Still, I doubted that my naughty little tabby would ever lie placidly on her side like this Persian was doing, and allow herself to be pulled and prodded for hours.

Cassie must have been having similar thoughts

because she gave a snort of laughter and said, "We had a cat growing up—a big ginger tom—and you would never have been able to wash him! I think we tried to once and he nearly ripped us to shreds."

"You have to start when they're kittens and get them used to it," said Mary. She looked down, fiddling with a brush. "Actually, I... I probably didn't need to groom Tabitha today but... I... I needed something to do."

"Were you all right last night?" I asked. "That was really why I stopped by. I wanted to check that you were okay."

She smiled gratefully. "Thank you. Yes, I did what you said and then went to bed. Aunt Audrey came to see me early this morning. She said she would help me with Mr Grimsby, our family solicitor, and also help me sort out Mummy's papers, and organise the funeral."

"When's that going to be?" asked Cassie gently.

Mary licked her lips nervously. "I... I'm not sure yet. Mummy had some very specific instructions for how she wanted things and I... I wanted to make sure I followed... maybe at the end of this week...? And I... I suppose I need to speak to the college too, about a memorial service..." She swallowed convulsively. "I... I just can't believe that she's really gone. I mean, I knew that her heart wasn't good—Dr Foster did warn us—but I suppose I just thought those pills would fix everything."

Mention of the pills made me think of the

71

conversation with my mother that morning and I said impulsively, "Mary, I hope you don't mind me asking but there was something I was curious about."

"Yes?" She looked at me enquiringly.

"You know your mother's angina tablets—the ones she had with her at the show—she kept them in a little enamel pillbox, didn't she?"

Mary nodded. "It was given to Mummy by her mother—my grandmother—and she really liked it. She used to keep her daily vitamins in there, then she started using it for her heart pills so that she could carry some with her wherever she went. She hated those metal foil packets that pills come in these days."

"Do you know how many tablets she normally carried in her pillbox? Like how many she had with her at the show yesterday?"

"She usually carried six with her. Mummy always said that was a good number."

"Can you..." I hesitated, knowing that this sounded like a bizarre request. "Can you find the pillbox and check?"

Mary looked slightly puzzled but she went obediently to the front of the house, with us following. In the foyer, she rummaged through a large leather handbag sitting on the hall table, then pulled something out and handed it to me. It was a beautiful circular Victorian pillbox, with a delicate enamel top and silver base.

I flipped it open and silently counted. There were six white tablets resting inside.

CHAPTER SEVEN

"What was that all about?" asked Cassie as we came out of Eccleston House. "Why were you asking Mary all that about her mother's heart pills?"

I told her about my conversation with my mother that morning.

"Well, couldn't Dame Clare have carried some more pills somewhere else? Like in a pocket or another box thingy?" said Cassie.

"You heard what Mary said just now when I asked that. She said her mother was very fussy and only carried the tablets in that pillbox."

"So… are you saying your mother was right and Dame Clare never got any pills from her own box?"

"Yes, which makes you wonder how she got the pill she was clutching in her hand when she died."

Cassie gave me a sidelong look. "You sure it was

a heart pill and not something else?"

"Well, her doctor identified it but..." I trailed off, remembering my mother's scathing comments about Dr Foster's abilities. What if the old doctor had been wrong? What if Dame Clare *hadn't* died of a heart attack?

I felt an uneasy feeling start to gnaw at the base of my spine. We walked in silence back to the car. As I approached the driver's door, I felt in my coat pocket for the car keys. They weren't there. I thrust my hand deeper into the pocket and discovered why: there was a ragged hole at the bottom where the seams of the fabric had come undone.

"Blast! My keys must have dropped out while we were walking around the garden earlier." I glanced back towards the house. "I'm going to have to go back and look for them."

"You want me to come with you?"

"No, I'll just be two secs. I'm sure they're somewhere along the path around the side of the house. I remember taking my coat off when we went into the house and if the keys had fallen out then, they would have been in the foyer. So they must have dropped out while we were looking for Mary in the gardens."

I hurried back around the side of the house towards the rear, retracing our steps from earlier. I had gone almost all the way to the back when I saw the glint of metal in the neatly trimmed grass at the edge of the path. *Aha!* I crouched down and scooped the keys up.

As I rose to my feet, a sweet perfume wafted over me and I looked around for the source of the fragrance. It must have come from the bank of old-fashioned roses growing alongside the path. I stepped closer to the flower bed and leaned down, inhaling deeply. They were gorgeous—somehow the smell of fresh flowers could never be captured in a bottle, no matter how expensive the label.

I straightened and looked around with pleasure. Unlike the landscaped formality at the front of the house, the gardens at the back had been left in a more informal style—in fact, much more like an English cottage garden. There were great swathes of delphiniums, foxgloves, and hollyhocks, and the sweet williams so beloved of the Victorians; rambling roses and a romantic wisteria in the corner, and bees humming busily through the fragrant blooms. The unseasonably warm spring we'd had meant that many of the flowers seemed to be blooming early. I pressed my nose to the rose petals again for one last sniff, then, smiling to myself, I turned back towards the path.

A man was standing right behind me.

He was so close—practically breathing down my neck—that I crashed into him as I turned around. I stifled a scream and staggered back into the soft earth of the flower bed, clutching a hand to my chest.

"Oh my God! You nearly scared me to death!"

He said nothing but stood there watching me. He was a tall, cadaverous-looking man in his fifties, I guessed, with the slightly stooped posture of someone who spent a lot of time bending over. He had deep-set eyes and a thin, lipless mouth. From the overalls he was wearing and the trowel he held in one hand, I guessed him to be the gardener.

"I... I was just admiring the roses..." I stammered, wondering why I felt compelled to explain. It wasn't as if I owed him an explanation. And yet something about the way he stood there, like a grim executioner, made me nervous.

I took another step back and felt my heel sink further into the soft soil, making me pitch backwards. He reached out and grabbed me, yanking me out of the flower bed. Then without a word to me, he dropped to his knees and began patting the soil back into place, rearranging it around the sweet williams which had been disturbed.

"Oh, sorry... didn't mean to step on them..." I trailed off, annoyed with myself for feeling the need to explain again.

What was it about the human psyche that made you feel compelled to speak when the other person remained silent? It was something clever investigators took advantage of in their interviews, I knew, and I was irritated to find myself falling into the same trap.

In any case, this isn't a criminal interview and

this man is just being plain rude! I thought, frowning down at his bent head. A voice called suddenly behind us.

"Joseph? Joseph, I thought—oh, there you are…" Mary Eccleston came into view around the side of the house. She paused at the sight of me. "Gemma? I thought you'd left already?"

"I had—except that I got to my car and realised that I had dropped my car keys so I came back to find them." I raised my hand and jingled the keys. "I found them by the path here and I was admiring some of your flowers when Joseph came up behind me." I couldn't quite keep the note of accusation out of my voice. "He gave me a bit of a scare."

Mary gave him a reproachful look. "Oh Joseph, Mummy said you must stop doing that." She turned to me apologetically. "Joseph is ever so quiet—he walks like a cat."

Joseph said nothing, his head bent, still intent on repairing the flower bed. There was an awkward silence, then Mary looked at me apologetically. "I hope you weren't hurt or anything, Gemma?"

"Oh, no, no, I'm fine. I think the flowerbed suffered more than me," I said with a chuckle.

Joseph turned his head and shot me a look filled with so much hostility that I was taken aback.

I cleared my throat. "Erm… Anyway, I must be getting on."

"I'll walk you back to the front of the house," Mary said, falling into step beside me. Once we were a bit farther away from Joseph, she said in an undertone, "I hope you weren't upset by Joseph. Mummy and I have got used to him but I know people can find him a bit strange. You see, he doesn't really speak, unless you talk to his plants. But he's a lamb really."

I couldn't think of anyone who had less resemblance to a lamb but I kept my thoughts to myself. And she didn't really say "talk *to* his plants", did she? It must have been a slip of the tongue, I decided.

"Don't worry, he didn't upset me—just gave me a bit of a fright, that's all," I reassured her. "Hey, listen... if you need anything—or just feel like you need someone to talk to—don't hesitate to give me a ring."

Mary looked surprised and pleased. She gave me a tremulous smile. "Thank you."

I walked slowly back down the drive to my car, my thoughts humming as busily as the bees had been back in the garden. I was remembering Mary telling me that Joseph had helped them load the car for the show yesterday morning. I wondered if he had known about Dame Clare's heart condition...

***

I was still feeling a bit low by the time I returned

to my parents' house. Cassie had kept up a stream of cheerful conversation on our way back, but once I'd dropped her off and was left to my own thoughts, I found myself sinking into a gloom again. I knew I just had to keep looking—I would find a place to rent eventually—but I couldn't help feeling demoralised. Oxford was so expensive... how would I ever find a suitable place within my budget?

As I let myself into the house, my spirits sank even further when I heard the clink of china and the babble of excited voices coming from the sitting room. *Uh-oh.* It sounded like my mother was having one of her Sunday afternoon tea parties. The last thing I felt like doing right now was making polite conversation with a bunch of well-meaning, middle-class housewives who all seemed to have an abnormal interest in my love life.

I crept along the hall, hoping to get past the living room doorway without being seen and escape upstairs to my room.

No such luck.

"Oh, darling! You're back!"

I stifled a groan and went reluctantly into the sitting room. When I stepped in, though, I was relieved to see that instead of my mother's usual crowd, there were four little old ladies sitting on the sofa around her. It was the Old Biddies—the Senior Command of Meadowford-on-Smythe: loud, bossy Mabel Cooke, eighty-going-on-eighteen Glenda Bailey, plump and food-loving Florence Doyle, and quiet, gentle Ethel Webb. Okay, so they were nosy and meddling in their own way, but somehow I didn't mind it so much.

"I thought you'd be back earlier, Gemma," said my mother.

"I stopped off to see Mary Eccleston," I explained.

"Ah!" Mabel pounced on me. "We were just talking about her." She sat forwards on the sofa, balancing a teacup on her knees. "Your mother has been telling us about your discussion at breakfast this morning and the Mystery of the Untouched Pillbox!" She made it sound like a Nancy Drew book.

My mother looked at me eagerly. "Did you mention it to Mary?"

"Yes, actually, I did," I admitted.

"And?" Five pairs of eyes stared avidly at me.

"It doesn't look like the pills were disturbed," I admitted. "There were six tablets in the pillbox and Mary said they always carried six with them when they went to shows."

"You see?" my mother said triumphantly. "I told you I am never wrong."

"But what does this mean?" asked Florence, helping herself to a jam tart from the tea tray.

"I'll tell you what it means," said Mabel. "It means that Dame Clare was *murdered*, just as I suspected!"

"Ooh!" Glenda squealed, although whether with delight or horror it was hard to tell.

"Hang on... Don't you think you're all rather jumping to conclusions?" I said weakly.

"Nonsense, darling. It makes perfect sense," said my mother. "I wouldn't be surprised in the least if that horrible woman was murdered."

Mabel nodded in agreement. "If you ask me, there is no shortage of people wishing to do her harm. Ask anyone in the village. Dame Clare was a tyrant and a bully and I should say that she will hardly be missed."

"Oh Mabel, hush! One shouldn't really speak ill of the dead like this," said Ethel.

"I'm only speaking the truth," said Mabel with a sniff. "That woman would have tempted a saint to murder. Heaven knows how that daughter of hers endured it for so many years. At least the poor child is free now."

Glenda gave a gasp. "Maybe it's her! The daughter!"

Florence nodded excitedly. "Yes, yes, *and* I shouldn't wonder if Mary inherits all of Dame Clare's money. That would be a double reason to murder her mother."

"Wasn't there a case where a son murdered his father by putting poison in his breakfast marmalade?" said Glenda excitedly. "It was to get his money—and the son was such a charming young man too."

"That was in a novel by Agatha Christie," I protested. "It was fiction, not real life."

"But that's the point—it *could* be true," said Mabel, completely missing the point of "fiction". "And Mary Eccleston would have been in the ideal position to poison her mother!"

"This is ridiculous!" I burst out. "Mary Eccleston is a really sweet girl; she's so shy and quiet. She's... she's as docile as a lamb! I just can't believe that she could have murdered her mother. I took her home from the fête yesterday and you should have seen how upset she was."

"Ah... but she could have been putting on an act for your benefit, couldn't she?" said Mabel quickly.

I thought back to Mary's clenched hands and pale face as she sat in the car next to me. "No, I don't believe it! No one could be that upset and just be acting."

"Oh, but that's why people win Oscars, isn't it, darling?" my mother chimed in. "Because they are such wonderful actors and actresses that they fool us all. I mean, Meryl Streep certainly never lost a child to the Nazis but she still made us cry in *Sophie's Choice*."

"Yes, but that's different," I insisted. "Mary is... she's not a professional actress! And even with actors and actresses, they say close friends and family can tell if they're being genuine."

"But you're *not* a close friend, dear," Mabel pointed out. "You don't really know Mary very well at all. In fact, none of us do. Mary Eccleston has always lived in the shadow of her mother. Nobody really knows what she's like."

"I still think it's a ludicrous suggestion," I said stubbornly. "This is all just speculation. You've got no real evidence against Mary."

"Aha." The Old Biddies and my mother exchanged a meaningful look.

"What?" I said quickly.

"Nothing," said my mother airily—a bit too airily. I gave her a suspicious look but she simply gestured to the tray on the table and said, "Would you like some tea and cakes, darling?"

Wow, my mother had really gone to town with the baking that afternoon. There was a full afternoon tea service in dainty bone china, accompanied by a selection of freshly baked scones, hot buttered crumpets, dainty little jam tarts, and slices of lemon drizzle cake, which all looked delicious. I was sorely tempted but shook my head.

"No, thanks, Mother. I don't want to spoil my appetite for dinner. Devlin's coming to pick me up around six. I'm just going to dash upstairs now for a quick shower."

"Oh. Yes. I'd forgotten about that." My mother looked like she wished she *could* forget about it. She compressed her lips. "Well, don't let him keep you out too late, darling. Make sure you're back by ten."

"Mother. I'm not a teenager anymore," I said impatiently. "I think at twenty-nine I'm entitled to stay out as late as I like. I've got the spare key so you needn't wait up for me."

"Yes, well... I just don't like the thought of you out alone on the streets at night with *him*." She made Devlin sound like Jack the Ripper.

I glowered at her. "Devlin is a perfect gentleman."

"Oh, but you just never know, darling, do you, what... er... habits Devlin might have picked up from his criminal associations—"

"*Aaaarrgghh!*" I contradicted my fine statement earlier by regressing straight back to my teenage years and storming out of the room.

CHAPTER EIGHT

Devlin had chosen a lovely little French crêperie in Little Clarendon Street for dinner and it was the perfect setting for a quiet, romantic meal. Unfortunately, my boyfriend didn't seem to appreciate the surroundings much. He spent most of the dinner looking down at his food, a frown on his face, and seemed to be lost in thought. Finally, as we were being served dessert—a delicious apple cinnamon crêpe—he looked up at me with an apologetic smile.

"Sorry, Gemma. I'm not being a very good dinner companion this evening."

"It's okay," I said, trying to be understanding. "Long day?"

He sighed and finished his glass of wine, then leaned back. "Yeah, and most of it pretty tedious and boring."

"Are you still sorting out the stuff from what happened at the fête?"

Devlin made a sound of frustration. "Yes. It's bloody annoying. To think that the CID is being beaten by a bunch of petty thieves!"

"Well, not that petty, from the sound of it. Didn't you say they could be an organised gang?"

"Yeah, it's looking that way. The thefts are just too well planned and executed."

"Did you find the quad bikes taken at the fête?"

Devlin shook his head. "No, and the Superintendent wasn't too happy about that, I can tell you. It was a huge embarrassment to have his top CID man there and for the bikes to be stolen from right under our noses."

"Well, you can't be everywhere all the time," I said reasonably. "You were dealing with Dame Clare's death at the cat show. Speaking of which..." I leaned forwards. "Are the police happy with the verdict on that?"

Devlin looked surprised. "Yes, why wouldn't we be?"

I shrugged. "I just wondered if maybe there was any... um... uncertainty about the cause of death."

"No, her doctor signed the death certificate. Death from natural causes. Heart attack."

"And you trust his opinion?"

Devlin looked at me curiously. "What's this about, Gemma?" Then understanding dawned on his face and he groaned. "Don't tell me: you've been speaking to Mabel Cooke and her friends."

"Well, not just them... my mother too... They all think that there's something fishy about Dame Clare's death at the show."

"What do you mean: 'fishy'? You're talking about 'foul play', aren't you? Mabel thinks it was murder... as usual," said Devlin dryly.

I grinned. Devlin was feeling less charitable than usual towards the Old Biddies because of an incident two weeks ago when they had got him and an entire SOCO team out to the village school to investigate a "suspicious mound" which had appeared overnight on the front lawn. Mabel had been sure it was a buried body. It had turned out to be a large marrow bone which Mrs Patterson's Newfoundland had stashed there for future enjoyment.

"The thing is, there *is* something that doesn't quite add up," I said.

"Which is?"

Quickly, I told him about the pillbox inconsistency. Devlin wasn't particularly impressed.

"Gemma, there could be any number of reasons to explain that," he said impatiently. "You can't jump to conclusions based on your mother's vague memory. She could have been wrong."

"My mother is never wrong," I said without thinking.

Devlin gave me a look.

I held up my hands. "Okay, okay, that's not true—but in this instance, I do think she's right. There *is* something odd about this whole thing with the angina pills... I mean, what if they were tampered with or... Do you still have the pill that Dame Clare was holding in her hand?" I asked suddenly.

"Yes, I believe so."

"Can you test it? Please? Just to verify what it is."

Devlin sighed. "All right. I'll ask them to check it tomorrow. But ten to one, Mabel and her friends are just making a mountain out of a molehill as usual." He sat back and changed the subject. "How did the house-hunting go today?"

I told him about my disheartening afternoon.

"Don't worry, you'll find somewhere eventually," said Devlin. "And if you don't... well, I've been thinking, Gemma, maybe you'd like to—"

"Would you like some tea or coffee?" The waitress paused by our table.

"Nothing for me, thanks," said Devlin.

"Me neither," I said. "That was delicious. Thank you."

We paid and left the restaurant, stepping out into a balmy spring evening. Devlin clasped my hand in his and we strolled down the wide pavement. Little Clarendon Street was one of the prettiest streets in Oxford at night, with quaint little boutique shops and cafés lining the street, and fairy lights strung across the space between the buildings, forming a sort of twinkling canopy above our heads. We walked slowly, reluctant to get back to Devlin's car and end the evening.

"You could come back to my place," Devlin suggested, his hand warm against my skin as he caressed the nape of my neck.

I sighed. "I'd better not. It's pretty late and you've got an early start tomorrow, even if I have the day off. Besides, I haven't seen Muesli much today. I've been out and busy all day. I should probably spend a bit of time with her before going to bed."

"Rejected in favour of a cat," Devlin teased. "Still, since it's Muesli, I'll forgive you. Okay, how about I give you a call tomorrow evening then? If I manage to get off on time, maybe we can grab some takeaway and go back to my place."

"Sounds great," I said with a smile.

A short while later, we pulled up outside my parents' residence and I glanced up at the elegant Victorian townhouse. There seemed to be a glow of light behind the thick drapes at the front bay windows. I felt a prickle of irritation, hoping that my mother hadn't stayed up to wait for me. This was ridiculous. I felt like I was eighteen again, creeping home after an illicit night out with the undesirable boyfriend. I laughed to myself. In a way, not much had changed.

"What's so funny?" said Devlin.

"Nothing. Just... something ironic..." I put my

hand on the door handle. "Thanks for a lovely evening."

Devlin leaned towards me and pulled me into his arms. I melted against him as his lips trailed gently from my earlobe down the side of my jaw, towards the corner of my mouth. I turned my head and our lips met, his mouth slanting across mine as he kissed me until I was breathless. His hands drifted down my side and I heard a soft click, then felt my seatbelt being released, freeing me to turn more fully into his arms. The windows of the car were steaming up. My pulse raced as Devlin pulled me even closer, his body hard against mine...

A loud rapping sounded on the glass next to us. *RAP-RAP-RAP!*

"What the hell—?" Devlin jerked up.

I looked at my window and yelped.

Four wrinkled old faces were peering through the fogged-up window, their noses squashed grotesquely against the glass. A gnarled, old hand rapped again on the glass.

"Gemma?" came my mother's voice. "Gemma, are you in there?"

Oh God.

Devlin muttered under his breath and looked away, running a hand through his hair as I hastily rearranged my clothing and sat up in the front passenger seat. I lowered the window pane to find myself staring at my mother, surrounded by the Old Biddies. They thrust their heads into the opening, jostling with each other to get a better view.

"Gemma? We heard the car pulling up but when you didn't come in, we came out to see what was going on. What on *earth* are you doing in the car?" my mother said.

Glenda giggled next to her. "I expect they are— what do the Americans call it—'making out'?"

I flushed, mortified. "We... we were just saying good night," I said, with as much dignity as I could muster.

Mabel glared at Devlin and wagged a finger at him. "If you spent less time snogging in cars, young man, and more time investigating suspicious deaths, we wouldn't have a potential murderer running around the village."

"Oh, don't badger the boy, Mabel," said Glenda. "He's allowed to have a night off! And besides, you know what they say—all work and no play makes Devlin a dull boy!" She giggled again.

Oh God. This isn't happening to me.

By now, lights were coming on in the street and neighbours were starting to peer out of windows and come out onto front doorsteps. I could just imagine the gossip that would be making the rounds tomorrow.

"Well! I think it's disgusting behaviour," said my mother, pursing her lips. "You should have been escorted to your door, Gemma, like a proper lady." She gave Devlin a dirty look. "A real gentleman wouldn't have been mauling you in a car in the middle of the street."

"Devlin was not mauling me!" I cried, exasperated. "We were just... Look, can you go in now, please? I'll be along in a minute."

My mother sniffed with disapproval but withdrew her head from the window, followed by the rest of the Old Biddies—although not before Glenda gave us a lewd wink.

"Sorry," I muttered to Devlin as I raised the window again. "I don't know what the Old Biddies are still doing here. They came for tea earlier and should have left hours ago..."

"Probably roped in by your mother to make sure you were escorted safely to your door like a lady," said Devlin with a wry chuckle.

I rolled my eyes. "I don't know which century she's living in! Honestly, this is ridiculous! I'm nearly thirty and I have absolutely no privacy... Living with my parents is driving me crazy! I need to get a place of my own!" I sighed and my shoulders sagged. "But I don't know how I'm going to find anywhere I can afford in Oxford..."

Devlin reached out and gave my hand a squeeze. "Look, Gemma... I wasn't sure about saying anything because I didn't want to rush you but... I was going to suggest this in the restaurant earlier: how about if you moved in with me?"

I stared at him. "With you?"

"Yes," said Devlin evenly. "I've got the space, we want to spend more time together, you want to get out of your parents' pocket... It seems like the perfect solution."

"You mean... live together?"

He shrugged. "You don't have to think of it like that, if you don't want to. Think of it as sharing a place with a friend." He gave me a sexy grin. "A very *good* friend."

"Don't answer me now," he added, as he saw me hesitating. "Take your time and think about it. But the offer is there if you want." He leaned across and gave me a quick kiss on the lips. "And now you'd better go in, Miss Rose, before I'm tempted to maul you again."

I laughed and gave him a peck on the cheek, then let myself out of the car and ran up the steps to the front door where my mother and the Old Biddies were hovering in the doorway, waiting for me.

CHAPTER NINE

I was up bright and early the next morning and came downstairs half expecting to find my parents at breakfast but, to my surprise, the house was empty. My father, I remembered, was out this morning—it was one of the few days when he still lectured at the University—but my mother had left me a mysterious note saying she was out "doing some investigating". Hmm... I had a slightly uneasy feeling about that. But I tried to ignore it and instead, as I set about rustling up some milk and cereal for breakfast, I thought again about Devlin's offer to move in with him. I felt a little thrill at the thought. Should I say yes?

Why not? Devlin was right—it was the ideal solution. We could spend more time together, I wouldn't have to worry about my budget, it would be easy for getting to work... and I wouldn't have the hassle with "pet-friendly" landlords either. Aside from the fact that Devlin's place was in the country, away from the main roads, Muesli absolutely *loved* him—and I knew that she had him completely wrapped around her little paw.

My mind began conjuring up a romantic daydream of cosy evenings with me cuddled up against Devlin on the couch, my head on his shoulder, his hand gently stroking my hair, as we watched TV together...

The sound of the kettle boiling brought me back to reality and I hastily pushed the daydream away as I made myself a mug of tea. *Mustn't rush into things*, I decided. *I must think about it some more.*

Mondays were my day off—although "day off" usually translated into a day catching up on emails and admin. This morning, though, as I sat down to do some dreary accounting, I realised that I had left some of the paperwork I needed at the tearoom. It wasn't really urgent—I could get the papers tomorrow and finish off the accounting in the evenings or when I was next off—but when I looked out of the window and saw the spring sunshine, I decided to cycle out to Meadowford to get them now.

Ten minutes later, as my bicycle headed out of Oxford and I breathed deeply of the fresh air, I smiled to myself. Getting through the long dark winter had been the hardest thing I'd faced since coming back from Australia. Somehow, the romantic memories of England had omitted all the cold wintry mornings and gloomy grey days, the freezing fog and the icy wind numbing your fingers and slicing right through your clothes into your very bones. And the relentless rain! It had only taken me a few weeks back in the country to finally understand why the English were so obsessed with the weather. Still, it looked like Spring had arrived at last: aside from a few April showers and one night of sudden frost, it had been bright and sunny in the past week, and the warmer weather seemed here to stay.

The village seemed unusually quiet this morning and I didn't see anyone I knew well enough to stop and chat. Surprisingly, I also didn't see the Old Biddies anywhere. I would have thought that they'd be out and about in the village first thing, catching up with the other senior residents on the gossip from the weekend.

I got to the tearoom, ran in and picked up the papers, then turned my bike around to head for home. But a part of me wanted to prolong the lovely excuse to be out enjoying the countryside so, instead of taking the usual route, I decided to take a detour which would go through some back country lanes. It would take a bit longer but hey—it was my day off, right?

It was only as I was freewheeling along a narrow lane surrounded on either side by neatly trimmed hedges that I realised I was very close to Eccleston

House. In fact, the hedge that ran alongside the road to my right bordered the rear of the property and, as I followed the curve of the road around the bend and the hedge thinned out, the house itself came into view. Seen from the rear, it wasn't as grand but it was still an imposing residence, with its classical proportions and Palladian architectural features—

Wait. What was that?

I squinted through the trees surrounding the property, then my eyes widened and stared.

No way. I must be seeing things.

The bike sailed closer and, through a gap in the trees, I saw four small figures climbing furtively into an open window.

I nearly crashed my bike.

It was the Old Biddies.

What on earth were they doing?

Hastily, I pulled over and jumped off my bike, then thrust it against a tree and sprinted towards the house. I arrived just as Glenda and Ethel were trying to shove Florence over the window ledge, while Mabel—who was already inside—was trying to pull her in.

"Push! Push! Harder!" ordered Mabel, tugging on Florence's hands.

"We... we are!" puffed Glenda as she and Ethel shoved themselves ineffectually against Florence's ample bottom. "I told you—you need to lose weight, Flo—"

"WHAT ARE YOU DOING?" I demanded, coming up behind them.

"Eeek!"

Glenda and Ethel sprang up guiltily; Mabel jumped and let go of Florence, who flailed her arms wildly, then pitched backwards and landed with a thump in the flower bed beneath the window.

"Gemma!" said Mabel, recovering with spectacular aplomb. "Er... how lovely to see you, dear."

"*What* are you doing?" I repeated.

"We were just... ah... ha-ha... er..."

"Admiring Dame Clare's windows," supplied Glenda.

"Yes!" said Mabel, nodding vigorously. "We heard so much about the... er... marvellous architecture of Eccleston House..."

"And we're taking a course on Georgian architecture at the community centre," Ethel chimed in.

Bloody hell, how can they look like such sweet, little old ladies and be such slick, remorseless liars?

"You weren't admiring the window, you were *climbing in* the window," I said tartly.

"I think we'd better tell her," said Florence, standing up and wincing as she rubbed her sore bottom.

"Oh, very well," said Mabel irritably. She drew herself up grandly and said, "We were conducting a search of the premises."

"You were breaking and entering!" I said. "Even the police can't search a property without a warrant—what were you thinking?"

"Oh, tosh!" said Mabel scornfully. "We were only going to have a nosy around, no harm done—"

"Yes, we only wanted to find out a bit more about the Ecclestons," said Glenda.

I looked beyond Mabel's shoulder. She seemed to be standing in some sort of small utility room. It was the room where Cassie and I had found Mary grooming the cat yesterday, I realised.

"What if Mary had come in and found you here?" I said.

"Oh, she's not home this morning," said Mabel, waving her hand dismissively. "We made sure of that. She's gone with Audrey Simmons to see the family solicitor. And your mother's distracting the maid at the front door—"

"My *what*?" I stared at them, aghast. "Don't tell me you've got my mother roped into this as well?"

"Oh, she's marvellous, Gemma," gushed Glenda. "She's got such an elegant way about her, nobody would believe that she's telling fibs about things—"

"Oh my God, I don't believe I'm hearing this," I muttered.

"You could help us, Gemma," Florence suggested hopefully, looking me up and down. "You're a lot thinner and lighter on your feet."

"Yes, yes, why don't you climb in and have a quick look around the house?" asked Mabel.

Glenda nodded eagerly. "Maybe even go upstairs—"

"No!" I said. "Are you mad? No, no, we're all leaving now and just hope that the Ecclestons haven't installed any security cameras!"

Five minutes later, four sulky little old ladies shuffled beside me as I led the way around the side of the house and back onto the front drive. I saw my mother as soon as we got there. She was standing on the front doorstep, chatting to an olive-skinned girl in an apron—Riza, the Ecclestons' maid. The girl was gesticulating wildly, obviously in the middle of telling a story:

"... and the Madam, she is very angry—shouting and screaming like crazy person. She said, *'You stupid girl! You always put it back the wrong way! How many times do I have to tell you? Are you an imbecile?'* Yes, ma'am, she say that," Riza recounted with relish. "And then she throws book at Miss Mary!"

"Oh my goodness, did she really?" said my mother with melodramatic horror. "And what did Miss Mary do?"

"She flip out, ma'am! First time I see that! She is always so quiet, you know, ma'am, so good to her mother, but this time, she go crazy!" Riza laughed, her eyes bright with malicious enjoyment. "Miss Mary, she stand up and shout back. *'I'M SICK AND TIRED OF BEING YOUR SLAVE,'* she say. And then she scream, *'I HATE YOU! I WISH YOU WERE*

101

DEAD!' and she run out of the room.*"*

"Really?" My mother sounded absolutely delighted. "And this was just the night before the fête? I wonder if—"

"Mother."

She whirled around and saw us standing at the bottom of the steps. Then her gaze slid past us just as I heard the sound of an engine coming up the drive. I turned around myself to see a pale blue Mini Cooper roll down the driveway and come to a halt in front of the steps. Mary and Audrey got out of the car.

"My goodness, this is quite a party here," observed Audrey with a laugh.

"Oh, we just came to see how Mary was doing," said my mother glibly as she came down the stairs to join us. I saw Riza scurry quickly off into the interior of the house.

My mother looked at Mary soberly. "My dear, I haven't had a chance to say how very sorry I am about your mother. Please accept my condolences."

The Old Biddies gathered around and repeated the sentiments. I restrained the urge to roll my eyes. Honestly! I couldn't believe their brazen hypocrisy when they had just been snooping around, trying to find evidence to accuse the poor girl of murder!

Mary murmured her thanks, looking slightly bemused. "Thank you... I... it's not really sunk in yet. Even in the solicitor's office, when they were discussing Mummy's will..."

Mabel cleared her throat delicately. "I suppose your mother has left you amply cared for?"

Mary flushed. "Yes... I knew about her will from before... I'm the sole beneficiary of her estate."

The Old Biddies waggled their eyebrows at each other.

I said quickly, hoping Mary hadn't seen them: "Is the college going to hold a memorial service?"

"Yes, I think so—but just a small one in the college chapel." Mary sighed. "They were all so shocked when I told them this morning. No one could believe that Mummy had died of a heart attack so suddenly—"

"I don't suppose there *was* any question that it was a heart attack?" said my mother.

Mary stared at her. "What do you mean?"

"Nothing, she doesn't mean anything by it," I said quickly. "Um... anyway, I think we should leave you now—"

"Mary, you've got to show them the note," said Audrey urgently.

The Old Biddies pounced. "What note?"

Mary hesitated, biting her lip.

"Mary..." Audrey pleaded again. "You can't just ignore it. You really ought to be reporting it to the police. Ask Gemma and the others. I'm sure they'll agree with me."

Mary swallowed, then said, "This morning, before we went to see Mr Grimsby, Aunt Audrey and I were in Mummy's room—you know, just to... Anyway, I was tidying up her dressing table and I found a note tucked into the top drawer."

"A note? You mean like a message?" I asked.

"Well, not a normal message. It was—" Mary swallowed again. "It was saying the most horrible things."

"Can we see?" asked Mabel eagerly.

Mary stuck her hand into her handbag and withdrew a piece of paper. Mabel grabbed it and the Old Biddies pored over it. I saw their faces change. Then they thrust it at me. My mother peered over my shoulder as I spread the paper out and slowly read the contents.

There were a series of words spread across the page but they were not written or even typed. Instead, they were made up of printed letters which had been neatly cut out of some magazine or newspaper and stuck on, one by one. There was something a bit creepy about that in itself, even before you read the words that the letters spelt out. In crude, vicious language, the sender had called Clare Eccleston some of the foulest names you could call a woman and added that she would soon be getting what she deserved.

At the bottom of the message was a picture of Dame Clare which must have been cut out of a University publication, for she was in her formal senior academic gown—except that her face had been disfigured, the eyes scratched out with savage ferocity and a big black "X" drawn across the mouth. There was no signature at the bottom.

I shivered. There was no question about it. Somebody out there had hated Clare Eccleston—maybe even hated her enough to murder her.

CHAPTER TEN

I took a shuddering breath. Even though it was not directed at me, there was something shocking and disturbing about such a letter. The hatred and vitriol practically oozed off the page and even touching the note made me feel a bit tainted. I handed it hastily back to Mary.

"When did this arrive?" I asked.

"I'm not sure—I think it was last Friday morning, the day before the fête. I remember bringing the mail in and there was an unmarked envelope with Mummy's name on it. I saw her open it and she looked a bit funny, but then she put it away and didn't say anything, so I didn't dare ask her about it."

"Do you know if your mother's ever received a note like this before?"

Mary frowned. "She did get some unpleasant letters in college last year."

"Same in style? With these cut-out letters?"

"No, those were different. They were typed on a computer... and the college authorities did find who had sent them in the end. It was a couple of students playing a nasty prank. They were disciplined and suspended for a term."

I looked again at the note held in Mary's hands. The paper itself was just the typical kind of cheap photocopy paper that you would get in any printer. It gave no clue as to the sender.

"I think Audrey is right and you should show this to the police, Mary," I said. "They might be able to trace who sent it."

"But... but why? I mean, Mummy is dead now so it doesn't matter anymore, does it?"

"It's just so horrible!" said Audrey, her face distressed. "Someone who could write something so nasty—It just suggests a... a disturbed mind. I'm worried for you, dear. What if they target you next?"

"Besides, it *could* have something to do with your mother's mur—I mean, death," said Mabel.

Audrey looked startled and Mary said in a scared voice, "What do you mean?" She turned to my mother. "You were asking me about Mummy just now—why do you think she might *not* have had a heart attack? *What are you all trying to say*?"

"We just think someone might have had a grudge against your mother, dear," said Ethel gently.

Florence nodded. "Yes, and they might have meant her harm."

Mary paled. "You mean—" She shook her head violently. "No! No! Mummy had a heart attack! I was there—I saw her! And we know she was trying to get her pills—"

"Ah, but that's just it," said Mabel quickly. "We don't know that for sure. Gemma told us that you checked and the tablets in her pillbox were untouched, so..." She trailed off suggestively.

Mary shook her head again. "No, I'm sure Mummy just had a heart attack! And as for the note—I'm sure it's just a silly thing. Just like those prank letters in college last year! It's *nothing* to bother the police about!" she said vehemently.

There was an awkward silence following this outburst. Then Audrey cleared her throat and said, resorting to the usual English solution for every social problem:

"Er... would you like a cup of tea?"

"No, thank you, we really must be going," I said quickly, before my mother or the Old Biddies could answer. I dragged my phone out of my pocket to check the time on the screen. "Heavens, look at the time! I have to—"

"Oh, that's little... Muesli, isn't it?" said Audrey as she caught sight of my phone screensaver. "What a gorgeous shot!"

She smiled down at the screen which showed Muesli sitting on a windowsill, her head cocked to one side, her green eyes bright and curious, and one little white paw raised as if she was waving.

I gave a sheepish laugh. "Yes, that's Muesli doing one of her tricks. I've taught her to high-five."

"That's delightful!" said Audrey. "In fact, I noticed at the fête that she is a very outgoing little cat. Hmm, I wonder..." She looked at me speculatively. "Would you be interested in having Muesli join the Therapy Cats programme?"

"Therapy Cats?" I said, giving her a wry smile. "That's not what I think it means, is it? I mean, there are times when I think Muesli needs therapy but I was hoping no one would notice."

Audrey gave a little laugh. "It's a new initiative of the Cotswolds Cat Fancy Club. You've heard of pet therapy, haven't you? It's been shown that spending time with animals has huge health benefits—not just the medical, like lowering your blood pressure—but also things like relieving stress, reducing loneliness and depression, and improving social interactions. It was my idea, actually," she said with shy pride. "There's a team in Oxfordshire which takes dogs into places but I knew there weren't any visiting cats and I thought—why not? And the cat club committee supported my idea. So the programme has been going for a few months now but we're still actively looking for volunteers."

"How lovely," said my mother. "I think it's a marvellous idea and I'm sure Muesli would make the perfect therapy cat. She is such a friendly, inquisitive little thing—I'm sure she would love going to visit hospitals and rest homes and such."

Yeah, and cause mayhem wherever she went, I thought. "She's very naughty, you know," I warned Audrey.

Audrey twittered. "Oh, the naughty ones are the best sometimes! Why don't you just bring her along for an assessment?" She added in a lower voice, darting an apologetic look at Mary, "Clare would normally be doing the assessments as she was the Programme Leader and she had far more experience with cats, of course, but since the... um... I've taken over the responsibilities."

And thank goodness, I thought. I couldn't imagine what it would have been like if my mother had to endure more of Dame Clare's contemptuous comments about Muesli.

We arranged a time on Thursday and then I hustled my mother and the Old Biddies down the drive before they could make any more suggestive comments about Clare Eccleston's death. My mother had parked her car just outside the property and I left her and the Old Biddies there, conferring in excited whispers, whilst I went back down the side lane to retrieve my bicycle. When I returned, I found my mother alone.

"Where are the Old Bid—where are Mabel and the others?" I asked.

"Oh, they've gone off in Mabel's car. She'd parked it around the corner. There's an amateur lawn bowls game on the village green that they wanted to get back for. Shall I give you a lift home, darling?"

I secured my bicycle on the bike rack at the back of the car and got into the passenger seat.

"Well! I think there have been some very exciting developments, don't you?" my mother said brightly as we started the drive back to Oxford. "Mabel says we might have picked up some Very Important Clues to the murder!"

I gave her an exasperated look. "Mother, we have no idea yet if Dame Clare's death was suspicious or not—there could be a perfectly logical, innocent explanation for everything so far. You and Mabel can't just go around telling everyone it's murder! You'll start all sorts of rumours, especially in the village, and frighten people."

"But, darling, there *is* something suspicious about Clare Eccleston's death!" my mother insisted. "I think the police are being remarkably foolish to accept the word of a fuddy-duddy village doctor."

Although she said "police", I knew she really meant Devlin and I bristled slightly. "There was no reason to suspect any kind of foul play at the fête. The police did exactly what they ought to have. You can't expect them to treat every sudden death as murder. People drop dead of heart attacks all the time."

"Yes, but there are just too many odd things in this case, darling. And Mabel says that most murders are committed by someone known to the victim—often members of the family who have something to gain!"

I groaned. "You're not still thinking that it could be Mary? It's a ridiculous suggestion, Mother! You saw her just now—the poor girl is distraught."

"Oh, but darling, I told you—she could simply be a very good actress! She has obviously come into a very large sum of money with her mother's death… *and* it sounds like she *knew* she would be the sole beneficiary of the will. What's more…" My mother paused dramatically. "You heard what Riza the maid said!"

"She just said that Dame Clare and Mary had a row the night before the fête. Lots of mothers and daughters have arguments—"

"Yes, yes, but Mary said that she wished her mother was dead!"

"But that doesn't mean anything! It's the kind of thing you say when you're angry. I remember when I was thirteen, I used to—" I broke off guiltily.

My mother, however, hadn't noticed. She was continuing blithely, "And Mary was very reluctant to show that note to the police—I wonder why? She kept insisting that her mother must have died naturally of a heart attack. It all seems very suspicious to me."

"Mother, why are you all so against Mary? She seems such a sweet, nice girl—"

"Murders aren't just done by unpleasant people, you know," said my mother. "Sometimes, the killer

112

is someone we like—but that doesn't change what they did."

Grrr. Don't you just hate it when your mother is right?

CHAPTER ELEVEN

"Darling, why don't you come with me to the hairdresser this afternoon?" my mother asked as we arrived back at the house.

I looked at her in surprise. "Me? Why?"

"Oh, I just thought it would be nice for you to get your hair done. You know—have a proper wash and blow dry. It'll be my treat." My mother looked at my short pixie bob with disapproval. "It's just so *unfeminine* having such short hair... but maybe Antoine can put a bit of curl in it or something."

I touched my hair defensively. "My hair is fine as it is."

"Why don't you just let him have a look, darling? He's such a splendid talent, you know, and in his hands, you'll look your absolute best!"

I gave her a suspicious look. "Why is it suddenly

so important for me to look my absolute best?"

My mother opened her eyes wide. "Well, don't you want to look your best, darling?"

"Um... well, yeah, of course. But..."

That was enough encouragement for my mother. Somehow, I found myself bundled into the car after lunch and accompanying her into town, where she presented me to Antoine with the sheepish embarrassment of someone presenting a badly matted dog at the groomer's.

"I know it's shockingly short, Antoine, but you're such a magician—do you think you could do anything?" My mother clasped her hands hopefully.

"*Mais bien sûr!*" said Antoine, whose own hair resembled a cross between a bird's nest and a Japanese flower arrangement. I couldn't stop staring at it in the mirror. If that was an example of his "talent", I shuddered to think what he would do to me.

But as it turned out, I was pleasantly surprised, and when I was released from the salon chair some thirty minutes later, I couldn't help admiring myself in the mirror. Antoine had given me a quick shampoo and rinse, then artfully blow-dried my hair so that it framed my face in the most flattering way, making my brown eyes seem larger and my neck graceful and slender.

"*Voila!*" he said, taking my nylon cape off with a flourish.

"Thanks, Antoine, it looks great," I said, turning

to eye my reflection this way and that.

"And now, *la maman...*" he said, escorting my mother to the chair I had vacated.

My mother was "getting her greys done" and so would be quite a while. I had plenty of time to kill. The hair salon was situated on George Street, right in the busy commercial heart of Oxford, and I decided to take a stroll around the city rather than sit in the stuffy waiting room. I hadn't had much chance to ramble around the streets of Oxford since I'd returned to England—working at the tearoom didn't give me much time off, and if I did come into town, it certainly wasn't to window shop! But my forced wait for my mother meant that, for once, I didn't have anything else to do, anywhere else to be, and I enjoyed my leisurely stroll around the city centre. I made my way through the hordes of tourists and down the pedestrianised central thoroughfare of Cornmarket Street, then into the bustling 18th-century Covered Market, where you could find a traditional fishmonger rubbing shoulders with a designer hat shop, an old-fashioned cobbler alongside an Oriental boutique.

Eventually, I wandered into Turl Street, a narrow cobbled-stoned lane full of historic charm, lined on both sides by several of the smaller Oxford colleges, as well as a selection of quaint shops and boutiques. I was delighted to see that some of these were still the same as from my student days; in fact, a few—such as the bespoke shoe shop and the traditional gentleman's tailor—had probably been here for a few centuries!

Just as I was reaching the end of the lane where Turl Street joined the High Street, I noticed a shop on my right and my steps slowed. It was a second-hand bookstore, specialising in rare and antiquarian books, and the shop window showed an inviting display of leather-bound books stacked next to an antique globe. What made me pause, however, was the logo on the sign above the door, accompanied by the words: "Edwin Perkins, proprietor."

I remembered seeing the same logo and sign at the village fête—there had been a second-hand book stall there—and I also remembered the pompous middle-aged man who had run up to Mary's car just before we left the fête. She had called him "Edwin"... could this have been the same man?

I went into the store. Inside the doorway, I paused, breathing deeply. *Ahhh.* There was nothing like the smell of books, particularly old books—that magical combination of oaky aged paper, the rich robustness of leather, the silkiness of binding, together with the fruity topnotes of faded ink, all combining to produce the perfect bouquet. And in here, you didn't just smell it—you were immersed in it. It was a tiny shop, the walls lined floor-to-ceiling with bookshelves and the centre holding tables heaped with more books, stacked haphazardly against each other.

I walked slowly down the aisle, trailing my hand reverently along the spines of the books on the shelves, occasionally pulling out a volume to flip through. *There is nothing as beautiful as an old book*, I thought, *lovingly caressed and read for years.*

Towards the back of the store were the more expensive rare and antiquarian books, locked up in glass cases, and in the corner, next to an old leather Chesterfield armchair, was a large writing desk. There was a man behind it and a quick glance told me that this was the same "Edwin" I had met at the fête. In fact, I thought he was wearing the same brown tweed jacket with matching waistcoat and olive-green corduroy trousers, together with a faded bowtie which made him look slightly ridiculous.

He glanced up as I approached and I saw something flicker in his eyes as he rose politely. "May I help you, miss? Are you looking for anything in particular?"

"Um... no, just browsing..." I paused, then added, "I'm sorry about what happened at the fête. It must have been very upsetting for you, being a friend of the family."

"I'm sorry? I'm afraid I don't follow..."

"Dame Clare Eccleston. We met when I was driving her daughter home after the—afterwards. Actually, we also met briefly earlier: you were just coming out of the cat show pavilion as I was going in. We... sort of had a collision. I was carrying lemonade."

"Oh, yes, of course..." He took his spectacles off and polished them busily. "I'm sorry. I didn't recognise you."

Liar, I thought. He had recognised me all right, the minute I entered the shop. I saw the way he had looked at me as I approached him—and unless I had been mistaken, there had been a flicker of apprehension in his gaze.

Why? Why should he have been nervous to see me?

"Have you been a friend of the Eccleston family for long?" I tried again.

"I knew Sir Henry Eccleston," he said shortly. "He had an interest in antiquarian books and collected first editions." He replaced his spectacles and said briskly, "Well, if you need anything, let me know. We have general second-hand books, as well as rare and first editions."

I nodded and started to turn away, then on an impulse, turned back to him and said, "I don't suppose you have any books on poisons?"

He stiffened. "Poisons?"

"Yes, I was thinking... something that might mimic a heart attack," I said, watching him.

"No, I'm afraid we don't have any books on that subject."

I raised my eyebrows slightly and glanced around the store. "You have a lot of books here— you don't have a single volume on poisons?"

"Not that I'm aware of," he said coldly. "I'm sorry I can't help you." His tone was final.

I gave up. I wasn't even sure why I had brought up the subject anyway. It had just been... a bit of a hunch. I turned to leave. Just as I was nearing the door, however, I came across a woman who was browsing one of the upper shelves. She put a hand out to stop me as I walked past her.

"Excuse me," she said in a low voice. "I couldn't help overhearing your question just now. I'm not sure if this is what you are looking for but I did see a few books on herbal remedies and such, including poisons, on that shelf over there." She pointed to her right. "They're just next to where I was looking for recipes."

"Oh, thank you. That's very kind of you."

"Perhaps Mr Perkins misunderstood what you were asking for," she suggested. "Or maybe he simply forgot that he had them." She laughed, looking around. "I probably also wouldn't remember if I had a shop with this many books!"

I smiled at her. "Yes, I'm sure you're right. Thanks anyway for letting me know."

I glanced over my shoulder and saw Edwin Perkins watching us from his table, his mouth compressed in a thin line. Ignoring him, I turned and walked over to the shelf the woman had indicated. Sure enough, there were a few books on homeopathic herbal medicine, such as a reprint of an 1880 publication called *Principal Homeopathic*

Medicines and an *Antique Apothecary Book,* and finally one entitled *Home Remedy Secrets—Potions to Heal and Harm.*

Curious, I reached up and pulled the last volume out. It had a faded cover, the edges curled and worn, and the pages yellowed with age. I opened it gently and skimmed some pages. There was a recipe for dandelion tea to clear up acne and eczema, and another for a comfrey salve to relieve aches and bruises. I flipped to another page and found a recipe for nutmeg oil which brought relief from rheumatic pain and toothache but which in higher doses could be lethal. Hallucinations, liver damage, and death. It seemed you could produce a whole pharmacy from your garden, as long as you had a bit of gardening expertise and knowledge of herbal remedies. With the right equipment, you could even make home-made, hand-pressed tablets. I wondered how closely they resembled the store-bought pills.

Thoughtfully I shut the book and slid it back into position on the shelf, then glanced over at the desk again. Edwin Perkins was still watching me.

Suppressing a shiver, I turned and left the store, stepping out into the afternoon sunshine with some relief. I didn't like to admit it—even to myself—but that man gave me the creeps.

I mulled over the whole episode as we drove home, barely listening to my mother chattering next to me. It wasn't until we were drawing up to the house that what she was saying filtered through.

"...and I told Helen I'm sure you'd be able to help Lincoln with choosing new curtains for his townhouse and you can discuss it together over dinner tonight—"

"Wait—" I turned to my mother. "What did you say? Aunt Helen and Lincoln are coming over for dinner tonight?" I was aghast.

Suddenly, I realised the real reason my mother wanted me to go with her to the hair salon, so that I would "look my best". She was up to her old match-making tricks again! Helen Green was my mother's closest friend and their joint greatest dream (and lifelong mission) was to see me married to her son, Lincoln. The thing was, I did like Lincoln a lot—he was a great guy—but as a friend, nothing more. It had taken me a while to understand my own feelings but I knew now that my heart belonged to Devlin. Ever since that day when we'd met as Freshers in our first week at Oxford, there had never really been anyone else but him.

My mother, though, wasn't so easily convinced. I had thought that she would have given up by now, but no, it seemed that she had simply been rallying her forces and planning new lines of attack. As for Helen, she was still full of indignation at my audacity in choosing Devlin, with his working-class roots, over her beloved son, an Eton-educated, upper-middle-class, eminent doctor. She had been decidedly frosty in her manner towards me lately and it made for a *lot* of awkward conversations. I thought with dread of an entire evening sitting across the table from Helen and Lincoln… I couldn't face it.

"I can't come," I said impulsively. "I won't be home for dinner tonight."

My mother looked at me in astonishment. "Why ever not?"

"Because I'm… I'm moving into Devlin's place." *So much for not rushing into it.*

"*What?*" For once, my mother forgot her own rule of "never say *what?*—say *pardon?*" She stared at me, an expression of absolute horror on her face.

"You mean… you're going to *live together?*" She made it sound like we were going on a killing spree together.

"Well, yes," I said, trying not to sound defensive. "Lots of couples do it nowadays. It's no big deal. It's an ideal solution. I'm having trouble finding a place to rent, Devlin's got loads of room… It would be really handy for me to get to work, as well as come into Oxford—his place is about halfway between here and Meadowford—and… it would be easier for us to spend more time together as well."

My mother looked like she had swallowed an incredibly nasty slug. I almost felt sorry for her. As we parked the car and went into the house, I felt guilt begin to weigh down on me. I thought of how excited my mother had been earlier and winced when I thought of how I must be ruining her evening. How was she going to explain things to Helen Green when they arrived? I felt terrible.

In the hallway, I hesitated, wondering if I should stay for dinner after all. I could always leave afterwards. At least that way, my mother would salvage a bit of her pride and it would be a sop to her feelings.

Then I stiffened my resolve. No. I had to do this. If I caved in now, I'd be back down the slippery slope of pandering to maternal approval. Whether my mother liked it or not, Devlin was in my life for good now.

CHAPTER TWELVE

Muesli peered excitedly through the bars of her cat carrier as we arrived at Devlin's place. As soon as we were in the house, I let her out to explore her new home. She took a few steps, then stopped and looked back at me.

"*Meorrw*?"

"New digs, Muesli," I said with a smile.

She vibrated her tail, then turned and trotted off. We watched as she made a wide circuit, weaving her way between Devlin's modular lounge suite and side tables, past the bookcases, rubbing her chin against the entertainment system in the corner, slipping behind the curtains to look out of the French windows at the darkness outside, then turning and scampering across to the gleaming stainless steel kitchen on the other side of the room.

Devlin lived in a converted barn—a huge, airy space renovated with modern furnishings but retaining much of its rustic charm. The ground floor was basically one large, open-plan room, with the kitchen at one end and living room at the other, as well as a laundry and downstairs toilet. Muesli trotted importantly up the open spiral staircase ahead of us as we took my things up to the mezzanine level where Devlin had his bedroom and en suite.

"I thought you might like to have the side of the bed nearest the bathroom. And I've cleared a couple of drawers for you," said Devlin as he set my case down by the built-in wardrobe. "But if you need more space, just let me kn—Gemma? Is anything the matter?"

I had stopped by my side of the bed and was fingering the bedspread nervously. Suddenly, the enormity of what I was doing hit me: *I was moving in with Devlin O'Connor.* Aside from the lingering guilt I still felt from my mother's disapproval, there was a stab of panic. Was this a good idea? Were we moving too fast? After all, we'd only really been "going out" (again) as a couple for a few months now—wasn't this rushing things?

"Gemma?" Devlin came over to me and put a gentle hand on my arm. "What's wrong?"

I blinked. "Nothing, I guess. Just..." I shrugged. "It feels a bit weird."

"It's not that different to when we were always sleeping over at each other's rooms, back in college. Only a much bigger room and—" Devlin grinned wickedly, "—a much bigger bed."

I blushed slightly and gave him a playful shove. He tumbled backwards on the bed, pulling me down with him.

"Mmm... I've been waiting for this moment... and this time, there's no mother, no Old Biddies to barge in the windows..." Devlin chuckled, his breath warm against my ear.

"Devlin, we can't!" I protested, laughing. "We haven't had dinner yet and—"

"To hell with dinner," he growled playfully, pulling me closer. But before I could reply, there was a thump as something landed on the bed next to us and the next moment, a little whiskered face thrust its way between us.

"*Meorrw!*" said Muesli indignantly.

I laughed and pushed myself up, away from Devlin. "I might be able to delay our dinner but Muesli isn't going to allow us to delay *hers!*"

"All right," said Devlin, sitting up with a good-natured sigh. "I guess I shall have to put off mauling you until after we've eaten."

He got up but I stayed where I was, sitting on the bed and thinking about what Devlin had said. He was right. This wasn't really any different to when we had been at college together and practically living in each other's rooms. And in a way, although it might have felt like we were moving a bit fast, we weren't really like most couples who had just begun dating. We'd known each other since we were eighteen and had spent almost every waking hour together when we were students at Oxford. For goodness' sake, we had almost been engaged! In some ways, Devlin and I knew each other better than most couples ever would.

"Hey…"

I looked up to see Devlin watching me and realised that my thoughts must have been clearly written on my face.

"Remember, you can check out anytime you like," he said gently. "Although I think Muesli might have something to say about it," he added, nodding at his bed and grinning.

I turned to look. Muesli had made herself comfortable in the middle of the duvet. Her loud purring filled the room. She certainly had no qualms about moving in with Devlin—in fact, she looked like she was in kitty heaven!

I chuckled in spite of myself. "The little minx. You know she hogs the bed at night."

"I'm looking forward to it," Devlin laughed. "Come on, let's go downstairs. Are you hungry? I thought we could rustle up some pasta for dinner."

"Sounds great," I said, following him back down the stairs.

As we cooked dinner together in the large, modern kitchen—boiling the pasta, simmering the tomato sauce, chopping up some fresh herbs—I listened to Devlin tell me about his day.

"By the way, I had that pill tested," he said. "The one that Dame Clare was holding in her hand when she died."

"And?" I looked at him eagerly.

"It's kosher. Perfectly legit, bog standard angina pill, such as would be prescribed by any doctor and dispensed by any pharmacy."

"Oh." I rocked back on my heels, disappointed. "I was so sure..."

Devlin gave a sigh. "Gemma, I told you not to listen to Mabel Cooke's over-imaginative—"

"But what if it's *not* just her imagination?"

"We've been through all this," Devlin said impatiently. "I can't start a murder investigation just because your mother thought a pillbox was in the wrong place—"

"It's not just that. A couple of other things have come up," I said.

Quickly, I recounted a carefully censored version of what had happened at Eccleston House that morning, glossing over the bit where I'd caught the Old Biddies breaking and entering. Devlin was no fool, however, and he gave me a wry look when I finished.

"Why do I get a feeling that there's more to that story than you're telling me? Never mind..." He held up a hand with weary resignation as I started to protest. "I don't really want to know. I'm sure it involves Mabel Cooke and her friends doing something they should probably get arrested for."

"So what about what the maid said?" I asked. "About the fight between Dame Clare and her daughter?"

"Do you really think Mary Eccleston could have killed her mother?"

"I—" I stopped. "I don't know," I said at last. "I just can't believe it... but then, maybe I don't *want* to believe it. You know, because I like Mary. But as my mother said—and I hate to admit it but she's right—just because I like Mary doesn't mean that she can't be a murderer. But still... I just can't believe it! For one thing, if she was the murderer, that anonymous note wouldn't make sense. If we assume that it was sent by the murderer, then that would be suggesting that Mary had sent the letter herself. But if she *had*, surely she would want everyone to know about it as much as possible, to make people think that her mother had enemies— that the murderer was a stranger, someone outside the family?" I shook my head. "But she didn't—she was really reluctant to tell us about it and when she finally did, she kept downplaying it; she said it was just another prank letter like the ones her mother got in college last year."

"Did you suggest that she report it to the police?"

"Yes, and she was adamant about not showing it to the police. I think if it wasn't for Audrey insisting that she show it to us, Mary wouldn't even have mentioned it. So I don't think she sent it herself—which means that the murderer is much more likely to be someone else."

"Did it look like a prank letter?"

I shrugged. "I don't know. I didn't see the ones Dame Clare received before so it's hard to compare. Audrey was pretty freaked out by it. It *was* a bit disturbing. I mean all anonymous letters are a bit creepy, aren't they? But it wasn't even the actual message—it was the way the person had cut these letters out and stuck them on—and then that horrible picture of Dame Clare with her eyes crossed out and her face disfigured like that..." I shuddered. "Audrey thought the person who had sent it must be unbalanced and I'm inclined to agree with her. You could really feel the... the hatred."

Hatred. I thought uncomfortably of what Riza had said and the image of Mary Eccleston standing there, screaming: "I *HATE* YOU! I WISH YOU WERE DEAD!" flashed across my mind. I pushed the thought away.

"I suppose I can see if my sergeant has time to interview Mary Eccleston tomorrow about the note," Devlin was saying.

"No, don't do that," I said quickly. "I would hate for Mary to think that I was telling on her, behind her back. She might still report it to the police herself."

"Fine. But in that case, there's not much else I

can do."

"But... surely this is enough now to start a murder investigation?"

"Based on what? Dame Clare died suddenly, that is true, but it wasn't an unexpected death. It was certified by her doctor that she had a weak heart and was likely to have a heart attack any time. There's no reason to suspect that her death was due to any other cause. That little bit of inconsistency with the pillbox doesn't really prove anything. The fact that she received an anonymous nasty message a few days ago *might* mean something—on the other hand, there are a dozen cases of school and workplace bullying each week, all involving nasty anonymous notes, and that's not even counting all the trolling that goes on on social media sites and online forums! Bloody hell, if we went by those parameters, we'd be having to treat half the deaths in Oxfordshire as murder!"

"Isn't there *any* way to check if Dame Clare did die of natural causes?"

"Only if we do a post-mortem."

"Well, can't you do that?"

"Not without justifiable reason. It costs time and expense for the forensic pathologist to perform a post-mortem. We don't do them unless there's a compelling reason to suspect that a crime has been committed. Or..." Devlin added, "if a family member requests it and is prepared to foot the costs for an independent pathologist."

I let the subject drop, although I couldn't stop thinking about it as we finished cooking the meal. It was only when we sat down to dinner and I realised how hungry I was that I finally allowed myself to be diverted. It was a simple meal but delicious, the pasta just perfectly *al dente*, the tomato sauce fresh and tangy, flavoured with basil and rich red wine. Devlin had also made a quick salad of lettuce leaves and crisp cucumber slices, drizzled with a bit of balsamic vinegar and olive oil, and this went beautifully with the pasta.

"Smart, handsome, and good in the kitchen... how did I get so lucky?" I teased Devlin as we finally sat back from our empty plates.

He grinned. "*And* I've got chocolate ice cream in the freezer."

"I think you're eligible for sainthood," I said with a laugh. I sprang up and started gathering the plates. "Here, I'll do the washing up. Why don't you go and relax in front of the TV?"

Devlin stifled a yawn, passing a tired hand over his face. "Thanks. That sounds like a great idea." He yawned again and gave his head a sharp shake. "It's been a long day. And I've got an early start tomorrow morning."

He wandered over to the living area and a little feline form trotted after him. Muesli had had her own dinner whilst we were having ours and was now obviously looking forward to having a good wash on the lap of her favourite detective. I smiled

to myself as I carried the dirty plates into the
kitchen. There was something about the cosy
intimacy of this domestic scene that made me feel
all warm and fuzzy.

"Do you want to set up a movie?" I called as I
turned on the taps at the kitchen sink. "I'll be done
here in ten minutes."

There was no answer from the living room but I
heard what sounded like movie credits coming from
the TV. Quickly, I stacked the dishwasher and
washed up the pots and pans, then gave the
counter a wipe. I smiled again as I suddenly
remembered my daydream about cuddling with
Devlin in front of the TV. And then I remembered
the romantic moment on the bed upstairs. I gave a
delicious shiver. No Mother, no Old Biddies, no
meddling or interruptions... *Oooh, I can't wait.*
Switching off the kitchen lights, I hurried across to
the living room.

Then I stopped short.

Devlin was lying sideways on the couch, his long
legs stretched out in front of him, his head tilted
back against the cushions and his eyes closed. He
was fast asleep. And curled up on his chest, her
head tucked into the crook of his neck, her face the
picture of contentment, was Muesli. She moved up
and down slowly as Devlin's chest rose and fell, and
her purring was almost loud enough to drown out
his deep breathing.

I went slowly towards them, feeling something

squeeze my heart at the sight of them together. Muesli opened one eye and gave a sleepy "*Meorrw...?*" then closed it again and snuggled closer to Devlin.

I don't believe it.

So much for the romantic anticipation. It looked like I would be spending my first evening in my boyfriend's house watching him cuddle with my cat.

CHAPTER THIRTEEN

"That man is back again."

I glanced up from assembling a tea tray and gave Cassie a harassed look. "What man?"

"You know, the chap who wants to sell us those novelty chocolate spoons."

I rolled my eyes. "Him again! Wasn't he here just last week and we told him we were too busy to see him?"

Cassie grinned. "Well, you have to hand it to him for persistence."

I looked over her shoulder and saw a small balding man in a shiny suit standing by the door. He had a case in one hand and a sycophantic expression on his face. He caught my eye and waved breezily, giving me a big smile.

"I haven't got time to see him now," I said

hurriedly. "The orders for that tour group haven't gone out yet and they're leaving in twenty minutes!"

"Well, shall I tell him to come back later today?"

I shook my head quickly. "No, it's going to be manic all day today." After the whole weekend off, it seemed like all the business we should have had was coming in one big flood. Not that I was complaining—it was great to be missed!—but it had meant a hectic day so far and it didn't look like we were slowing down any time soon. It was nearly three o'clock, a time when the lunch rush usually died down and we normally had a chance to catch our breaths before the next horde arrived for "afternoon tea"—but today, every table was still full and there was even a couple standing by the front door right now, waiting to be seated.

"Tell him to come back later in the week," I said as I picked up the tray, carefully balancing the weight of the heavy teapot at one end with the teacups and plate of scones on the other, and carried it over to an American family by the window.

They had that enviable self-confidence and friendly manner most Americans seemed to possess and I found myself enjoying a short chat with them as they told me about their home state of Minnesota. Then it was a mad dash to serve the tour group before they were due to leave. I breathed a silent prayer of thanks again for our new baking chef, Dora. She might have been a bit prickly at times and too proud for her own good, but she was usually fantastic under pressure, whipping up the most delicious cakes and baked goodies, all without turning a hair on her neat grey head. Although... I frowned to myself. There seemed to have been a few problems in the kitchen lately—I remembered Cassie mentioning it to me—some mistakes and accidents that Dora had had, which seemed very unlike her... A new group of tourists cut short my train of thought and I hurried to offer menus and seat them.

By the time I returned to the counter, I was relieved to see that everything seemed to be under control for the moment. Then the front door jingled again as someone entered and I looked over, reaching automatically for a menu. But I paused as I recognised who had just come in. It was Audrey Simmons—and she didn't look like she was in the mood for tea and scones.

"Hello, Audrey." I went over to greet her. "How nice to see you. Would you like some tea?"

She shook her head, her face strained and anxious. "No, actually Gemma, I came to have a word with you, if you've got a moment...?"

"Sure. What's the matter?" I said, putting a gentle hand on her arm and drawing her to one side.

"Is it true?" she said. "That Clare could have been murdered? Your mother was hinting at it when you all came to Eccleston House, wasn't she? And I've just been in the village post shop and everyone's talking about it. Apparently, Mabel Cooke and her friends have been telling everyone that they have proof that Clare didn't die of a heart attack after all—that her death was due to 'foul play'!"

Grrr. I thought of my mother and the Old Biddies reproachfully. What were they doing, going around spreading rumours like that?

"Well, I..." I hesitated. "There does seem to be some suspicion surrounding her death. There was that odd thing about her heart pills... and then there was that letter Mary found yesterday."

"Yes, I've been thinking about that," said Audrey. "It was horrible... horrible... I had trouble sleeping last night thinking about it! I don't think Mary realises how serious that letter is. I've been trying to urge her to report it to the police but she keeps refusing." She sighed. "I love Mary dearly but she can be like an ostrich sometimes—she thinks if she can just shove something out of sight, it will go away. But I don't think so—that letter was just vicious... and if it's true that Clare was murdered, then we must show it to the police! That letter might be a clue to catching her killer!"

"Did Dame Clare have any enemies?"

"Well..." Audrey looked uncomfortable.

I gave her an encouraging smile. "You're her oldest friend. I'm sure you knew a lot of what went on. And Dame Clare... er... made her presence felt. Perhaps she rubbed someone up the wrong way?"

"Clare always meant well," Audrey said defensively.

"Oh, I'm sure she did," I agreed. "But perhaps not everyone appreciated her good intentions?"

Audrey shrugged. "She wasn't very popular, that's true. People often didn't like her manner. There were a few problems at St Cecilia's College... but these things happen, of course, especially in a community as big as a college, with so many staff and students."

"But no one in particular who you think might have wished Dame Clare harm?"

Again, Audrey looked uncomfortable. "Well, I did think of this yesterday, but I didn't like to mention it in front of Mary. She's led a very sheltered life, you know, and she's quite sensitive. And she likes Joseph."

"Joseph?"

"The college gardener. He also does some work at Eccleston House from time to time."

"Yes, I've met him. I thought he was a bit... er... odd."

"Oh my goodness, yes, I've never warmed to him. But I have to say, he's a fantastic gardener. Not just in terms of digging things up and pruning things, but really knowing a lot about plants—their history and uses and everything. Clare kept telling me to get him to come and redo the Vicarage gardens and I wonder now if she might be right—things are getting so wild and with the spring pruning and the new bedding—"

"So something happened with Joseph?" I said, bringing her gently back on track.

"Yes, it was very silly really. It was to do with a flower border in the rear quadrangle, just by the college chapel. Joseph had been nurturing some dahlias in a greenhouse and Clare wanted him to transfer them to the border, but he refused. He said that although we've had a really warm spring, it was still too early and a cold snap might kill them. Anyway, Clare overruled him— she told him he would lose his job if he didn't do as she said. Clare could be a bit... um... high-handed sometimes when she wanted to get her own way." Audrey gave an apologetic laugh.

That's a polite way to describe a woman who sounded like a nasty bully, I thought. Aloud, I said, "What happened?"

"Well, unfortunately Clare was wrong and Joseph was right. The flowers all died in that sudden frost we had last week—if you remember? Joseph was livid. Honestly, I'd never seen anyone so furious and upset. You'd think that a member of his family had died! I happened to be over at St Cecilia's that day—I had gone to discuss something with Clare about the village fête—and I walked in on them having a dreadful row. You could practically hear them shouting from the other side of the quad. I was quite shocked because aside from anything else, I had never heard Joseph speak before. I'd almost thought that he was mute!"

I frowned. "But surely... he could just plant them again? It seems a bit extreme—you don't think he could want to harm Dame Clare just for that?"

Audrey gave me a look. "You don't know Joseph. He's very... odd, as you said. And he really loves his plants—almost like... obsessed. I don't think he sees them like we do. He's a bit of a loner and... well, his plants are everything to him." She brightened slightly. "It's what makes him such a brilliant gardener, though. There's nothing he doesn't know about plants and flowers. And such an amazing nose—he can identify different species of rose just by scent, you know. I said to Clare once that she ought to get him to put all his knowledge down in a book but she just laughed. She said Joseph was too stupid to write a book." Audrey grimaced. "Clare could be a bit tactless sometimes when she said things."

Bloody hell, talk about understatement of the year. The more I heard about Clare Eccleston, the more I was beginning to dislike her—and the more I was beginning to agree with Mabel Cooke that many people might have had reason to want her dead. I glanced sideways at Audrey and wondered how she could still think of her friend so fondly. They said love was blind—maybe childhood friendships were too. I knew that I would overlook a lot of things in Cassie. Having said that, Cassie wasn't a megalomaniacal tyrant...

The front door tinkled again at that moment and we looked up to see the Old Biddies walk in. I had been wondering where they had been—usually, they were the first in the tearoom every morning. But from what Audrey had said, it sounded like they had been busy holding court at the post office today. They certainly looked very self-satisfied as they trundled in, taking off their hats and coats.

"... I think Ruth is going to regret moving into the retirement village—you mark my words!" Mabel was saying as they came up to the counter.

"Well, *I* think she is going to have a *fabulous* time. There will be art classes and Scrabble competitions and *tai chi* and theatre visits to London... The retirement village even has its own pool and bowling green. Think of all the gentlemen she is going to meet!" Glenda giggled. "And Ruth told me that they have dances every Saturday evening! Oh, I do hope she'll take me as a guest."

"I just wish she could have donated her books to the library, instead of selling them off," said Ethel with a sigh. "It's such a wonderful collection, built up over a lifetime. It seems such a shame..."

"Well, you can't really blame her when that bookseller was offering that kind of money," said Florence reasonably.

"Hmmph! I don't trust that Edwin Perkins," said Mabel with a sniff. "He may be the best second-hand bookseller in Oxford but I still think—"

"Edwin?" Audrey said breathlessly next to me. "Is

Edwin Perkins here in Meadowford?"

I looked at her in surprise. Her cheeks were flushed and her eyes suddenly bright with excitement.

Ethel nodded. "Ruth Harding has decided to move into the retirement village now that her husband has passed away. We've just been over at her house, helping her with some packing. But there is no space for all her books in her new home so she called Mr Perkins to come and value her collection."

"Is he still there?"

"Yes, we'd only just left and he was still discussing one of Ruth's first editions with her."

"Oh, excuse me... I must try to catch him... I need to speak to him about... er... the village fête for next year..." Audrey hurried out of the tearoom.

Mabel watched her go sardonically. "She's wasting her time," she said.

"What do you mean?" I asked.

Glenda giggled. "Don't you know? Audrey has been in love with Edwin Perkins for years. She is always baking things for him and going into Oxford to visit his bookstore, and finding excuses to involve him in the village events. It was she who got him the stall to sell second-hand books at this year's fête, you know..." Glenda wrinkled her nose. "Though I must say, I really don't know what she sees in him. He walks with that dreadful stoop and he is so thin... I do think men look better with a bit

144

of weight on them. I mean, a 'beer belly' is so much sexier than a bony chest, don't you agree, Gemma?"

"I... er... I hadn't really given it much thought," I said weakly. "So, um... does Edwin return her feelings?"

Mabel snorted. "Not when he has younger fish to fry."

Glenda leaned towards me and, like a schoolgirl passing a secret in the playground: "Edwin is in love with Mary Eccleston."

"With Mary?" I spluttered. "But she's... she's young enough to be..."

"Exactly," said Mabel, nodding. "Well, they do say there's no fool like an old fool."

"It's quite sad watching him, actually," said Florence, shaking her head. "Almost embarrassing. The way he used to hang around them all the time, like a starving old dog hoping to be thrown a bone."

"I thought it was quite sweet," Ethel spoke up. "He is so devoted to her—he really would do anything for her. And although there *is* a big gap in their ages, well, Mary is so shy and naïve, sometimes I wonder if an older man would suit her better."

"Well, he's not likely to get a chance to try his hand, is he?" said Florence.

Glenda giggled. "He might, now that Clare Eccleston is dead."

I raised my eyebrows. "Did Dame Clare not approve of Edwin's feelings for her daughter?"

"Not approve?" Mabel guffawed. "She laughed him out of town! Called him a dirty old man behind his back—and to his face!—and delighted in humiliating him by telling everyone about the way he hung around Mary. Said he was like an old dog sniffing arou—" Mabel clamped her mouth shut suddenly. I glanced around. A man had just entered the tearoom. It was Edwin Perkins.

CHAPTER FOURTEEN

He stood on the threshold for a moment, surveying the room with a kind of fastidious appraisal, then he came towards the counter. I reached for a menu and stepped forwards to greet him but before I could say anything, Mabel's booming voice cut in:

"Good to see you again, Edwin. All finished up at Ruth's?"

"Yes," he said stiffly. "Mrs Harding and I have concluded our business; I thought it would be salubrious to have a cup of tea before returning to Oxford and I had heard this place recommended."

"Oh, yes, people come from far and wide to eat at Gemma's tearoom," said Florence proudly. "Best scones in Oxfordshire!"

"Yes, well, perhaps we should let Mr Perkins

decide for himself," I said, slightly embarrassed. I smiled at him. "Would you like a table by the window?"

"No, this one will do," he said, indicating a table near the counter. "I don't intend to stay long. Just a pot of tea, please."

"Are you sure you wouldn't like something with your tea?" I said. "We have a large range of cakes and buns, as well as, of course, our signature dish: freshly baked scones with home-made jam and clotted cream. We also do traditional finger sandwiches, in a range of flavours."

"Well, I..."

"Try the Victoria sponge," Glenda piped up. "It's very good. Although perhaps not quite as good as Mary Eccleston's..." She giggled.

A faint line of colour showed along Edwin's cheeks but his expression remained impassive. He glanced down at the menu. "I'll have a plate of cucumber sandwiches, then."

I went back to the counter to put the order through. Meanwhile, the Old Biddies had found something new to occupy their attention: they were poring avidly over a copy of today's local newspaper.

"Look at those eyes..." said Glenda with a mock shiver. "One can tell he's a criminal."

"And his mouth! My mother did always say never trust a man with thin lips." Florence nodded sagely.

"Well, *I* think he looks rather ordinary," said Ethel in her gentle voice. "That's what makes it even more frightening—that he can look like anyone we know. Only fancy, he was there at the fête, walking around and no one even realised that there was a master criminal in our midst!"

"What are you looking at?" I said, my interest piqued.

"It's that chap—the one who's the leader of the gang of thieves that has been causing havoc lately," said Florence. "They're calling him the 'Agri-Crime Boss'. Nate Briggs."

"Oh?" So this was Devlin's nemesis. I leaned over for a better look, half expecting to see some kind of cliché of the evil mastermind: a swarthy face, perhaps, with dark demonic eyebrows and a creepy moustache.

Instead, I saw a fresh-faced, very ordinary-looking young man, probably no more than thirty years of age, with sandy hair and a ruddy complexion. The picture had been snapped in a supermarket car park and he was looking off camera, with a vacant, relaxed expression on his face. Ethel was right: he looked like any one of a dozen other young men you might see out and about in Oxfordshire. You'd never look at him twice in the street. It was difficult to believe that this unassuming young man was the leader behind a clever gang of criminals that was keeping the police on their toes.

"They even stole two quad bikes at the fête, from right under the police's noses!" Mabel gave me an accusing look. "Your Inspector O'Connor ought to be ashamed of himself."

"Yes, well, Devlin was a bit distracted by Dame Clare's collapse at the cat show—he couldn't be in two places at once," I said defensively.

"Hmph." Mabel sniffed. "Well, at least it seems that he has finally seen sense and is now appealing to the public for their help. I have always said that the police ought to rely more on the local residents' knowledge—we have eyes and ears on the ground that they can never match!"

"The police have put out an appeal," Florence explained, pointing to the article beneath the photo. "They're asking for anyone who might have information about Nate Briggs or who might have seen him—especially at the fête last Saturday—to come forward."

Cassie came past the counter, muttering to herself: "...hope we've got extra supplies of sticky toffee pudding. Can't believe all three tables wanted the same thing! Maybe I'd better check with Dora and see if—"

"Cassie—" I grabbed my friend as she was about to step into the kitchen. "Remember those pictures your brother took? He was sending you some while we were out house-hunting on Sunday."

She made a face. "Yeah, wish I could forget them."

"He's got more, hasn't he? Aside from the ones of you—and that one of me in the cat pavilion. You said he was going around the whole fête taking pictures of people."

She nodded. "Liam's building up a range of 'types' for his portfolio. He said the fête was an excellent place for that—you get all sorts coming and the crowds are so large that people don't always notice when they're being photographed, so everyone looks natural."

"Well, he might have inadvertently photographed this 'Agri-Crime Boss'!" I said. "I'm sure the police would like to see his pictures. Even if Liam didn't catch Nate Briggs directly, he might still have got him somewhere in the background." I thought for a moment, then added, "In fact, if Liam doesn't want the hassle of going down to the police station, he can give the pictures to me and I'll show them to Devlin tonight."

"Okay, I'll ring him now. I think the pictures might still be on his camera..." Cassie paused. "But wait—he's probably in Oxford. Do you want to go back into town just to get these photos? Seems a bit of a pain when you would have just gone straight back to Devlin's place after work."

"Oh, that's okay. I was thinking of popping back to my parent's house before returning to Devlin's, so I'm heading into North Oxford after work anyway."

Cassie grinned. "Guilt trip? Because you left in a huff yesterday?"

I squirmed slightly. She was right. Even though I

still felt that I had been completely in the right and my mother completely in the wrong, I hadn't been able to shake off the feeling of guilty remorse all day.

"Yeah, maybe a little," I said sheepishly. "I thought I'd pop back and... um... maybe apologise."

Cassie laughed. "You're so predictable, Gemma. Okay, let me ring Liam..." She put the call through and I could hear an excited babble the other side.

"Yeah, he's happy to meet you," said Cassie, chuckling as she ended the call. "And he's well chuffed to be 'helping the police with a criminal investigation'. In fact, he was planning to meet a bunch of his friends tonight and I'll bet you he's going to be bragging to them no end." She grinned at me. "I think you've made his week."

"Where does he want me to meet him?"

"He'll be in school until five and then I think a group of them are going to the 6:15 p.m. movie at the Magdalen Street cinema—so I told him to pop over to your parents' place around 5:30 and wait for you there. His school is just around the corner. Is that okay?"

"Perfect. I might leave a bit earlier today so I don't keep him waiting. Do you think—"

I felt a movement at my elbow and turned in surprise to see Edwin Perkins standing next to me. He had left his table and was looking slightly flustered.

"I'm afraid I have to cancel my order," he said

curtly. "I need to get back to Oxford sooner than I thought."

"Oh, the sandwiches should be ready in a minute—"

"No, no, I have to leave now." He pushed past me and headed out the door.

Cassie and I looked at each other in bemusement.

"What on earth got into him?" said Cassie.

I shrugged and walked over to the tearoom windows. I was just in time to see Edwin hurrying away down the opposite side of the street. He had a mobile phone pressed to his ear and he was talking into it urgently. *Hmm...* Maybe he *had* been telling the truth and he really had forgotten

an appointment in Oxford—and was now calling his client to apologise... But something about his sudden departure made me uneasy.

CHAPTER FIFTEEN

The rest of the afternoon passed fairly uneventfully, although I found myself unable to get the subject of Dame Clare's "murder" off my mind. I mulled over things as I took orders and served trays of tea and cakes around the tearoom. I kept returning to the discrepancy about the pills and, in particular, the one that had been found clutched in the dead woman's hand...

It had been so tempting to think that the pill which had been found in her hand might have been a "fake"—a doctored tablet which had contained poison instead of the real medication. Maybe Dame Clare had taken one already and was still holding the second one when she collapsed. She might have thought that she was taking angina pills when instead she was taking a lethal replacement...

And maybe she had asked her daughter to fetch her some pills from her pillbox and Mary had given her mother the poisonous fake pills instead? That would explain why the pills in the pillbox had remained untouched.

But my mind shied away from that thought. Besides, it didn't make sense. Mary hadn't seemed at all concerned when I asked to check the pillbox—and if she really *had* given her mother some fake, poisoned pills, wouldn't she have taken the trouble to remove the same number of real pills from the box? It would have been easy to do and would have removed the chance of people noticing a discrepancy.

In any case, this was all irrelevant now since Devlin had confirmed that the pill *was* a genuine angina tablet after all. It was definitely *not* poisonous. So that scratched that theory out. But that still didn't explain the discrepancy. The fact that the six tablets in the pillbox had been untouched meant that Dame Clare must have got that pill in her hand from somewhere else... or... or...

... Or someone had placed the pill in her hand after she had collapsed!

I felt a surge of excitement. Yes! That was it!

The pill was a decoy, designed to mislead. It gave the suggestion that Dame Clare had suffered a heart attack: after all, that was the natural conclusion anyone would come to when she was found dead, with an angina tablet clutched in her hand. It would lead people to assume—as we all did—that the poor woman had been feeling chest pains and had been on her way to take some medication, but had been too late.

So why would anyone want to do that? Why would someone want people to believe that Dame Clare had died of a heart attack?

Because they didn't want to raise suspicion that she might have died of something else.

And in fact, they had almost succeeded. Dr Foster had signed the death certificate, citing natural causes, and if it hadn't been for my mother's observation about the pillbox and the Old Biddies' meddling and habit of seeing "murder" everywhere, no one would have questioned it. Dame Clare would have been buried and the murderer would have got away with it.

On a sudden hunch, I picked up my phone during a quiet moment and put a call through to Lincoln Green.

"Hi Gemma," he said. He sounded pleased to hear from me and I was relieved.

"Hi Lincoln—I haven't caught you at a bad time, have I?"

"No, I'm just about to start a ward round but I've got a moment to spare." There was a pause, then he added, "My mother and I were sorry not to see you at dinner last night."

"Oh, yeah... I'm sorry about that," I said,

embarrassed. "I... um... something came up at the last minute..."

Lincoln laughed. "It's okay, Gemma. To be honest with you, I was a bit relieved when I found out that you wouldn't be there. It's been awkward enough... well, you know my mother didn't take your... um... that is, you know she was very disappointed that things didn't quite work out between us the way she had hoped."

My face was flaming and I was glad he couldn't see me. "Lincoln... I'm... I'm sorry. You know that I—"

"No, no, that's what I meant. You don't need to apologise, Gemma. Honestly. There are no hard feelings at my end and I'm very pleased we're still friends. I was just trying to say that actually your absence last night... er... made things easier for me too."

I felt a rush of gratitude and affection for him. "Thanks, Lincoln, for being so understanding."

"So what can I do for you? I'm sure you didn't ring me up just to tell me how embarrassed you are again," he teased.

"I was actually hoping to pick your brain," I said. "Listen, is there a way for someone to fake a heart attack?"

"What you mean? Why would anyone want to fake a heart attack?"

"Well... maybe if... maybe if you wanted to get rid of someone but you didn't want it to look like murder—"

"You're thinking of that death on the weekend, aren't you? At the Meadowford village fête? It's been in all the papers. She was quite a well-known figure around Oxford, you know, being a senior academic at one of the colleges."

"Yes," I said. "There have been one or two things which are a bit... odd about Dame Clare's death. She was taking angina pills—I don't suppose they could trigger a heart attack?"

"The drugs used to treat angina are nitrates such as nitroglycerine and they *can* be fatal, in theory, if one uses a large enough dose. But that isn't the heart medication that one would normally think of in terms of being potentially toxic and dangerous."

"But there's another one that is?" I said quickly.

"Well, the most commonly prescribed heart medication is probably digoxin—what's often called 'digitalis' by the general public. It's prescribed for congestive heart failure and it works on the heart muscles to increase contractions. It's very effective and beneficial in small doses, but it's potentially very lethal if the dosage is exceeded. An overdose could cause tachycardia, arterial fibrillation, atrioventricular block—"

"Which could lead to a heart attack?"

"Yes, a large overdose could definitely lead to a sudden heart attack."

"Is it easy to get hold of these drugs?

"Digoxin is by prescription only and the amounts

dispensed are very carefully monitored, as you can imagine. But it's actually possible to make a large supply of the same drug from the flower itself."

"From the flower?"

"Yes, you know, the foxglove. You find it in a lot of English gardens. It's where the drug initially came from. I still remember the lecture we had about it as medical students. It was considered a landmark event in cardiac medicine. An English apothecary-surgeon named William Withering discovered the potency of digitalis and he was the first to use foxglove concoctions to treat people." Lincoln laughed. "Nowadays, he would probably have got a patent for the drug and become a multi-billionaire... Actually, he sounded like a really decent chap. They said he personally treated two or three thousand poor patients every year, which meant that he only earned about a thousand pounds a year—compared to his colleagues who were all making something like five thousand pounds a year. That was a lot of money in those days."

"So... if you had the foxglove plant, you could get access to the same drug?"

"Yes, although not in the pure form, of course— but I believe it's fairly easy to extract the active ingredient."

I thought back to the day at the cat show. "If someone was poisoned by digitalis, what kinds of symptoms would they show? Would it be similar to a heart attack?"

"Yes, I suppose some of the symptoms could be interpreted that way," Lincoln mused. "Which would make it a very clever poison to use. The victim would feel nauseous, have an irregular pulse, be confused and uneasy—which are a bit similar to symptoms of a heart attack, such as nausea, sweating, and light-headedness..."

"And would you have to give someone a lot to kill them?"

"No, that's what makes it so lethal. Digitalis has a very narrow therapeutic index. That means that the difference between a 'safe' dose and a 'toxic' one is very small. Even a small overdose can be fatal. And it works really quickly too. Death can be immediate, although if the poison is taken with food, it can take a bit longer due to the oral absorption time." Lincoln's voice was concerned. "This sounds serious, Gemma. Have you spoken to Devlin about it?"

"Yes, but he's not convinced that there are any grounds for suspicion in Dame Clare's death," I said.

"I'm surprised—Devlin is normally so astute," said Lincoln with grudging respect.

I sighed. "The problem is that, this time, the woman's doctor was there and he certified that death was due to natural causes."

"Really? Who did that?"

"Dr Foster from the village. You know him?"

"Yes, though not very well. I've seen his name on some of my patient charts as he is their usual GP." Lincoln gave a polite cough. "He's... uh... coming up for retirement, I believe."

"Would you trust his judgement?"

"Well..." Clearly Lincoln didn't like criticising a colleague. "Let's just say that many of us feel that he probably should have retired well before now."

I gave a frustrated sigh. "That's what I've been hearing from my mother and other village residents. They don't think much of his abilities at all and they don't trust his verdict. I wish I could get a second opinion on Dame Clare's death."

"Well, post-mortem would be a sort of second opinion, wouldn't it?"

"Yes, I know, and I've been trying to persuade Devlin to ask for one but so far he's refused. He says I have to provide him with a compelling reason to request one and what I've got so far isn't enough." I gave another frustrated sigh. "I'm almost tempted to contact the forensic pathologist myself and try to persuade *him*—except that I've seen him a couple of times before at crime scenes and he's a bit of a grumpy old man. I don't really fancy my chances—"

"Actually, Dr Maxwell has gone on long service leave," said Lincoln. "There's a locum pathologist in his place who is very good and who might be very willing to listen to you, I think."

"I don't know," I said doubtfully. "I mean, I

haven't even met him; I can't just—"

A loud clatter came from the kitchen, followed by raised voices. I looked around in consternation. *What is happening in there?*

"Sorry, Lincoln, I've got to go," I said hurriedly.

"Okay, well, if there's anything else I can do to help, just give me a call."

"Thanks," I said gratefully.

I hung up and dashed into the kitchen, where I found Dora and Mabel standing back from the central wooden table, both of them surveying the mess in the middle with wary dismay. It looked like a small volcano had erupted there, with bits of flour, dough, and liquid splattered everywhere and a cracked glass bowl lying on its side.

"It's all your fault!" Dora burst out, looking at Mabel accusingly. "If you hadn't come in, trying to meddle as usual—"

"I did not touch a thing!" said Mabel indignantly. "It was you! You poured that lemon mixture into the batter and the minute you tried to fold things over, everything just exploded!"

"Oh my goodness, was anyone hurt?" I said, rushing forwards.

"Not this time, but that doesn't mean we might be so fortunate next time," said Mabel, giving Dora a dark look. "What if the bowl had shattered and glass shards had flown everywhere? And it is not the first time this sort of thing has happened. Don't glower at me so, Dora—you know it's true. Cassie has been telling me about your 'accidents'. You need to do something about it."

"What accidents?" I said, looking from one to the other. I vaguely remembered now that Cassie had mentioned something last week about being worried about Dora... and earlier this week too... but I had been so busy at the time, I hadn't paid much attention.

"Dora has been making all sorts of strange mistakes and having accidents in the kitchen," Mabel said. "Entire cakes have had to be chucked out because they've come out tasting horrible or the oven was set to the wrong temperature and they've been completely burnt, and one even exploded in the ov—"

"Everyone makes mistakes sometimes," said Dora quickly. "Especially when they're trying new recipes. It is to be expected!"

Mabel frowned and pointed at the mess on the table. "This is more than just a small mistake. Look at it!"

"What were you trying to make?" I asked.

"A lemon tea cake," muttered Dora. "It's a new recipe I saw. I was simply following the instructions and then everything just burst apart all of a sudden!"

"How long has this been happening, Dora?" I asked gently.

Dora compressed her lips, a mixture of embarrassment and annoyance suffusing her face.

She answered reluctantly, "A few weeks. But it's just been a bad spell, that's all. Sometimes you get a run of bad luck or are a bit clumsy with things. It doesn't mean anything."

Mabel gave me a knowing look and tapped the side of her head. "Brain's not what it used to be," she said in a loud whisper.

Dora bristled. "There's nothing wrong with my brain! And you're hardly of an age to be commenting on other people's brain function!"

Mabel drew herself up with superior pride. "My brain is as sharp as it was when I was a twenty-year-old girl. I take great care to keep it active and nimble."

I hastily interceded. "Let's not jump to conclusions. But, Dora, I have to agree with Mabel—if things have been going wrong for a while, you shouldn't just ignore it. Maybe you should see a doctor?"

"I don't need to see a doctor," said Dora quickly. "There is nothing the matter with me! Maybe I've been a bit distracted lately, that's all. It's... it's probably the changing of the seasons. And maybe I've had a touch of the flu."

"*Have* you had flu?" I said, furrowing my brow in an effort to remember. I couldn't recall Dora even having a sniffle in the last few weeks.

"Well, no," Dora admitted. "But perhaps I had some virus without realising... you know, you can get these things..."

"All the more reason to see a doctor," I said. "If it's a case of money, I can—"

"It's not money," said Dora stiffly. "I can afford to see a doctor. In any case, consultations at the village GP clinic are free of charge on the NHS."

"Well, then in that case, I'm going to make an appointment for you with Dr Foster now. And I'm personally going to take you to see him tomorrow afternoon. No arguments," I said, for once standing firm.

Dora looked as if she would protest, then she gave in grudgingly. "Oh, all right. But I'm sure it's all a lot of fuss for nothing."

"And in the meantime, you're not doing anything else today," I said. "I don't care what you say— you're going to stop now and go home and put your feet up. I can—"

Cassie burst into the kitchen. "Gemma!"

I swung around. *What now?*

"It's Liam! He's been mugged and his camera has been stolen!"

CHAPTER SIXTEEN

I had been hoping to get back early enough that evening to surprise Devlin with a home-cooked meal. Instead, I found myself spending most of the evening, tired and hungry, at the police station, sitting with Cassie and her brother whilst the police questioned Liam and took his statement. He had been jumped on by two hooded thugs just as he was turning the corner into the street where my parents lived. They hadn't really hurt him and had grabbed his camera and nothing else, but Liam had been so furious that I think the constable taking his statement had to do a lot of judicious censoring of the language used. Things weren't encouraging though. Liam's brief description of the "thugs" hadn't been very useful and I could see from the expression on the constable's face that they didn't hold out much hope of catching the thieves or retrieving the camera.

"This sort of thing happens a lot around here, especially with all the tourists wandering around Oxford with their expensive cameras hanging off their shoulders, just waiting to be nicked," said the constable, rolling his eyes. "Easy target for thieves. People come to England and think it's not a third world country so it must be safe—oh, it's pretty safe from violent crime, all right, but you still get petty theft. And anywhere there's a bunch of tourists, this kind of thing is rampant. The tourists are all jet-lagged and bumbling around in a strange new environment—"

"I'm not some gormless tourist," said Liam indignantly. "I wasn't just wandering around like a plonker. I *live* in Oxford. And those two bastards weren't random pickpockets, I tell you—they came straight for me!"

"Yes, well, we've got the camera serial number and product description and all that, and it will be entered in the stolen items database," said the constable. "Chances are, they'll try to sell it online. Canon DSLRs are the most popular, and Nikons too... but your model is quite fancy as well. I'd keep an eye out on the online classified sites, if I were you."

Still fuming, Liam left the station with Cassie. I asked at the reception and was delighted to find that Devlin was working late and still in the CID offices. It meant that twenty minutes later, instead of cycling back alone, I found myself being driven home in the sleek comfort of his powerful Jaguar XK. As Devlin drove and listened, I told him about what had happened to Liam.

"Don't you think it's weird that they took his camera but not his wallet?" I said as I finished the story.

"Not necessarily. His wallet was probably tucked deep into a pocket, whereas a camera is an easier item to snatch and grab. And besides, a teenage boy might not be carrying much money anyway, whereas a fancy camera would be quick cash. You don't know how many reports of stolen cameras we get all the time—"

"Yes, the constable who was taking Liam's statement mentioned that. But this wasn't in one of the tourist spots down in the city centre. This was in a quiet side street in a residential suburb." I paused, then said, "I don't think it was just some random petty theft."

Devlin took his eyes off the road for a moment to glance at me. "What do you mean?"

"Liam was coming to meet *me*, actually. He was planning to give me the SD card from his camera, with the photos he'd taken from the fête. You know, because of that police appeal in the newspapers. I was going to show you the pictures tonight—I thought there might be something in them; apparently Liam had been going around the whole fête, taking pictures of people for his portfolio. I thought he might have caught a picture of your 'Agri-Crime Boss'—you know, Nate Briggs—without realising it." I leaned forwards. "I think his camera was stolen on purpose! They didn't want you—the police—to see the photos!"

Devlin raised his eyebrows. "That's a bit far-fetched."

"It all fits!" I insisted. "In fact, Cassie and I were discussing the whole thing in the tearoom this afternoon, in full earshot of everyone there."

"Who was 'everyone'?"

I gave a frustrated sigh. "We were busy so I wasn't paying that much attention. I think there was a group of German tourists by the window and a young American couple next to them... There was another large group at the big table in the centre— from Eastern Europe, I think—I wasn't quite sure if they were one family... and there was a Japanese couple sitting by the fireplace; I remember because they had the most gorgeous little baby in a stroller—big black eyes and a tuft of black hair, just like a doll... and I think there were a couple of village locals sitting near the counter—Frances Moore and Judith Powell, and old Mr Bernard with his niece who's visiting Oxford... and... and Edwin Perkins!" I said suddenly.

"Edwin Perkins?"

I nodded eagerly. "Yes, the second-hand bookseller. He's got a shop in Oxford—and he'd come to Meadowford to value a book collection belonging to a friend of the Old Biddies, who's going into a retirement home—the friend, I mean, not the Old Biddies..." I could see Devlin looking slightly lost. "Anyway, the point is—he was in the tearoom at that time. I remember now because he suddenly rushed off. I was surprised because he'd ordered some tea and sandwiches, but he just got up and left before his order even arrived. He said he had an urgent meeting or something in Oxford which he'd forgotten about, but I remember seeing him talking really urgently on the phone as he was walking away from the tearoom."

"He could have simply been ringing the person he was having the meeting with, to apologise for being late," Devlin pointed out. "And according to the description that Liam gave, I doubt either of the thugs who attacked him was Edwin Perkins. They were young men wearing hoodies."

"Yes, but they could have been hired thugs *sent* by Edwin," I said. "That was probably why he was calling someone so urgently as soon as he left the tearoom. He heard me and Cassie talking about the photos and he was hurrying to inform his accomplice and tell them to get hold of the camera before it fell into the hands of the police."

"Accomplice? Hired thugs?" Devlin gave me an impatient look. "Gemma, you're making Edwin Perkins sound like some kind of criminal ringleader. He's just a second-hand bookseller in Oxford.

Besides, why would he even care about the pictures falling into the hands of the police?"

"Because... because the photos might show him doing something incriminating!" I said. "I'm sure of it! He must have overheard us talking and panicked. That's why he left the tearoom so quickly. He had to find a way to intercept Liam and get hold of that camera."

"Yes, but what incriminating thing would he be worried about, for God's sake? Selling a second-hand novel for retail price?"

"Evidence of him poisoning Dame Clare," I said promptly.

Devlin groaned. "Not that again, Gemma."

"Why not? He's a possible suspect."

"I thought last time you said the daughter was the suspect?"

"The Old Biddies and my mother think it's Mary but I don't agree. I think it's much more likely to be Edwin—or maybe even Joseph, the creepy college gardener."

"Who?" Devlin was starting to look confused and irritable now. "Who on earth is Joseph?"

I launched into a rambling account of my meeting with Edwin at the fête, followed by my trip to his bookstore in town, and the Old Biddies' gossip about Edwin's humiliation at the hands of Dame Clare. Then I told Devlin about my encounter with Joseph in the Ecclestons' garden and Audrey's account of the gardener's anger at the loss of the college flowers.

"So you see, they both had a grudge against Dame Clare and they both could be possible suspects," I finished triumphantly.

"Possible suspects? You're talking as if there is an ongoing murder investigation when there isn't one."

"Well, there ought to be!" I said peevishly. "I think I've given you more than enough reason to start one."

"What you've given me is a bunch of wild theories and speculation, based on circumstantial evidence—if we can even call it that."

"Why won't you at least consider the possibility that Dame Clare could have been murdered?" I burst out in frustration. "It's like you're determined not to take me seriously. *Lincoln* believes me."

"Lincoln?" said Devlin, his voice cool. "You spoke to him about this?"

"Yes, I rang him today, actually," I said, trying not to sound defensive. "And he was very interested. And supportive. He told me that it's possible to fake a heart attack with the use of certain heart medication, such as digitalis. If Dame Clare was poisoned with that, then Dr Foster could have made a mistake—especially if he's not very sharp—and put it down as death due to natural causes. Lincoln thinks the best thing to do would be a post-mortem to double check."

"I'm not ordering a post-mortem just because

Lincoln Green thinks I should," Devlin growled.

I felt my temper flare in response. "Why do you have to be so stubborn? You're just doing this on purpose!"

"I'm not doing anything on purpose," said Devlin through gritted teeth. "I'm simply doing my job— which means not jumping to start murder investigations based on the whims of little old ladies with overactive imaginations and a doctor who should keep his nose in the ICU where it belongs!"

The car pulled up smoothly outside Devlin's house. He got out and slammed the door. I followed suit and stalked into the house after him. Muesli came running up to greet us, vibrating her tail in greeting, then stopped short as if sensing the hostile atmosphere.

"*Meorrw*?" she said, tilting her head and looking up at us curiously.

Devlin gave her a quick pat, then stalked into the kitchen. He took a bottle of red wine out of the pantry and opened the cupboard where the glasses were kept.

"Drink?" he asked curtly.

"No thanks," I said, just as brusque. I realised suddenly that the problem with living together was that when you had a fight, there was nowhere to get away from each other for a while and cool off.

Devlin opened the fridge. "It's a bit late to start cooking a big meal but there's some—"

"I'm not very hungry," I said tightly. "I'm... I'm

going upstairs. I think I'll take a shower, wash off the grime of the day."

I bent down and scooped Muesli up, then turned and started up the stairs to the mezzanine level.

"By the way, Gemma..." Devlin's voice made me pause. "The pile of clothes on the chair by your side of the bed—are you planning to do anything with that?"

"What do you mean?"

"Well... are they going in the wash?"

"No, they're not dirty. They're things I took out this morning which I tried on then decided not to wear. And a couple of things from yesterday too."

"Well, if they're not dirty, why don't you put them back in the drawers or the wardrobe?"

I shrugged. "I don't know... I just couldn't be bothered. I'll sort them out at the end of the week."

"Why not sort them out now?" said Devlin impatiently.

"Why does it matter?" I said in exasperation. "You're not using that chair anyway."

"I just don't see why you need to have them all out, piled in that mess, when it wouldn't take you two minutes to put them away."

"You're not exactly perfectly neat and tidy either," I snapped. "You left a whole bunch of CDs on the table beside the TV in the living room."

"That's different," said Devlin quickly. "There are certain CDs that I always listen to and it's a lot quicker having them out than having to search

174

through the whole collection each time."

"But it's the same thing!" I said. "They look really messy strewn all over the side table. It would only take you two minutes to slot them back with the others. You could arrange them together at one end of the shelf, so that you could find them easily when you want."

"It's just easier this way," said Devlin irritably. "I've always left them out like that and it's been fine." He didn't actually say *"before you moved in with me"* but the implication was there.

I paused, stung and hurt. Devlin picked up on it immediately.

"Gemma... I'm sorry, that came out wrong," he said, coming quickly to the foot of the stairs and looking up at me. "You know I love having you and Muesli here. This is your home now, as much as mine."

I looked away, not meeting his eyes.

"*Meorrw...*" said Muesli forlornly, looking from one of us to the other.

Devlin sighed and ran a hand through his hair. "Look, I think we're both tired and a bit short-tempered tonight. Why don't we take a time-out and start again? You go and have a shower and when you're done, we'll have something to eat. Maybe watch a bit of TV, then have an early night..." He gave me a crooked smile. "What do you say?"

I felt slightly mollified. "Okay," I said at last, dredging up a stiff smile in return.

"*Meorrw!*" said Muesli approvingly, then she wriggled out of my grasp and dropped down, scampering back down the stairs to join Devlin.

I scowled at her. *Traitor.*

CHAPTER SEVENTEEN

Things were still decidedly cool between me and Devlin the next morning as we both got ready for work. It reminded me of when we were students and had a fight—we were always both more than capable of holding stubbornly to our end of the argument. It's one of those hard truths in life, isn't it, when you realise that just because you love someone doesn't mean you'll always agree and get along? I knew it was probably just silly pride, but I felt like I had to stand my ground. I suppose Devlin felt the same. Still, he hesitated as he was about to leave the house and turned back to me.

"Um… I might be late again tonight," he said.

"That's okay."

"If you want to have dinner yourself first—"

"Actually, I think I might have dinner with my

parents," I said. "Since I didn't manage to go yesterday, with what happened to Liam and having to go down to the police station, I thought I might pop in tonight."

"Yes, good idea," said Devlin, perhaps a shade too quickly. Maybe he was thinking, like me, that a bit more time apart would help to heal the breach. Didn't they say that absence makes the heart grow fonder?

He hesitated again, then leaned suddenly towards me and kissed me on the lips. I softened and slid my arms around his neck, kissing him back.

"Maybe we can watch a movie together when I get back," Devlin suggested with a smile when he raised his head at last.

I smiled back. "Sounds good."

When he had gone, I went up to the bedroom and, feeling more charitable now, I tackled the pile of clothes on the chair by the bed, folding them and putting them back in the chest of drawers or hanging them back in the wardrobe. Then I checked Muesli's food and water and got ready to leave.

Because the tearoom didn't open until late morning, I usually had a bit of time to myself in the mornings, particularly if I got up earlier. It was now just past eight o'clock and I had a couple of hours to kill. In spite of mellowing slightly towards Devlin, my frustration about the murder investigation—or lack thereof—rose up again. I just couldn't abandon it. I knew in my gut that something was wrong about Dame Clare's death and I had to find a way to prove it.

I thought back to the conversation I had had with Lincoln yesterday. He was right: the best way to prove "foul play" was to have a post-mortem. But how could I convince Devlin to agree? Then I remembered something else: Devlin had said that a family member could request further examination of the body...

Of course! I could ask Mary! If she put in the request, that would bypass all of Devlin's objections. And surely she would be keen to find out the truth about whether her mother had been murdered?

Galvanised into action, I called Eccleston House, only to be told by Riza that Mary was at St Cecilia's College. I debated for a moment, then headed out, cycling eagerly towards the college situated on the east side of Oxford. St Cecilia's had the distinction of being the last women's-only college in the University and was hanging on precariously to this title. For someone brought up with equal rights for women as the norm, it was weird for me to think of a time when Oxford was a male only-domain. But women hadn't actually been allowed into the University until the early 19th century. And even then, they had to attend special women's-only colleges and weren't given proper degrees. Still, things had certainly reversed since then and all the other women's colleges, such as Lady Margaret Hall and St Hilda's College, had slowly gone "co-ed". All, that is, except for St Cecilia's. And somehow, I didn't think that St Cecilia's would hold out for much longer either.

I pulled up outside the imposing Victorian stone façade of the college, which was partly covered by a blanket of ivy and was one of the most beautiful frontages of any of the University buildings, especially in the autumn, when the ivy leaves turned into a rippling sea of orange and gold. St Cecilia's was not one of the largest Oxford colleges but it more than made up for this with its beautiful grounds, in particular the garden surrounding the college chapel.

A stony-faced porter stopped me as I entered through the college gates. "No visitors today," he said. "We have had a bereavement at the college and it is not open to any outsiders."

"Oh, I'm not a tourist. I'm a member of the University," I said quickly, pulling out my wallet and flashing my old university card. "I'm here to see Mary Eccleston, Dame Clare's daughter."

He thawed slightly. "Ah, in that case..." He nodded his head towards the rear of the college. "I believe you might find Miss Eccleston in the college chapel."

"Thank you," I said and started in the direction he had indicated.

I hurried across the main quadrangle, taking

care to follow the unspoken Oxford custom of not walking on the grass, and made my way down a connecting colonnade into a second quad, which was paved with large flagstones. I had been to St Cecilia's a few times when I was a student and I remembered now that the chapel garden was entered through the archway at the far end of this second quad. I looked around as I walked, admiring the tall casement windows and the symmetrical line of the decorative Dutch gables. I remembered coming here for tutorials and parties, and enjoying the different atmosphere of an all-female college.

Glancing around now, it didn't seem like very much had changed. That was one of the things about Oxford—it had a timeless quality about it, perhaps because the buildings were so ancient and the University rituals and traditions extended back centuries. Oh sure, there were modern changes and developments, but the heart of Oxford remained somehow the same. It was one of the few places you could return to, no matter how long you had been away, and always feel like you were stepping back in time.

I passed through the archway and stepped out into the beautiful garden that surrounded the college chapel. *Wow.* I could see why it was Joseph's pride and joy. Everywhere I looked, there were gorgeous flowers already in bloom, the different varieties artfully arranged so as to display to their best advantage, and the colours blending in perfect harmony. Around them were planted mature trees with graceful spreading branches and neatly trimmed shrubbery which formed an elegant backdrop for the flowers.

As I began to walk down the path towards the chapel, I noticed a bank of plants lining the flower border on my right: tall, elegant stalks each bearing rows upon rows of bell-shaped flowers in various shades of purple and lavender, and the occasional cluster of creamy white. My interest sharpened as I realised what they were. *Foxgloves.* They were blooming unusually early, perhaps as a testament to Joseph's skill. There was something at the base of them: a hunched-over shape which moved slightly. Then I realised it wasn't some*thing*—it was some*one.* Curious, I left the path and went closer.

It was Joseph. He was crouched beside the border, his hands moving lovingly as he carefully scooped out small depressions in the soil in front of the foxgloves and deposited a series of seedlings, gently patting the earth back around them. I could hear a voice murmuring and I was shocked to realise it was Joseph talking. Like Audrey had said, I'd almost thought Joseph to be mute—I'd never heard him utter so much as a word before. But he was speaking now. And with another shock, I realised that he was speaking *to the plants.* In a soft, cooing tone, he was talking to them, giving them words of love and encouragement, such as you would hear a mother tenderly telling her child...

I shifted back, feeling suddenly embarrassed to be listening to this. Like I was spying on someone during their intimate moments with a loved one— which was ridiculous when you thought about it. For heaven's sake, the man was talking to plants!

My sudden movement must have caught Joseph's attention because he jerked his head around and fixed those deep-set eyes on me.

"Oh, s-sorry!" I stammered. "I thought... I mean, I didn't mean to..." I trailed off helplessly, half embarrassed and half annoyed that I felt the need to explain myself again.

He said nothing, remaining kneeling in the dirt, glaring up at me.

This is ridiculous. I mustn't let myself be intimidated by a barmy college gardener!

Standing up taller, I said as calmly as I could: "I was looking for Mary. I had been told that she was in the college chapel?"

He stared at me for a moment longer and then, still not saying anything, he made a strange jerking motion with his head towards the building behind us.

"Ah, she's there? Great. I'll... um... just go along and see her now."

I walked as quickly as I could to the chapel entrance, conscious of his eyes boring into my back the whole way, and relieved when I could finally disappear into the small sandstone building. I paused for a moment, letting my eyes adjust to the dimness within. Like the rest of the college, the chapel was on a modest scale—nothing like the grand cathedral of Christ Church College or the Gothic splendour of Magdalen College chapel. Nevertheless, it was beautiful in its simplicity, with its soaring arched ceilings and the white walls highlighted only by a few narrow stained-glass windows.

For a moment, I thought the chapel was empty, then I realised that there was a lone figure sitting in the very first pew. It was Mary. She was sitting very still, with her head bowed. I hesitated, suddenly feeling embarrassed again at intruding on another person's private moment. I turned, planning to leave her in peace, but my rubber-soled shoes squeaked on the wooden floor and she glanced around.

"Gemma?"

"Hi..." I said weakly. "Sorry, I didn't mean to disturb you..."

She rose and came towards me. I wondered if she had been crying and felt suddenly the archetypal English horror of having to confront such raw emotion in public. But as she came closer, I saw to my relief that her face was calm and composed.

"I'm sorry," I said again. "I didn't realise you were... It's not important, I can come back another time..."

"No, that's okay," she said. "I wasn't really doing

anything. It's just nice to sit in the chapel sometimes. It's quiet and peaceful... and nice to be alone for a bit. I mean, everyone has been really kind to me, but I... I feel like I don't want to talk about Mummy's death anymore... Do you know what I mean?"

"Yes, of course," I said gently. "I can understand completely."

"Was there any particular reason you were looking for me?" asked Mary.

"Er..." I hesitated. After what she had just said, how on earth could I bring up the subject of a post-mortem on her mother's body? I scrabbled around for something else to say. "Um... I was wondering if you wouldn't mind giving me that recipe for your Victoria sponge cake. I've been telling Dora, my chef at the tearoom, how delicious it is and she's very keen to try your version."

"Oh, sure," said Mary, a smile lighting up her face. "I'd be delighted to share it. I don't have it here at the college though. If you give me your email, I can send it to you tonight. I'll have a look for it when I get home."

"No rush, no rush," I said. I turned to leave the chapel. "Thanks. I'll leave you now..."

But she fell into step beside me, following me out into the sunlit garden. "I'll come with you. I wasn't planning to stay much longer anyway. It's nice to see you again, Gemma," she added with a shy smile.

I smiled back, feeling like a worm inside for even suspecting her of her mother's murder. Surely this sweet, shy girl couldn't have murdered anyone?

"The porter at the gate told me that the college was officially in mourning," I said as we walked slowly along the path. "Has there been a memorial service already?"

Mary shook her head. "No, they want to wait until after the funeral, which will be on Friday."

Yikes. That meant I was running out of time. I bit my lip. It was not the right time to ask now—but would it ever be the right time? I took a deep breath and said:

"Mary, I did actually come to ask you something specific."

"Yes?"

"I was wondering..." I hesitated, then said in a rush. "Would you... would you consider requesting a post-mortem on your mother's body?"

She stopped walking and stared at me. "A post-mortem?"

"Yes, there's some uncertainty over her cause of death—whether it might have been a heart attack, after all. I think it's important to confirm that and the only way of knowing for sure is if a forensic pathologist performs a post-mortem."

Mary looked at me in horror. "You want to cut up Mummy's body?"

I winced. "Well, it's not exactly like that. I'm told it's a very discreet cut and they restore everything—

"

"No!" she cried. "I can't do that to Mummy! She would have hated it! Strangers cutting her open and looking inside her—"

"It would just be one stranger really—the pathologist," I said hurriedly. "And they'd only be interested in her body—they wouldn't really be looking at her as a person—" I broke off, cursing myself. *Argh! What a dumb thing to say.*

But really, everything seemed to be the wrong thing to say. I would have to just stop tiptoeing around the subject, I decided grimly. I took another deep breath and said:

"Mary, if there's a chance that your mother could have been the victim of... um... foul play, wouldn't you want to know?"

Her eyes widened. "You think Mummy could have been murdered?"

I hesitated, then thought: *What the hell. In for a penny, in for a pound.* "Yes, I do. I think the heart attack was just a cover-up, a decoy."

"But Dr Foster said—"

"Dr Foster may have been wrong," I said bluntly. "That's why we need a post-mortem. So we can double-check and see if your mother might have been poisoned."

"Poisoned?" Mary's voice rose even higher. "But who would want to poison Mummy?"

I didn't want to say that half of Meadowford village, not to mention the cat show competitors and people here at the college, probably wanted to poison her mother. I tried to evade the question. "Look, we don't need to go into all that now—the first step is to conduct an autopsy to confirm things."

"Do the police suspect someone?" asked Mary. "Is that why they want to do a post-mortem?"

"Um... well, actually the police haven't ordered one," I admitted. "They're still... uh... gathering evidence to support the case. But it's crucial that one is done. And you, as a family member, can request for the body to be examined, without having to wait for the police to open an investigation. It would have to be an independent pathologist and at your own expense," I added. "But... I hope you feel that it's money well worth spending."

"No, I won't do it," said Mary suddenly. "No, it's not the money—I don't mind spending that—but it's disrespectful to Mummy and I can't do that to her. She would hate it—I just know she would—and I can almost hear her voice..." Mary shuddered. "She would never forgive me."

She threw a scared look over her shoulder, as if half-expecting her mother's ghost to suddenly materialise out of nowhere and start berating her.

"If your mother was murdered, she would want you to help the police catch the killer," I said desperately.

"But you just said that the police didn't think there was enough evidence," Mary pointed out. "If they did, they would have started a murder investigation, wouldn't they?"

Reluctantly, I nodded.

"If the police think there is a good reason to do it, then I'll go along, but otherwise, no," said Mary. "I won't let Mummy be cut open just because of some gossip that's going around the village."

I looked at her with new eyes. Mary Eccleston was not as naïve—nor as much of a meek little lamb— as I had thought her to be.

I sighed, defeated. "Okay. But will you please think about it again, especially as the funeral is on Friday?"

Mary nodded and, with that, I had to be satisfied. She walked me to the college front gate and watched as I mounted my bicycle and pushed off. I glanced back as I cycled away and saw her standing there: a small, plump figure silhouetted in the open archway. There was something lost and lonely about her, and I felt a wave of sympathy again.

But mixed in with the pity was something else—a flicker of unease, a feeling of doubt for the first time. I thought back to that vehement refusal to ask for a post-mortem. No matter how much I might like her, I was aware that Mary Eccleston only had to hold out for two more days and then her mother would be safely buried underground, with the chance of an autopsy very unlikely, and the chance of discovering if she had really been murdered gone.

Oh, everything Mary had said made complete sense—she was behaving exactly as a dutiful daughter would have, in such a situation—but I couldn't help thinking that it was also a very convenient attitude to have if you had poisoned your mother and didn't want the truth to come out.

CHAPTER EIGHTEEN

I cycled back from St Cecilia's, feeling very despondent. This case seemed to be going nowhere and I could see that soon, with Dame Clare's funeral, the chance to catch the killer would be lost forever. Once she was buried, it would be even harder—I'd have to fight to get an exhumation order, never mind a post-mortem.

I sighed impatiently. *Oh, why did I care anyway?* The woman had been a horrible, obnoxious tyrant and had probably deserved everything she got, if the gossip was to be believed. Why was I so keen to find her killer?

Because justice needs to be done, answered a voice in my head. Regardless of who the victim was and how unpleasant she had been, she did not deserve to be coldly murdered like that. And the killer did not deserve to get away with it. And if I had it within my power to see justice done, then I knew I should do everything I could to make it happen. I couldn't let it go, just because there were a few hurdles. I had never been a quitter and I didn't intend to start now.

Besides, I thought wryly, *on a purely practical level, if I don't do something about it, my mother and the Old Biddies probably will.* I shuddered to think what they would come up with next in their bid to investigate the case.

I arrived at the tearoom to discover that my fears were well justified. It was still half an hour until we officially opened but, as I cycled up outside the tearoom, I could see through the large front window pane that there was a group of people huddled over a table by the window. I parked my bike in the adjoining courtyard, which used to serve the stables that gave the Little Stables Tearoom its name, and hurried inside through the back door. Cassie and Dora were in the kitchen, getting a few things ready, but I barely called a greeting as I whisked past and out to the dining room. There, I found my mother and the Old Biddies talking excitedly to each other.

"Mother?" I said, going up to them. "What are you doing here? I didn't realise you were coming to the tearoom."

"Oh, I'm on my way to the garden centre to see about that sale," my mother said. "I thought I'd pop in, seeing as I was passing by, and have a little chat with Mabel and the others—" She looked around furtively and lowered her voice in a dramatic fashion, even though there was no one else in the tearoom. "—about The Case."

"Gemma, did Inspector O'Connor say anything to you last night?" asked Glenda eagerly. "Are the police going to start a murder investigation?"

"No," I said, trying to hide my frustration. "Devlin says there isn't enough evidence to justify—"

"Codswallop!" declared Mabel. "Young people today think they know everything. You tell your Inspector O'Connor that I was already a grandmother when he was still in nappies. In fact, I could have been *changing* his nappies. I have half a mind to go to the CID offices and tell him myself—"

"No, no, don't do that," I said hastily. "I don't think the police would appreciate it. You know how they feel about civilian interference."

"They should be thankful that we are offering interference." Mabel glowered. She waved a dismissive hand. "Never mind, we do not need the police. We can conduct the investigation ourselves. You too, Evelyn. You may join our team," she said grandly to my mother.

"Er... wait—what?" I said. "No, no, I don't think that's a good idea. Look, you can't go around breaking into houses and things—you'll get arrested, even at your age!"

"Why on earth do you think we would be breaking into houses?" said Mabel haughtily.

Because that's what I caught you doing last time, you old coot, I thought. Aloud, I said, "Please, don't get involved. I'm working on it—I just need a bit more time. I'm sure I can convince Devlin to order a post-mortem on Dame Clare's body—"

"Why don't you just ask the pathologist, darling?" my mother spoke up.

"What?" I stared at her. "Mother, I can't just go to see him and ask him if he would cut up a body for me, as if I'm asking him to cut up some teacakes!"

"Why not?" asked my mother.

I opened my mouth to answer, then paused and shut it again. She was right—why not? Hadn't Lincoln suggested something similar? Yesterday, during our phone call, he'd said I could try approaching the pathologist myself. And it was known that forensic pathologists sometimes went out on a limb and did things on their own initiative in a murder investigation. Well, they did in books, at any rate, I thought with wry humour. Anyway, what did I have to lose? Nothing at this point.

I turned quickly to the Old Biddies. "Listen, can you and Cassie manage without me here for a bit this morning?"

"Well, of course, Gemma," said Glenda in surprise. "But what—"

"I'll tell you later!" I promised and, leaving them looking after me perplexedly, I dashed back out of the tearoom.

I decided to catch the bus rather than cycle—there was a direct one to the hospital—and I was soon on it, rehearsing in my head what I was going to say. When I got to the hospital, however, I lost my nerve slightly. Suddenly the thought of marching into the morgue, and demanding an autopsy from a pathologist I hadn't even met, seemed very daunting.

I know—I'll go and find Lincoln first. That way at least I'd get the name of the new pathologist and maybe even an idea for how to introduce myself in the most positive way. I made my way up to the Intensive Care ward, only to find that Lincoln wasn't there.

"Dr Green? He's just gone down to the hospital canteen, actually," said one of the nurses at the ICU reception counter. "It's on the third floor. If you go down now, you should be able to find him. There won't be many people there at this time of the morning."

"Thanks," I said, already turning and making for the lifts.

I found the canteen relatively easily and hurried in, scanning the room for a sign of Lincoln's tall figure. I saw him instantly, to my right just as I came in the room, and I started eagerly towards him—then jerked to a stop.

He was leaning against the wall, his body relaxed, his head tilted to one side in a slightly teasing manner, laughing and looking down at a pretty Oriental girl who was standing next to him. From the white coat and scrubs she was wearing, she must have been a doctor, although she looked too young to be even out of medical school. Her hair was jet black and silky straight, pulled back in a low ponytail, and it matched her black almond eyes. She had that enviable smooth glowing skin that all Asian women seemed to possess, with a faint smattering of freckles across her high cheekbones. Her head was tilted back too, looking up at Lincoln and laughing with him as she balanced her tray against one shapely hip.

They're flirting, I realised. And something wriggled uncomfortably inside me.

Suddenly, I changed my mind about speaking to Lincoln. The last thing I wanted to do was intrude on this intimate tête-à-tête. But at that moment, a clatter of crockery across the room made Lincoln look up and his eyes fell on me.

"Gemma!" he said with a smile. "What are you doing here?"

Reluctantly, I approached them. "Uh... hi Lincoln," I said uncomfortably. "Sorry to bother you..." I glanced at the girl, who was looking at me curiously. "I... um... was hoping that you might be able to help me. I wanted to try and speak to the locum forensic pathologist—you know, you said he might be open to listening to me—but I wasn't sure about just going down to the morgue... I was thinking maybe you could give me his name?"

"I can do better than that," said Lincoln with a laugh. He put a hand under the elbow of the girl standing next to him. "Let me introduce you to Dr Josephine Ling. Jo is the forensic pathologist who will be taking over Dr Maxwell's job while he's away on long service leave."

I couldn't help but stare. *This* was the new forensic pathologist? The girl looked like she belonged in a Chinese teenage cheerleading team! Then her gaze met mine and I saw the vivid intelligence in those dark eyes—and I quickly revised my opinion. In spite of her looks, this was no empty-headed China doll.

"Hi, nice to meet you," she said, holding a hand out towards me. She had a soft, musical voice. "What was it you wanted to ask me about?"

"Um..." I hesitated, assessing her, wondering what her reaction would be. Then I tossed caution to the winds. "I'd like you to do a post-mortem on a woman who died last Saturday," I said. "I think she might have been murdered."

"If you think that, shouldn't you be reporting it to the police?" asked Jo.

"I have—that is, I've told Inspector Devlin O'Connor—"

Her eyes lit up. "Oh, Dev! He's great. Such a brilliant investigator."

I eyed her warily. *Dev?*

Jo was continuing, "Wait... last Saturday—was this at that village fête out in the Cotswolds? Wasn't

197

Dev there himself? I heard there was a thing with the Agri-Crime gang…"

"Yes, he was. He arrived just after Dame Clare collapsed and he pronounced her dead."

"Well, surely if he had thought that there was anything suspicious—"

"The thing is, the woman's GP was at the fête as well and he certified that she had died of natural causes. She had had a heart condition and it was put down as a heart attack."

Jo raised her eyebrows. "He didn't feel the need for a post-mortem to confirm?"

"It was Dr Foster from Meadowford-on-Smythe," Lincoln put in.

Jo's eyebrows climbed even higher. "Ah." She looked at me again. "But Dev is normally very sharp about these things. If he doesn't feel that there needs to be an investigation—"

"Devlin could be wrong!" I burst out. I felt slightly disloyal questioning his judgement in public like this, but I was getting desperate. "I'm not sure he's taking the evidence seriously enough."

"You have evidence?" said Jo quickly. "What sort of evidence?"

Quickly, I told her everything I knew, from the inconsistency with the pillbox to the anonymous letter that Mary had found to Edwin Perkins's suspicious behaviour to Joseph's possible grudge and finally the general belief that Dame Clare had many enemies who wouldn't have hesitated to do her harm. When I finished, Jo shook her head sceptically.

"I can see why Devlin is reluctant to turn this into a murder investigation," she said. "All the so-called 'evidence' seems highly circumstantial or tangential and could all have other interpretations."

My heart sank.

She chewed her bottom lip for a moment, thinking to herself. Then she gave me a conspiratorial grin. "Still, I believe in a woman's intuition. I think you're on to something... Okay, I'll do it."

"Really?" I said, delighted. "Can you do it tomorrow? Because she's being buried on Friday."

She considered. "I should be able to swing it. But just be aware that it's not like a cookery show where I can go into the kitchen and say: 'Here's one I made earlier!' I can't just do it on the side and then produce the results to give to the CID. It's got to go through official channels. I'll tell you what I'll do though," she said with sudden enthusiasm. "I'll speak to Dev and tell him that I support your suspicions and get him to officiate everything."

Uh-oh. I hope Devlin won't be annoyed that I've gone behind his back, I thought uncomfortably.

"You might find him really difficult to convince," I said to Jo. "I've already tried speaking to him several times—"

"Oh don't worry, leave Dev to me," she said with a wink. "And I'll tell him that I'll stay late on my own time to do it, so there won't be any question of overtime expenses and impinging on other cases."

"Thanks," I said, surprised and grateful. "That's... that's really nice of you."

"I told you she was great," said Lincoln with an admiring smile.

"Flattery will get you nowhere, Dr Green," said Jo with a laugh and a playful shove at Lincoln's arm. "Now, are you going to help me eat this muffin or not?"

She indicated her tray which contained—in addition to the chocolate muffin—a pasta salad, a tub of yoghurt, a muesli bar, a packet of crisps, a large banana, and a cup of tea. I stared at the crammed tray and then at Jo's slim, petite figure. Where did she put all that food?

"I'll just grab a coffee," said Lincoln, heading towards the canteen counter. He looked back at me. "Would you like to join us, Gemma? Can I get you something?"

"N-no, that's okay," I said quickly. "I've got to get back to the tearoom. But thanks. And thank you," I said, turning back to Jo. "I really appreciate it."

She smiled at me. "No problems. I'll try to squeeze it in tonight, so you'll hopefully have a preliminary report by tomorrow morning."

I left Jo and Lincoln still talking and laughing together in the canteen, and walked slowly out of the hospital to catch my bus back to Meadowford. I was aware of a funny mix of feelings—there was relief and gratitude, but also something a bit like irritation. On the one hand, I was delighted and grateful that Jo was willing to stick her neck out for me. But on the other, her confident takeover of the situation rankled a bit. Like the way she had talked so easily of handling Devlin—or "Dev", as she called him. I frowned. The nickname implied a level of intimacy that I was surprised they had, given that she had only just come to fill in the locum position. And then there was the way Lincoln hovered around her, like a Labrador eager for a pat... and they had *definitely* been flirting when I arrived...

Come on, Gemma, I thought with a wry smile. *You're just jealous! Admit it!*

Okay, so maybe I was. Just a tiny bit. And a tiny bit peeved. Oh, don't get me wrong—of course, I was happy for Lincoln if he had found someone else; I wasn't trying to be "dog in the manger" about it. But... I'm only human. And I guess every girl likes to think that the chap who fancied her wouldn't have moved on *that* quickly and easily. Besides, Jo Ling was the type of girl who would make any woman's hackles go up. She was just so bloody *perfect*—smart, charming, confident, and highly skilled at her job, all while managing to look like some kind of Asian fashion model too!

I shook my head and gave a self-deprecating laugh. All right, maybe I was more than just a teeny bit jealous. Who wouldn't be of that gorgeous creature? Still, if that gorgeous creature helped me prove that Dame Clare had been murdered, I would be eternally grateful to her.

CHAPTER NINETEEN

It was slightly quieter in the tearoom that day, which was just as well because I had to leave early. I had made an appointment for Dora with the village GP and I was making sure that she kept it by practically marching her to the door of the clinic.

"Oh, for goodness' sake! You'd think I was a child, the way you are treating me," Dora grumbled as we left the tearoom together and walked slowly down the cobbled lane to the other side of the village where the GP clinic was situated. "I said I would go and I am going! I don't need you to hold my hand."

However, when we arrived at the clinic and I was about to bid her goodbye, Dora suddenly reached out and caught my arm.

"Um, Gemma... Would you... Do you mind

coming in with me for a bit?" she said, licking her lips. "I mean, if you don't need to rush off—"

"Oh sure, I'd be happy to," I said with a smile. "I'll sit with you in the waiting room until you go in."

"No, actually, I'd like you to come in with me— that is, if you don't mind," said Dora. She swallowed again and I saw the whites of her eyes. "I... um... It would be nice to have a friend with me... if it's bad news."

"I'm sure it won't be that," I said quickly. "It's probably something really simple and the doctor will fix you up in no time."

Inside, we found a waiting room full of what seemed to be sniffing, coughing people and wailing babies. Like most general practice clinics, the appointments were running late and the receptionist informed us apologetically that Dr Foster wouldn't be able to see us for at least another half an hour. Resigned, we went to find seats to wait. I sat down between a lachrymose man with a dripping red nose and a middle-aged woman who was coughing fitfully into her handkerchief, and reflected wryly that it would be a miracle if I left the clinic without catching something. Dora sat on the edge of her seat, her back ramrod straight and her eyes darting nervously around the waiting room. I tried to interest her in the few magazines that were scattered on the table next to us—just to help her take her mind off things—but obviously, the latest celebrity diets and photos of rock stars sunbathing nude on their yachts weren't distracting enough.

Finally, the door next to the reception desk opened and Dr Foster stepped out. He looked even more doddery than he had at the fête, his spectacles sliding off the end of his nose and his white hair slightly rumpled. He called Dora's name and she jumped up like a frightened animal, turning desperate eyes on me.

"I'm here," I said reassuringly, rising and accompanying her into the doctor's inner office.

"I hope you don't mind but I have a first-year intern with me today," said Dr Foster, sitting down at his desk and indicating the young man hovering behind him. "Now then, what can I do for you, Miss Kempton?"

Dora began to speak haltingly whilst Dr Foster made notes on a notepad next to him.

"Hmm... Yes, I see..."

"... and I've been getting terrible headaches," Dora confessed. "Especially at the end of the day, after I've been baking for a while... I find I can't see things... when I look down, everything looks blurred. And... and..." She took a deep breath. "I've been making mistakes."

"What kind of mistakes?"

"Baking mistakes," said Dora, with all the grim horror of someone announcing a global stock market crash or threat to national security.

Dr Foster looked bemused, obviously not

understanding why a baking mistake should be such a grave problem.

"Dora is a very good baker," I explained. "She never makes mistakes."

"Well, now, everyone makes mistakes now and then," said Dr Foster with a smile.

Dora drew herself up with great pride. "*I* don't."

"Now, my dear..."

"Mainly with the new recipes, mind you," added Dora quickly. "I haven't had such trouble with the old ones. But I've been trying some new recipes and I just don't understand—they've come out too sweet or the dough's too wet or even... even tasting absolutely disgusting sometimes! And things getting burnt in the oven... I never make mistakes like that." She fidgeted, looking down at her hands, then looked up again, her eyes scared, "I think... I think there is something wrong with my head. Perhaps something in my brain..." She swallowed convulsively, then said in a rush, "Do you think it might be a tumour, doctor?"

The old doctor frowned. "Hmm... hmm... well, one never knows until one has had the proper tests and such. It is certainly possible..."

"But there could be a simple explanation too, right?" I said quickly, seeing Dora's white face.

"Perhaps, perhaps..." said Dr Foster vaguely. "Have you been having trouble tasting anything?"

"No... I mean, the things haven't tasted very good but I could certainly taste that!"

"Hmm… quite so… and you can distinguish the flavours on your tongue? Sweet, salty, sour?"

"Yes."

"And your hands? Have you been finding yourself dropping things a lot or not having the strength to grip things properly?"

Dora looked down at her calloused hands and shook her head slowly. "I don't think so. I do drop things sometimes but probably no more than usual. I am finding it hard pouring things out properly in a measuring jug though—I just can't seem to get the levels right…" She looked up at him anxiously. "I've never had trouble doing that before."

"And how long have you noticed these… ah… difficulties occurring?"

"It's been coming on so gradually, I can't really remember. You know in the beginning, you just put it down to carelessness or maybe bad luck…" Dora thought for a moment. "Perhaps a couple of months or so now?"

"Hmm… hmm… I see… Now, I'm just going to check a few things…" the old doctor said as he began taking medical equipment out of a drawer.

Dora watched apprehensively as he started to examine her. I sat quietly to one side and tried to give her an encouraging smile every time she looked my way. I could see her getting more and more anxious as the doctor said nothing other than an occasional "Hmm…" and her anxiety began to rub off on me. Could it be something serious after all?

Finally, Dr Foster sat down again opposite Dora. "Miss Kempton, I think we may need to send you for further tests at the hospital—perhaps a full neurological exam," he said gravely.

"Oh my God!" Dora covered her mouth with a hand. "You think... you think...?"

"I think at this stage, we may have to treat it as something serious that requires—"

"*Ahem*... excuse me, sir?" The intern cleared his throat and spoke up for the first time.

We all turned to stare at him. To be honest, I had completely forgotten that he was there. The young man flushed slightly under our gaze but continued doggedly:

"I wonder if I might suggest something... before Miss Kempton is sent to the hospital... Just... just something which may have been overlooked?"

Dr Foster's brows drew together. "Overlooked? Overlooked? What are you going on about, young man?" he blustered. "You are here to watch and listen and learn, not to interfere—"

"What were you thinking of?" I interrupted, looking at the intern encouragingly.

He flushed again, then said, in a hesitant voice, "Well, I did wonder if... if Miss Kempton's eyesight had been checked...?"

Dr Foster stopped in the middle of his tirade and looked dumbfounded for a moment, then said gruffly, "Well, yes, of course... of course, that was the next thing I was going to suggest..." He turned back to Dora, picked up a leaflet from his desk and handed it to her. "Can you read that for me, please?"

Dora looked at the piece of paper, then moved it farther and farther away, until her arm was stretched to its utmost. She squinted and said irritably, "Well, certainly... except that this print is most ridiculously small. Really! It is disgraceful the way they do things nowadays—I am sure text was printed much larger when I was younger but companies will do anything to cut corners these days—I suppose they're trying to save paper and—"

"Miss Kempton, can you read it?"

Dora squinted again, then said stiffly, "I... um... well, not all of it."

Dr Foster leaned towards her. "I think you need to get reading glasses."

Dora looked at him suspiciously. "I'm sorry?"

The doctor chuckled. "My dear, *that* is your problem. You have all the symptoms of presbyopia—otherwise known as 'old eyes'."

Dora was indignant. "My eyes are fine! I have always had excellent eyesight."

"Well... *ahem*... you know, old age does get to us all," said the intern diffidently.

Both Dora and Dr Foster turned around to glare at him. I felt quite sorry for the intern.

"He's right," I said. "And it makes perfect sense, Dora! That's probably why you've been having so many accidents! In fact, if you misread the recipe ingredients in particular and think that the measures have an extra zero or something, that would account for a lot of things! You'd be adding ten or more times the amount needed—which could end up tasting awful or even cause some kind of chemical reaction, which might explain all the explosions!"

"What a lot of nonsense!" Dora said.

"You have to admit—you are finding it much harder to read recipe instructions, right? And the numbers on the measuring jug?"

"Well, I... yes, sometimes... but that's because the lighting in the tearoom kitchen is just dreadful," said Dora. "I'm sure I'd be fine if it was brighter in there."

"It's not that dark," I protested with a laugh.

Dr Foster acknowledged my comment with a smile. "Presbyopia is worse in dim light—it is one of the classic symptoms."

Dora shook her head emphatically. "No, no, you don't understand. I know people's eyesight tends to get worse as they get older. I had several colleagues—other college scouts—who had to get reading glasses when they got into their forties. But *I* never needed them. My eyes were always perfect," Dora said proudly.

"Not everyone ages the same way," Dr Foster said. "It is true that most people start developing presbyopia around the age of forty but it varies. Some people don't need glasses until much later and a few lucky ones don't ever need them. I knew a lady who lived to her late nineties, who could still read perfectly fine with no visual aids. But that is extremely rare."

"What causes it?" I asked, thinking worriedly of my own still youthful eyesight.

"Well, my dear, it *is* just aging really. It's the lens in your eye. It gets less elastic as you get older, so it isn't as flexible any more. This means that when you look at something close to you and your eyes need to refocus, your eye muscles aren't able to bend the lens so well anymore and everything becomes blurred. It also leads to eyestrain—which can lead to headaches." He turned to Dora. "That would explain why you have been getting headaches, especially after a day of struggling to read recipe instructions and numbers."

"Yes, even the dials on the oven," I said. "That would explain why things end up overcooked and burnt, because you set it at the wrong temperature without realising."

Dr Foster patted Dora's hand in an avuncular fashion. "My dear, you need to go and see an optician and get yourself some prescription reading glasses. And then you'll be fine. There is no shame in that—we all need a little help sometimes and it will make all the difference."

"Oh, all right," said Dora grudgingly.

"There's a good optician in Oxford," I offered. "My mother goes there. I can help you make an appointment, if you like."

Dr Foster beamed. "Good, good... Well, I'm glad we've cleared that up and it was nothing serious. I knew it wouldn't be—when you've been a doctor for as many years as I have, not much gets past you."

I caught the intern's eye and we exchanged a surreptitious grin.

"Yes," Dora agreed with some relief. The colour had come back into her face. "I had been worrying that it might be something awful," she confessed. "Well, you know, with all the things that have been happening recently and people being struck down suddenly, like that lady at the village fête—"

"Ah, yes, poor Dame Clare..." Dr Foster tutted, shaking his head. "That was really very unfortunate. Of course, I did warn her family—her daughter, Mary, and even Mr Perkins when he was asking me about her heart condition—"

"Mr Perkins?" I sat up straighter. "Edwin Perkins? He was asking about Dame Clare's health?"

"Yes, he is an old friend of the family," said Dr Foster. "A most conscientious man. He was very concerned about her—and quite rightly too. He came to me one day and spoke to me in confidence, asking me about Dame Clare's prognosis."

"What did you tell him?" I asked eagerly.

"Well, I told him the truth, of course. That she had a heart condition which—combined with her weight and diet—put her at potentially high risk for a heart attack or stroke at any time. However, I did assure him that it wasn't definite; with the right management and care, Dame Clare could have lived for many more years to come."

"It was nice of Mr Perkins to be so concerned."

"Yes, yes, very commendable of him. But I suppose as an old friend of the family, he felt a certain responsibility, now that Sir Henry has passed away. He even wanted to make sure that she was on the right medication. Of course, I assured him that that was the case."

"Mr Perkins was asking about Dame Clare's medication? That's very... conscientious of him," I said carefully. "Was he worried that she might take an overdose or something?"

"Funny you should say that," said Dr Foster, furrowing his brow. "That is exactly what he did ask me about! He wanted to know what the dangers were of her taking an overdose of her angina medication. I assured him that as long as she followed instructions, it should be very safe. Now, if she had been on digoxin, that would have been a different story, of course. Very narrow therapeutic index, these digitalis compounds. One can overdose so easily and the effects can be fatal."

"Did you tell Mr Perkins that?"

"Oh yes, certainly, but I assured him that Dame Clare was quite safe because she *wasn't* on digoxin."

"When did he come and speak to you about

this?" I asked.

Dr Foster frowned. "Last week, I believe." He sighed and tutted again. "Who would have thought that only a few days after I spoke to him, the dear lady would collapse and die?"

CHAPTER TWENTY

My phone rang just as Dora and I were leaving the GP clinic. I let her walk on while I took the call. It was Devlin.

"Hi Gemma—I heard from Jo Ling that you've been speaking to her about Dame Clare."

"I wasn't trying to go behind your back or anything," I said hurriedly. "I just happened to bump into Jo by accident; I was... um... looking for Lincoln to ask him something and he happened to be with her so he introduced us. We got talking and—well, she agreed with me that the circumstances surrounding Dame Clare's death could be suspicious."

"Yes, that's what she told me too—and I think it might be worth doing a post-mortem after all."

"You... you do?" I said in surprise.

"Well, the way Jo explained it to me—it does seem to be a reasonable next step. And I respect her expertise and judgement in such matters. If Jo feels it's worth investigating further, I'm happy to sanction it."

But obviously not if I feel it's worth investigating, I thought resentfully. Aloud, I said, "That's great. So when will the post-mortem be? The funeral is on Friday so we don't have much time—"

"That's all right, Jo's got things sorted. She's contacted all the people who need to give approval and sweet-talked them into agreeing with everything. I'll have to put in the official report, of course, but she's basically done all the legwork for me." Devlin laughed. "When Jo decides she wants something, she makes it happen! And she's volunteered to stay late tonight to do the post-mortem in her own time, which is bloody nice of her. It means I don't have to worry about trying to squeeze it into the caseload tomorrow or delay the funeral."

"What about Mary Eccleston? Don't you still need to let her know that you will be conducting an autopsy on her mother?"

"Yes, Jo said she would take care of that too."

Was there anything that Jo Ling couldn't take care of? I suppressed the dour thought and reminded myself that I should be grateful. I was getting what I wanted.

"That all sounds fantastic. Good old Jo. So when

will she have the results?"

"The preliminary report should be ready tomorrow morning. And in fact, I think I might join her for the post-mortem this evening. You don't mind, do you?" said Devlin. "I'll be late getting back—but if it *is* murder, then I think it's important that I'm there. It'll be helpful to hear Jo's first impressions. She's got a very astute way of looking at things."

I tried to ignore that sharp niggle of jealousy. "Um... yeah, sure. So I guess I'll see you when I see you..."

I hung up and stared at the screen. I should have been glad, I knew, that progress was being made on the case at last. The post-mortem was the single most important thing—it would prove that Dame Clare had been murdered and probably give us clues as to how. I should have been grateful to Jo for pulling all the strings needed to make this happen.

All the same, I couldn't help a faint feeling of resentment at the easy way she had achieved everything I had been struggling to do in the last few days. Devlin had even scoffed at the whole murder theory until Jo suggested it. Why should he respect her judgement so much more than mine?

***

The whole episode left me in a pretty grumpy mood, and I was unexpectedly pleased when I remembered that I was supposed to have dinner with my parents that evening. It would be better than going home by myself to sit in Devlin's empty house and brood. Even my mother at her most exasperating would still be a welcome distraction.

I arrived at my parents' elegant townhouse in North Oxford to find the comforting smells of an old-fashioned roast permeating the air and the familiar sight of my father at the head of the table, which was beautifully laid as usual with linen tablecloth, sparkling glassware, and gleaming cutlery and crockery. My mother was just wheeling her little serving trolley into the dining room, ready to serve the first course of soup.

"Hi Dad," I said, giving him a quick peck on the cheek before sliding into my usual seat.

He nodded and smiled absent-mindedly at me. "Hello, dear. How nice to see you. Is the tearoom going well? And how are you settling in at Devlin's place?"

A warm feeling flooded through me. The questions might have been different but his gentle, interested manner was the same as when I had sat down at the table twenty years ago, ten years ago... and he had asked me about school, about university... Meanwhile, my mother hovered on my other side, asking if I had washed my hands and saying my shirt collar needed proper ironing. I smiled to myself, for once not minding her fussing. *It's nice to be independent*, I thought, *but sometimes, it's really nice to come back to the nest too.*

My mother seemed to be bursting to tell me something all through dinner and as soon as dessert had been eaten and my father was comfortably settled in the sitting room with a cup of tea, she hustled me into the kitchen and said dramatically:

"Darling, I think I have found A Clue!"

"A clue to what, Mother?"

"To Dame Clare's murder, of course!" she said. "I've talked it over with Mabel and the others, and they all agree that it is something of Vital Importance."

"What is it?" I asked, curious in spite of myself.

"Well, you know I went to the garden centre this morning? They were advertising a sale and I wanted to pick up some begonias... although it occurred to me that some water lilies would be a lovely addition to the water feature at the tearoom and I—"

"What?" I said in alarm. "No, no, I don't need any water lilies for the water feature, thank you!"

It was bad enough having to live with that monstrosity without getting any more accessories for it! The hideous purple elephant water feature was my mother's proudest purchase since her discovery of online shopping and it was the bane of my life. I was still trying to figure out a way to sell it on eBay without my mother finding out.

"Oh, but darling, they have the most wonderful aquatic section there—gorgeous miniature water lilies, club rushes and water violets, and British natives like starwort—and they come already rooted in a mesh basket, with aquatic compost so you can just place them directly—"

"No, Mother," I said hastily. "I really don't need any water lilies at the tearoom. Thank you. Anyway, what does this have to do with your clue?"

"Oh yes, the clue—well, I was walking down the aisle for the bedding plants and I must say, darling, they had the most gorgeous fuchsias and dahlias too... I had been thinking of getting some Begonia Sunset Yellow for my hanging baskets but the display there made me wonder if Fuchsia Bella Rosella might be better... Of course, the Busy Lizzies always look fabulous too—"

"*Mother!* What does this have to do with Dame Clare's murder?"

"Hmm? Oh, Dame Clare... yes, well, when I arrived, I couldn't remember the exact deal I had seen in that newspaper supplement so I picked up a copy from the pile by the front door to refresh my memory. And that's when I noticed it!"

"Noticed what?"

"My fingers were stained the most horrible blue!"

"And?" I looked at her in puzzlement.

"Well, I remembered the last time my fingers had

got so horribly stained, with exactly that shade of blue..." She paused dramatically. "When I was looking at the anonymous note!"

I frowned. "The note that Mary Eccleston showed us?"

My mother nodded. "Yes, I found the most dreadful stains on my cream skirt that day and I couldn't understand where they had come from. Horrible, ugly blue streaks... and then I realised that it was on my fingers as well. I hadn't noticed at the time but I must have got it on my hands when we were looking at that note. You see, the letters that were cut out to form the words in the note—I think they were cut out from a copy of the garden centre supplement."

"Yes, you could be right," I said, suddenly interested. I remembered that morning when I had sat with my mother at breakfast and she had first pulled the garden centre supplement out of the newspaper. She had complained then about the cheap paper and poor ink quality. And I remembered now that I had noticed my own fingers being stained after that visit to Eccleston House, although I hadn't paid it much attention at the time.

"And that means the person who sent the anonymous note to Dame Clare—who might have been her murderer—" my mother added breathlessly, "—is probably someone who shops at the garden centre."

I frowned. "That doesn't narrow the field *that* much. I mean, people go to that garden centre from all around—and if the supplement had been inserted into local newspapers and then distributed all over the county, anyone in Oxfordshire could have had access to copies."

My mother looked crestfallen at my lack of enthusiasm for her "important clue" and I felt slightly bad.

"It's still a good finding, Mother," I said encouragingly. "Taken together with some other things, it might be very valuable. Do you know if Mary has reported the note to the police yet?"

"I believe she hasn't decided yet."

"She really should show it to them," I said, with a frustrated sigh.

"Yes, that's what Audrey says too. She is really very worried about this whole thing, you know, and she thinks it's wonderful that Mabel and I have taken the investigation into our own hands, since the police aren't doing anything about finding Clare Eccleston's murderer."

"Well, they *are* doing something about it now," I said and I told my mother about the post-mortem that was happening that evening. "This will confirm whether Dame Clare died of natural causes and, if not, what the cause of death was. And then the CID can start an investigation."

"Well, I'm glad the police are finally taking this seriously!" said my mother with some asperity. "And

I am sure that when the autopsy is done, they will discover that Dame Clare was horribly poisoned."

"Mother, until we know the results of the post-mortem, you can't jump to conclusions like that," I protested. (Okay, it was a bit hypocritical since I was thinking the same thing myself. Still, I felt that I had to offer a voice of caution.) "They may yet find that she died of a heart attack."

"No," said my mother complacently. "She was poisoned."

CHAPTER TWENTY-ONE

As usual, my mother turned out to be right. Devlin rang me as soon as he got to work the next morning and said, with a grudging note of respect in his voice:

"I hate to admit this but Mabel Cooke and your mother were right. I had the preliminary report from Jo waiting for me on my desk. Clare Eccleston did not die of a heart attack. Well, she did, but not in a natural way. She was poisoned—which caused her heart to go into cardiac arrest."

"What was the poison?"

"We won't have details until we get the results from the lab, but Jo says she did a tox analysis of the blood, urine, and stomach contents, and managed to identify that a cardiac glycoside was present. We'll need to wait for further testing with gas chromatography and mass spectroscopy to determine exactly which one."

"A cardiac glycoside? Could it be digitalis?" I asked as an image flashed uneasily in my mind of a bed of tall, elegant foxgloves standing in the gardens at Eccleston House—*where Mary had easy access to them*, I thought, then I pushed the thought away. Instead, I reminded myself that there was also a glorious border of foxgloves in the beautiful chapel gardens of St Cecilia's College, where Joseph the gardener tended them with loving care. I thought of my mother's "clue" from last night. A gardener like Joseph would probably spend a lot of time going to garden centres...

Devlin was speaking and I pulled myself with an effort back to the present.

"Yes, according to Jo, digitalis—or digoxin, the purified drug form—would be the most common one," he said.

"Could she tell how the poison was administered?"

"Most likely through ingestion. And from the amount of poison in Clare Eccleston's system and how quickly she collapsed, the woman probably took it no more than half an hour before her death. There were no needle marks on the body but Jo said the stomach contents showed remnants of what looked like sponge cake, which had barely been digested."

"Oh, yes, that's right," I said. "It was Victoria

sponge cake. She was having some just before the judging started. Mary, her daughter, had baked a couple for the cake stall at the fête and Dame Clare had insisted on eating some—but wait..." I frowned. "It can't have been the cake. We all had a slice—and none of us got sick."

"What do you mean?"

"Well, my mother and me and Audrey—and Mary herself—all had a slice of the same Victoria sponge cake. So the poison can't have been in the cake, surely, otherwise it would have affected us all?"

"Maybe it was only in the piece that Dame Clare had. I presume you all had individual plates?"

"Yes. Mary cut the cake up and handed the slices out to each of us."

"Was there anyone else in the vicinity?"

I thought back. "There was another competitor— a lady with Siamese cats called Theresa Bell. She was at the table next to us. In fact, she was offered a piece of the cake, but she refused."

"She refused, did she?" said Devlin quickly.

"Yes, and funnily enough, the reason she refused was because she said it might have been poisoned," I said with an ironic laugh. "She was a weird woman. When we first arrived, she told me that someone was trying to kill her."

"She said what?"

"Yeah, she took me aside and told me that someone was trying to harm her and her cats; she kept going on about past attacks on her at other shows and how everyone was in a conspiracy against her, that everybody was all out to get her. It was all very melodramatic. She even accused me of trying to poison her cats' water just because I had been standing next to their cage..."

"Sounds to me like she has a persecution complex," mused Devlin.

"What's that?"

"It's... well, I guess you could call it a type of mental disorder. We covered it briefly in our CID training. Basically, it's when someone has an irrational and obsessive feeling that they are the victim of hostility from others. It's like a form of paranoia, I suppose, although the people who suffer from it genuinely believe that everyone is out to get them."

"And if someone has this, do you think they might lash out first in what they think is self-defence? Like... 'get them before they get me'?"

"It's possible," said Devlin. "If someone is suffering from a persecution complex, they will often get suspicious—usually without any real basis—that others are exploiting or harming them and they will read demeaning or even threatening meanings into random benign remarks that other people make. So they're more likely to react angrily because they're always on the defensive already."

"Theresa did mention that she thought Dame Clare had tried to poison her Siamese cats at the last show," I said excitedly. "Maybe she decided to poison the Dame as a way to counter-attack first?"

"We're jumping to conclusions here," said Devlin in a warning tone. "I'd have to interview this woman myself first to make up my mind about the persecution complex. I'm only going on what you've told me so far about her behaviour that day." He paused, then said, "But first, I need to speak to Mary Eccleston. She is currently the top suspect."

"It can't be Mary!" I said. "She's such a sweet, shy girl—and she was so upset that day, when her mother died...I just can't believe it's her."

"Gemma, you can't afford to let your emotions cloud your judgement. It's well known that most murder victims know their killers and that a family member is often the culprit. In addition, Mary has the most to gain from Dame Clare's death. I did some quick asking around this morning and I believe she is the sole beneficiary of her mother's estate. She is now a very rich young woman."

"Yes, but money isn't the only reason people commit murder," I said quickly. "Dame Clare sounds like she had a lot of enemies. The woman was an absolute cow and I think there were lots of people in the village—not to mention St Cecilia's College—who would have happily plotted her death."

"Anyone in particular?"

"Well, Audrey Simmons from the village was telling me about the college gardener..."

"The college gardener? The one you mentioned

before?"

"Yes, Joseph. I don't know what his surname is. Remember I told you I'd met him a couple of times? He does some extra work at Eccleston House from time to time."

"Yes, I vaguely remember you telling me about him, but I have to admit, I wasn't paying that much attention. Not with regards to a suspect in a murder case anyway."

"He's a really odd bloke. A bit creepy."

"Creepy in what way?"

"Oh, nothing sexual. Just... very weird. He never speaks, for one thing, and he never looks you in the eye—and he's got a strange obsession with his plants."

"Well, he *is* a gardener," said Devlin with a laugh.

"No, no, it's more than that. It's almost as if he sees them as... well, as human. Like... like I came across him at St Cecilia's and he was talking to a bunch of seedlings."

"Talking?"

"I know, it sounds crazy but that was exactly what he was doing. He was having an entire conversation with them and talking to them, as if they were people or something. It was really bizarre."

"Well, that does sound a bit strange but there are probably all sorts of men out there with unusual passions and hobbies. Doesn't make them murderers."

"Yes, I know, but Joseph has a motive too." Quickly, I recounted the story that Audrey had told me about Dame Clare and Joseph's huge fight over the planting of the border by the college chapel.

"You're not seriously suggesting that a man might have murdered someone just because of some dead plants?" said Devlin sceptically. "And how would he have got hold of the poison?"

"There are foxgloves growing all over the college gardens," I said quickly. "And loads at Eccleston House too. Given his expertise, I'm sure Joseph would have the knowledge of how to harvest them and extract the active ingredient."

"Was he at the fête?"

"No," I admitted. "Not as far as I know. But that doesn't mean that he couldn't have been there. There were a lot of people milling about; he's a quiet, nondescript, middle-aged man—I imagine that he could have easily got lost in the crowds."

"What you're saying is that he doesn't have an alibi for the time of the murder—that he could have somehow slipped unnoticed into the cat show pavilion and added poison to the slice of cake on Dame Clare's plate."

"Yes."

"Okay..." I heard the sound of a pen scratching, then Devlin said: "And anyone else on the day who was behaving suspiciously?"

"Well, I don't know about behaving suspiciously

at the show, but there *is* someone who had been behaving suspiciously before the show. And afterwards too."

"Who's that?"

"Edwin Perkins."

"Perkins... the bookseller chap? The one you thought might be some kind of crime boss who set thugs on Cassie's brother?"

I flushed. "Well, you have to admit that was a weird coincidence. And it's also a coincidence that he happens to be a family friend of the Ecclestons."

"But we come back to the same thing: motive. Why would Edwin Perkins want to murder Dame Clare?"

"Well, it could be revenge. I heard from village gossip that Edwin is besotted with Mary Eccleston. And I also heard that Dame Clare opposed any chance of a relationship—in fact, she took great delight in humiliating him very publicly about it."

"You're thinking that he murdered her because she humiliated him?" Again, Devlin sounded sceptical.

I shrugged, even though I knew he couldn't see me. "You're the one who told me before that people commit murder for all sorts of trivial reasons. And when it comes to things like love and relationships, people can get really sensitive, can't they? In fact, I can just imagine someone of Edwin's pompous, stuffy personality would take a public humiliation really badly and decide to get revenge for it."

"Hmm…"

I could hear from Devlin's tone that he still wasn't convinced.

"Or…" I said, suddenly thinking back to that day in the tearoom with the Old Biddies gossiping and hearing Ethel's voice again, saying: *"He is so devoted to her—he really would do anything for her…"*

"Maybe he did it for Mary," I said.

"How do you mean?"

"Maybe he killed Dame Clare out of 'love' for her daughter. You don't know what a tyrant Clare Eccleston was—and poor Mary was completely abused by her. Maybe Edwin couldn't bear to see her being treated like that anymore and thought that by getting rid of her mother, he'd be setting Mary free. In fact, it would have been a double bonus because it also meant that there would be no one stopping her from having a relationship with him. Assuming she wanted to, that is."

Devlin made an incredulous noise. "Mary Eccleston is twenty-five years old. Surely she doesn't need her mother's permission to date someone?"

"You haven't seen her with her mother," I said. "It wasn't a normal relationship. I mean, I thought *my* mother was a bit overbearing at times but bloody hell, she's nothing compared to Dame Clare! That woman was an absolute bully and Mary's entire life was dominated and controlled by her mother. I think she got so used to being meek and submissive—I don't think it ever entered Mary's head to defy her mother."

"She defied her mother the night before the show," Devlin pointed out. "I remember you mentioning that the Ecclestons' maid overheard the mother and daughter screaming at each other."

Bugger, why does Devlin have to have such a good memory? "Yeah, that's right," I admitted.

"Did the maid say what she had actually overheard? Like anything Mary said?"

I hesitated, not wanting to tell him.

"Gemma?" Devlin's voice was sharp. "What is it? There's something you're holding back."

"It's nothing," I said. "I'm sure it doesn't mean anything—just a childish thing."

"What is it?"

"The maid overheard Mary screaming at her mother: *'I'M SICK AND TIRED OF BEING YOUR SLAVE—I HATE YOU! I WISH YOU WERE DEAD!'*— just before she stormed out of the room."

"I... see."

"But surely that doesn't necessarily mean anything?" I said. "I mean, it's the kind of thing teenagers are always screaming at their parents and nobody expects them to all be murderers."

"They might if the parents turn up dead the next day and the teenager stands to inherit everything, plus had the best opportunity to administer the poison. In any case, Mary's not a teenager."

233

"I just can't believe it's Mary..." I said miserably.

Devlin's voice softened. "Well, for what it's worth, I promise I will give the other suspects you mentioned equal consideration. In fact, I might go and question Edwin Perkins first, before I interview Mary."

"Make sure you ask him what he was doing in the cat pavilion," I said.

"I thought you said you didn't see him in there."

"No, I didn't see him *in* the pavilion but I bumped into him just as he was coming out of the tent and I was going in. I was on my way back with two glasses of lemonade and I practically crashed into him. He seemed to be in a big hurry—I'd like to know what he was doing in there. If we're saying that Joseph could have slipped into the cat show and added poison to Dame Clare's cake unnoticed, the same could be said for Edwin."

"Yes, very good point. Well, Mr Perkins and I are going to have an interesting chat," said Devlin grimly.

"Devlin, about Mary... Will you be asking her to come down to the station?"

He was silent for a moment, then said, "No, in view of her recent bereavement, I'll keep things friendly and casual for the time being. I'll question her at home this afternoon."

"In that case, can I come? Please? It would just be like if she had a friend or relative staying with her, who happened to be there when you arrived," I pleaded. "And she might be more willing to talk if she feels like she has a friend with her."

Devlin hesitated, then said, "All right. But don't think you're going to make a habit of this, Gemma. You know I really shouldn't allow civilians to get involved in an investigation..."

I grinned to myself. "Oh, totally! One-time exception only!"

CHAPTER TWENTY-TWO

I hurried over to Eccleston House as soon as I could get away from the tearoom that afternoon. Devlin was already there when I arrived, sitting in the spacious drawing room opposite Mary, who was perched on the edge of sofa, looking like a frightened rabbit. Her face lit up as I was shown into the room by Riza.

"Gemma!" She jumped up, a tremulous smile breaking across her face, and hurried over to me.

"I was just passing by and thought I'd pop in to see how you were doing," I said smoothly.

Mary gripped my hands tightly. "Oh Gemma, they're saying that Mummy was murdered!"

I squeezed her hands reassuringly and threw a questioning glance towards Devlin.

Mary noticed my look and made an effort to

compose herself. She led me over to join Devlin on the sofa and said, "Inspector O'Connor wants to ask me some questions about Mummy and what happened at the cat show on Saturday."

I sat down next to Mary and nodded encouragingly. "You should tell him everything. Have you shown him that anonymous note?"

Mary hesitated, glancing quickly at Devlin, then back to me, then she shook her head.

"What note is this?" said Devlin, with a perfect pretence of ignorance.

Mary hesitated again, then rose and went over to an old-fashioned writing desk at the side of the room. From the top drawer, she pulled out a plain A4 envelope and handed it to Devlin.

"I put it in there," she said. "I found it with Aunt Audrey when we were going through Mummy's papers the day after the fête. It was a really nasty shock to find it."

Devlin opened the envelope and peered inside, then he took some latex gloves out of his pocket and put them on before carefully extracting the piece of paper. Silently, he read the message spelled out by the cut-out letters. I noticed that the dark blue ink from the cut-out letters had bled a little and smeared across the paper, blurring the words.

Devlin looked back at Mary. "Do you have any idea who might have sent this?"

Mary shook her head. "There were some anonymous letters sent to Mummy at the college last year... Everyone thought that some of the students had sent those. But they weren't this... this nasty—they were more like prank letters. And they looked different. They had been typed on a computer, whereas this one looks like someone cut out letters from something and stuck them on."

"My mother thinks the letters could have been cut out from the local garden centre supplement," I spoke up. "The print is in the same blue ink and it stains your fingers when you handle it. We both noticed that our fingers got this strange blue stain on them, the day Mary first showed us the note, but we didn't realise the significance of it until my mother went back to the garden centre yesterday and picked up a copy of the same supplement again—and got the same stain on her fingers."

"Hmm, very interesting," said Devlin. He slid the letter carefully back inside the envelope. "I'll take this in as evidence and have Forensics go over it, although I don't hold out much hope for things like fingerprints since it's been handled by so many people. Who else has seen this note?"

"Well, aside from Aunt Audrey and me, only Gemma, her mother, and Mrs Cooke and her friends," said Mary.

"That's a lot of fingerprints already." Devlin laid the envelope aside and leaned forwards slightly. "Mary, there's evidence that your mother was poisoned and we believe it was via the cake she was eating, just before the judging began. A Victoria sponge cake, I believe?"

Mary frowned. "Yes, but I baked the cake myself. Besides, we all had some and we were all fine!"

Devlin held up a hand. "Yes, I know—which is why I think the poison might have only been in the slice of cake that your mother had on her plate. Someone must have tampered with it. Did you notice anyone hovering around your table, especially near your mother's plate?"

Mary looked bewildered. "I... I don't know. I mean, I wasn't really watching the plate. We were so busy getting Camilla ready for the judge... and there were so many people around us..." She trailed off.

"Did you see anyone else at the show that you knew?" said Devlin, changing tack.

"Well, I suppose we knew a lot of the competitors there vaguely—"

"No, I meant someone you knew well, like a close friend, perhaps?"

Mary shook her head. "No, not really. As I said, I wasn't paying that much attention but I don't remember seeing anyone. I suppose we knew Theresa Bell fairly well—she was the lady with the Siamese cats at the table next to us—we'd seen her quite a few times at other shows, but I wouldn't say she was a friend." She gave an embarrassed laugh.

Devlin persisted. "Did you not see Edwin Perkins at the show?"

"Edwin?" Mary looked surprised. "Yes, I saw him as Gemma and I were leaving—"

239

"No, I meant before that. During the actual cat show—in the pavilion. Did you see him there?"

"Oh no, I definitely didn't see him in the pavilion."

Devlin nodded. I looked at him curiously but he didn't elaborate. Instead, he said, "What was in the cake?"

"Just what is usually in the recipe: flour, eggs, and butter for the sponge bases, strawberry jam and fresh whipped cream for the filling. Oh, and some fresh strawberries as a garnish, and some icing sugar on top of everything."

"The icing sugar," I said suddenly. "It would be really easy to mix something into that and dust it on top of the cake. You wouldn't even notice and the sweetness of the sugar would probably mask any bitter taste."

Devlin nodded grimly. "Yes, I was thinking the same thing. Someone could have had the poison ground up in powdered form and mixed it in with icing sugar, then carried in a small container—like a small bottle of talcum powder. Then if they slipped unnoticed into the show, and managed to get to the side of the Ecclestons' table when no one was looking, they could have easily sprinkled some poisoned icing sugar over the piece of cake."

"But I didn't see anyone do that!" said Mary.

Devlin didn't reply but I knew he was thinking: *Because you could have done it yourself.* And he was right. In fact, Mary was the person with the most opportunity to tamper with the piece of cake; she had been the one who was cutting up the pieces and serving them around.

As if echoing my thoughts, Devin said, his voice changing, "Mary, I believe you and your mother had an argument the night before the show?"

Mary flushed. "Wh-what do you mean?" she stammered.

"You were overheard," said Devlin baldly. "Apparently you shouted at your mother that you were sick and tired of being her slave and that you wished she was dead?"

"B-but I didn't mean it..." Mary cried. "It's just something you s-say when you're cross..." She gasped. "Do you think I killed Mummy? I would never want Mummy to die!" She burst into tears.

Devlin looked slightly taken aback. I put an arm around Mary and gave him a reproachful look over the top of her head. Although she was twenty-five, in many ways, Mary still had the emotional vulnerability of a ten-year-old child.

"I'm sure the Inspector didn't mean anything like that," I said soothingly, patting Mary's arm. She sniffled and gulped as I grabbed a tissue from the box on the table and handed it to her. We waited while she blew her nose and regained control of herself.

"I'm sorry," she said in a small voice at last. "I don't think I want to answer any more questions now."

Devlin stood up. "I'm sorry I upset you, Miss Eccleston, but it's important for me to ask these questions if we are to find your mother's killer."

She nodded but didn't reply.

Devlin handed her his card. "If you think of anything else that might help, please don't hesitate to get in touch or..." His eyes strayed to me. "Maybe you'd prefer to speak to Gemma instead? That would be fine too."

Mary nodded again and took the card, then saw us to the door. I gave her a quick hug and followed Devlin out of the house. We walked slowly down the drive, our shoes crunching on the gravel.

"I need to head back to the station; I'm afraid I'm going to be pretty late again tonight. There are quite a few things I need to tie up on other cases," said Devlin regretfully as we paused by his Jaguar parked outside the gates to the property. "But I can give you a lift back to the house—"

"No, it's okay—I'll cycle. The exercise will be good for me. By the way, why did you ask Mary that question about Edwin Perkins and whether she'd seen him at the cat show?"

"Because that was his pretext for being in the pavilion. I questioned him earlier this afternoon and he said he went into the cat show pavilion to say hello to the Ecclestons—but when he got there, they were obviously so preoccupied with getting the cat ready for judging that he decided it was a bad time and that he would go back later." He gave me a dry smile. "A perfectly plausible explanation."

"Except that Mary said she never saw him," I said quickly.

Devlin inclined his head. "Yes, and I'm sure when I speak to Edwin again tomorrow and challenge him about that, he'll say something like he didn't approach them because he didn't want to disturb them, so they never saw him."

"How convenient," I said sarcastically. "What about his conversation with Dr Foster about Dame Clare's medication?"

"He repeated exactly what he told the doctor— that he was a concerned family friend and wanted to make sure Dame Clare was taking her medication safely."

I rolled my eyes. "He's got a ready answer for everything."

"Well, you have to consider the possibility that his answers are the truth."

"What do you mean?"

Devlin gave me a sideways look. "There are other people who could have tampered with Dame Clare's piece of cake much more easily... such as her daughter."

"I just can't believe Mary did it!" I glanced back towards Eccleston House. "She seems so genuinely upset."

"Appearances can be deceiving," said Devlin.

I sighed. "That's what my mother said. She said people can be really good actors and that just because we like them, it doesn't mean they can't be a murderer."

"Well, for once, I have to agree with your mother," said Devlin dryly. "Especially with regards to how skilful people can be at putting on an act. I've interviewed people who you would never believe were cold, ruthless criminals. They're able to cry at will, look vulnerable, and generally pull at your heartstrings. They are actually master manipulators and know how to push your emotional buttons. So no, you can't just go on your own feelings anymore. Evil people can be nice and likeable too."

I looked at him thoughtfully. "You've become a real cynic, Devlin O'Connor."

He shrugged and gave a crooked smile. "Occupational hazard."

I felt a pang of sadness. Maybe my mother was right after all about spending too much time with the darker side of humanity. It did rub off on you. Oh, not in the way she thought—someone with Devlin's integrity would never go over to the "dark side"—but still, it could steal a piece of your soul.

***

I cycled slowly back to Devlin's place in the gathering twilight, enjoying the balmy spring evening and the sound of birds settling down for the night. To be honest, I was also enjoying the thought of an evening alone. Maybe I was a sad loner but I was actually looking forward to some solitude. Oh, it would have been nice to spend an evening with Devlin, of course, but somehow, the thought of having the house to myself gave me a sense of guilty pleasure. It would be so nice to have some "space", some "me-time".

Of course, "me-time" included Muesli-time. I got back to Devlin's house to find the little tabby cat waiting impatiently for me.

"*Meeeeorrw! Meeeeorrw!*" she said plaintively as she twined herself around my legs as soon as I walked in the door.

I felt a twinge of guilt. At least when I was living with my parents, Muesli had often had company during the day. But now with both me and Devlin working such long hours, she was spending the entire day alone. And while I knew that she usually spent most of it happily snoozing on Devlin's sofa, it still made me feel a bit bad. Sometimes I wished that there was a way I could take Muesli in to work with me. She used to come to the tearoom daily before I adopted her and had kept everyone busy with her naughty antics. *Perhaps I ought to check into that again*, I thought, *and see if there is a way I could have Muesli with me at the Little Stables...*

In the meantime, as a bit of a sop, I decided to spend half an hour playing with her. Like a typical cat, Muesli had completely ignored all the expensive cat toys I had bought her and instead preferred to chase a bit of scrunched up newspaper tied to a piece of string. I picked up her favourite toy now and flicked it around in front of her.

"*Meorrw!*" Muesli cried happily, darting after the end of the string. She grabbed the newspaper and somersaulted, clutching it in her front paws.

I laughed, jerking the string along the floor, pulling the newspaper end out of her claws and twitching it up in the air. I always tried to be quicker than Muesli but I could never quite match her reflexes. She dashed after the string and pounced, rolling over and kicking excitedly with her back legs, as if disembowelling imaginary prey.

She looked so funny that I burst out laughing again. Then I grabbed my phone and tried to take a picture of her rolling on her back.

"*Meorrw...*" Muesli flipped over to her other side and tilted her head, looking up at me upside down.

"You little minx! Are you posing?" I said with a chuckle as I snapped a few more shots. Like most cat owners, I already had dozens of pictures of Muesli on my phone—Muesli in similarly playful poses, Muesli curled up sleeping, Muesli looking pensively out of the window, Muesli sitting by the door, asking to be let out... it was embarrassing how many pictures I had of my cat. Six months ago, I would have made fun of pet owners with pictures of their animals everywhere and now here I was with my cat as my phone screensaver. I gave a self-deprecating laugh. And I never even used to think I was a "cat person". Talk about ironic.

Finally, I stopped and sat up, flicking to my photo gallery to look through the pictures I had just taken. I scrolled through them, smiling to myself. Then I paused.

Hang on... this picture was of Muesli and me together... I hadn't taken it. Where was it from?

Then I remembered. Of course, it was the picture Cassie's brother, Liam, had taken at the fête. She had sent it to me on my phone. I had meant to print it out and put it in a frame, then I totally forgot about it. I tilted my phone, looking at the photo admiringly. Liam was a great photographer. The image was crisp and sharp with even the background showing pretty good detail. It had been taken in the cat show pavilion and had perfectly captured the chaotic atmosphere as everyone rushed to do the final grooming and get their cats ready for the judging. I could see the Ecclestons' table in the background behind me and Muesli, with Dame Clare half in the picture and a bit of Mary too. They had their backs to the camera and you could just catch a glimpse of the snowy white fur of Camilla, their Persian cat, on their table next to them.

Then my gaze sharpened on another section of the photo. I zoomed in. *Wait a minute... wasn't that...? Yes!*

In the background, at the other end of the

Ecclestons' table, was a plate with a fork covered in jam and fresh whipped cream propped alongside the last few mouthfuls of Victoria sponge. *Dame Clare's half-finished plate of cake,* I realised.

But what had caught my attention was the hand that was just visible, reaching down towards it. Doing what? Adding poison?

The owner of the hand was obscured by the angle the photo had been taken; in fact, *I* was blocking the person from view. I sighed in frustration. *What bad luck!*

Still, at least I knew it didn't belong to Dame Clare or Mary—they were plainly visible on the other side of the table. So who did the hand belong to? Those thin, bony fingers and the nails an unattractive shade of lavender....

Lavender nail polish!

Suddenly, I knew who it was. My mind flashed back to the day at the show... me standing by the Siamese cat cage while Theresa Bell accused me of trying to poison her cats... she had wagged her finger at me and I had remembered noticing her nail polish then and thinking how hideous the colour was, especially against her sallow skin...

I looked back down at the photo on my phone screen. There was no doubt about it. That was Theresa Bell's hand. So the question was—what had she been doing to Dame Clare's cake?

CHAPTER TWENTY-THREE

I could barely wait for Devlin to get home and pounced on him as soon as he came through the door.

"It's Theresa! It's Theresa Bell! She had her hand in the cake plate... and she was acting all weird... and she hates Dame Clare because she thinks the Dame tried to poison her cats at the last show... and she wouldn't eat the cake herself... and maybe she faked that whole stolen necklace scene so she could deliberately crash into—"

"Whoa, whoa, Gemma," said Devlin, catching hold of my wrists gently and holding me still. "What are you going on about?"

I took a deep breath and started again. "I think the murderer is Theresa Bell. You know Cassie's brother was taking pictures at the fête and his camera got stolen? Well, he'd sent one of the photos over earlier—it's one of me and Muesli—and I just happened to look at it again this evening. In the background, you can see the cake plate that Clare Eccleston was eating from, with a bit of cake left on it... and you can also see a hand reaching towards it. Look!" I thrust my phone under his nose and pointed to the zoomed-in picture.

Devlin frowned, staring at the image on my phone screen. "How do you know this is Theresa?"

"I can tell from her nail polish! She had this awful shade of lavender nail polish on her fingers—I noticed it that day at the show—and look, you can see it there clearly in the picture."

Devlin scratched his head. "I don't know... Couldn't another woman have had purple nail polish too?"

I gave him an impatient look. "You don't know women. Most of us wouldn't use lavender nail polish. It's not popular, trust me. Especially not that shade. Pale pink, yes, or bright fuchsia or mauve or wine... or even strong purple, I suppose, if you're a teenage girl—but that pale, plastic-y shade of lavender? Uh-uh." I shook my head decisively. "In fact, I remember being in a store in Oxford and seeing a bargain bin full of bottles of that colour and the shop girl said to me that she doesn't understand why the manufacturers make that shade because it never sells, year after year."

"Okay, okay, you've convinced me," said Devlin,

raising his hands in mock surrender. "So what are you saying—that Theresa was the only person likely to have such unusual taste in nail polish?"

"I'm just saying that the chances of someone else at the show picking that colour were pretty slim. I mean, it could happen, I guess... but I doubt it. And Theresa was at the table right next to us, she had a hostile connection with Dame Clare... *and* she refused to eat the cake. It all fits!" I looked at him eagerly. "Have you questioned her yet?"

Devlin made a rueful face. "I tried. I didn't get a chance to tell you earlier: I went to see Theresa Bell before visiting Mary this afternoon. But I hardly got a foot in the door before she started screaming police harassment. I tried to explain that she *wasn't* being treated as a murder suspect—that she was just helping with enquiries—but I could hardly get a word in edgewise, especially after her Siamese cats joined in the caterwauling as well."

I had to suppress a smile at the image. "But surely, you've got the law on your side? You could force her to answer your questions."

"I can't force her to do anything. The police can ask you questions but you are not obliged to answer them."

"That's ridiculous," I said in frustration. "You said yourself that someone with a persecution complex is likely to lash out—and we know that there was bad blood between Theresa and Dame Clare—and now we've placed her at the scene of the crime, actually tampering with the victim's food... Surely that's more than enough to arrest her on suspicion of murder?"

Devlin shook his head impatiently. "Yes, but even if she was under arrest, she has the right to remain silent. In any case, I have to be a bit careful, especially with a suspect as sensitive as Theresa Bell. The last thing I want to do is march in and forcibly drag her to the station, especially if I don't have conclusive proof that she committed the murder."

"What about the photo? Isn't that evidence?"

"But what does the photo really show? All we can see is a hand reaching towards the plate—a hand that *might* belong to Theresa Bell, based on your assumption that no other person at the show would wear the same colour nail polish. That's not something that would stand up in court. And if it turns out that Theresa Bell wasn't guilty after all..." Devlin made a grimace. "I'd be accused of police harassment of a poor innocent woman and there would be a lot of unpleasant negative publicity, which is the last thing the CID needs right now. We're still recovering from the 'Agri-Crime' fiasco at the fête—and then having failed to pick up that Dame Clare's death was suspicious... well, all in all, it's been a very bad week for police PR. The Superintendent has warned us all that we have to watch our step very carefully, particularly when we're in the public eye."

"Okay, how about if I speak to her?" I suggested.

"You?"

"Yeah, she might not react so badly to me. I'm not the police. I'm no one official. I'm just a sympathetic fellow resident of the village—well, sort of, via my tearoom. And Theresa was fairly friendly to me at the cat show, if you discount the bit when she accused me of trying to poison her cat's water," I said, grinning. "In fact, she was practically confiding in me about her troubles... I think she would talk to me."

Devlin sighed. "Look, I know you want to help, Gemma, but I can't have you questioning suspects in a murder case. You're a member of the public. You shouldn't really get involved."

"You let me sit in on your interview with Mary Eccleston."

"Yes, and I probably shouldn't even have done that," said Devlin grimly. "Besides, *I* was doing the questioning that time, you were simply listening. This would be totally different. No..." He held a hand up as I started to protest again. "This isn't a place for amateurs."

"I suppose you'd be happy for *Jo Ling* to speak to her," I muttered before I could stop myself.

Devlin's brows drew together. "What's that supposed to mean?"

"Nothing," I said shortly. Then I took a deep breath. I didn't want to fight again. "I'm just trying to help."

"Yes, I know—and I appreciate it. But you've just got to let the police do their job, okay, sweetheart?" Devlin gave me a smile which melted the last of my resentment. "I'll figure out a way to question Theresa—even if it means I have to go through a lawyer. It might add a bit of a delay but don't worry, I'll get there in the end."

I followed him to the living area where he flopped down on the couch with a big sigh. He leaned back and rubbed his neck tiredly. I felt a tug of pity for him. Devlin worked so hard. Now that I was living with him, I could see just how much of himself he gave to his job. I reached out and gently massaged the back of his neck for him.

"Mmm..." He closed his eyes appreciatively

"*Meorrw?*" Muesli's little grey head popped up suddenly between us. She jumped up on the sofa and climbed into Devlin's lap, purring with delight.

He opened his eyes and smiled at Muesli, then turned his vivid blue gaze on me. "By the way, can you send me a copy of that photo?"

"For evidence?"

He laughed. "Well, I suppose I ought to have a copy for that, yes, but actually, I was thinking just for me. It's a really lovely picture of Muesli and I'd like a copy to keep."

I rolled my eyes. "I can't believe it. And here I thought you were going to say something really romantic, like you wanted a picture of *me* to keep with you at all times."

"I *do* have a picture of you."

I stared at him. Devlin flushed slightly and looked embarrassed.

"Where?"

He nodded reluctantly at his wallet on the coffee table. "In my wallet."

I reached across and flipped the wallet open. On the rear of the central leather flap was a picture slot and to my surprise, I saw a picture of myself tucked in there. It had been taken when I was glancing over my shoulder, a laughing smile on my face, my eyes glowing. It was obviously an old photo, slightly faded and with the edges worn. I realised from my long hair that it must have been taken when we were at Oxford together, eight years ago.

"But... this is an old photo," I said. I looked back up at him.

"Yeah, well..." Devlin looked away, his cheeks reddening.

"You mean... you've kept this in your wallet all these years?" I whispered.

He turned back, his eyes meeting mine. "Always," he said at last.

I stared at him, my heart too full to speak. Then I leaned slowly towards him and our lips met. Softly, tenderly, then with greater passion. Devlin's arms slid around me. Muesli meowed indignantly as she was jostled off Devlin's lap but for once we were too busy to hear her.

CHAPTER TWENTY-FOUR

Devlin left very early again the next morning and I decided to get to the tearoom earlier than usual too. Dora would normally be there well before we opened, to get a start on the day's baking, and I was keen to see how she was doing with her new glasses. She had gone to see the optician in Oxford yesterday and picked up a pair of temporary reading glasses while waiting for the prescription ones. I hoped that she was already finding things much easier.

My phone rang just as I was leaving the house and I was surprised to hear my mother's voice on the line.

"Darling! I was just making sure that you hadn't forgotten about this afternoon."

"This afternoon?" I said blankly.

"Muesli's assessment!"

"Uh... assessment?"

"We'd arranged with Audrey Simmons to take Muesli down to the Vicarage at 5:30 for her Therapy Cat assessment, remember?"

Yikes, I thought. I had completely forgotten about that. It was going to be a tight squeeze. I would have to dash back here first to pick Muesli up and then go back to the village... it meant that I would have to try and leave the tearoom early again today and...

"Darling? You haven't forgotten, have you?" My mother's voice was reproachful.

"No, no! Of course not!" I lied quickly. "5:30. No problems. I'll be there with Muesli."

Perhaps I could use the visit as a chance to ask Audrey about Theresa Bell, I thought as I mounted my bike and started cycling towards Meadowford. Even though I had let the subject drop last night, I hadn't been able to stop thinking about that photo and Theresa Bell's hand reaching towards the cake plate.

There *had* to be a way to find out the truth. If only Devlin would let me approach Theresa! I was sure I could get some valuable information out of her—information that the police could then use to investigate her further. It was so stupid not letting me try, just because of some silly belief that amateurs shouldn't get involved. Bloody hell, I'd helped to solve three murder cases by now! Surely, I wasn't really an "amateur" anymore—and besides, it wasn't as if I was suggesting I should go in to tackle a dangerous hostage situation... I was only going to ask Crazy Cat Lady some questions!

I chafed at the thought of just sitting back, doing nothing, waiting for Devlin to wade through the official channels and get past Theresa's objections. It seemed so... so *pathetic*, just giving up like this! Unbidden, the thought rose in my mind: *Jo Ling would never just give up and accept the situation because there were a couple of obstacles in her way...* Was I going to concede defeat so easily?

I couldn't put the affair out of my mind and it made me distracted and slightly irritable at work all day. I could see Cassie looking at me reproachfully several times as I slipped up on orders or made vague, unhelpful replies.

"I'll do that table," she said at last, taking an order pad off me as I came back with the wrong order for the third time. "You know what? Why don't you take the rest of the afternoon off, Gemma? I know you're supposed to take Muesli for her therapy assessment this afternoon, so you're going to have to pop back to Devlin's place anyway to pick her up and you'll need extra time for that. Why don't you just leave now?"

"Now?" I looked at the clock. "But it's only 2:45."

"So? We've passed the lunchtime rush hour now and I can manage the teatime crowd with the Old Biddies helping me." She nodded towards Mabel and her friends, who were trundling around the tearoom, serving tea and cakes and gossiping happily with friends and strangers. She gave me a dark look. "Besides, it's not as if you'd be much help anyway."

"Oh Cass, I'm sorry," I said sheepishly. "Have I been really bad?"

"You've been a nightmare," said Cassie with the blunt honesty you only get from really close friends. "But it's okay—we're all allowed to have 'off days'. Just make sure you're back to your cheerful, efficient self tomorrow!" she said with mock sternness.

I laughed and gave her a quick hug. "Thanks, Cassie. You are the best. Okay, I'll push off now. Oh, but I'm still meeting you and Seth at the pub later tonight, right?"

Cassie nodded. "Seven o'clock at the Eagle and Child. I'll see you there."

***

Stepping out from the tearoom, I felt a bit like someone playing truant from school. I started mounting my bike to cycle back to Devlin's place, then I paused. It was still barely three o'clock. I didn't need to get Muesli until nearly 5:30. There was no reason to go straight back now...

Without realising it, I dismounted and began wheeling my bike towards the other side of the village. *I'm only going to take a look*, I promised myself. I wasn't planning to speak to her or anything—but I just wanted to see where Theresa Bell lived...

I'd asked the Old Biddies for Theresa's address before I left and I found her house at the other end of the village, just a few doors down from the Vicarage. It had once been a farmer's cottage, I think, although a modern extension had been added on to one side. The two halves didn't quite blend and it looked like someone had picked up two completely different houses and smooshed them together. On one side of the new extension, there was an enormous enclosure, almost the same height as the house itself, with wire mesh completely enclosing the garden inside.

Curious, I went closer and realised that it was a custom cat enclosure. There were several Siamese cats inside, some strolling around the flower beds, some grooming themselves on top of the various wooden platforms, and some lounging in the late afternoon sunshine. They all turned and looked at me as I came up to the side of the mesh, their slanted blue eyes wide and curious.

I tried to see if I could recognise the two that were at the cat show but they all looked indistinguishable to me: a group of sleek caramel and coffee-coloured cats, with startling blue eyes and darker points on their ears, legs, and tails. One large Siamese came boldly up to the mesh and sniffed me curiously.

"MAAAA-OOOWWW?"

"Hello!" I smiled and crouched down. Away from the tense atmosphere of the cat show, these cats seemed a lot friendlier. I'd found them totally unappealing on the day of the fête but now, I had to admit, they were growing on me: their wedge-shaped heads, exotic looks, and long, lean bodies—so different from Muesli—and yet attractive in their own way. And it was obvious that they had Personality with a capital P! These were cats with attitude... and since I shared my life with a cheeky little bundle of trouble, I had a soft spot for spunky, mischievous cats.

"Hello—what's your name?" I said softly, putting my hand out to let the cat sniff me through the mesh.

"WHAT ARE YOU DOING TO MY CATS?"

I jumped and sprang up. Turning, I found Theresa Bell standing behind me, her arms akimbo and her eyes hard and suspicious.

"N-nothing!" I said, feeling a sense of déjà vu. "I was just saying hello. I was walking past and happened to see the enclosure—and I was admiring your cats. I never knew much about Siamese cats before and never realised how lovely they could be."

"Oh." She thawed slightly and came towards me. "Well, I am glad you've finally realised how special they are. There is no other breed as wonderful as the Siamese!"

"Yes, I don't think I've ever seen ones as beautiful as yours."

She softened even more and preened slightly. "Yes, well, my cats are the very best of their kind— although they are often overlooked and slighted at cat shows." She frowned. "They would win every show, you know, except that people are against me and will do anything to attack me and harm my cats."

"Uh, yes..." I interrupted her hastily before she started down that track again. "Do you do anything special to keep them in such great condition? I have a cat too and I'd love to pick up some tips."

Her eyes widened suddenly in recognition and she said, "You're the girl with that moggie at the cat show! The one with the funny name—Cornflake, wasn't it?"

"Er... Muesli, actually. Her name is Muesli."

"Yes, well, there's not much you can do with a common moggie," she said, looking at me with pity. "But I don't mind sharing some of my tips with you. Of course, you know that your Cornflake won't ever have the same glossy pelt as my cats but I suppose you could make it look a bit better."

I bit my tongue on the sharp retort and said instead, "Thanks. That's really kind of you."

"Would you like to come in?" said Theresa suddenly. "I was just about to make myself a cup of tea—would you like one as well?"

"Oh...." I hesitated, thinking of Devlin's warning about not speaking to Theresa Bell. But it wasn't as if I had come specially to question her about the murder, I reasoned—this was just a social chat about cats and *she* was the one who was inviting me in. I'd be stupid to refuse, especially when some useful information just might slip out in conversation...

"Thanks, I'd love a cuppa," I said with a smile and followed her into the house.

Inside, it was as if I had stepped into some kind of Siamese cat theme park—there were Siamese cat cushions on the sofa, Siamese cat coasters on the coffee table, Siamese cat paintings on the wall, Siamese cat porcelain figures on the shelves—even a Siamese cat miniature grandfather clock with a swinging pendulum tail! I sat down gingerly in an armchair covered with a Siamese-cat-patterned fleece throw and watched as Theresa brought in two mugs decorated with playful Siamese cats and a plate of biscuits. I was almost disappointed that the biscuits weren't Siamese-cat-shaped as well.

As I sipped the tea and nibbled the biscuits, Theresa gave me a few grooming tips, then launched once more into her favourite subject: the conspiracy against her and her cats, which prevented them from winning more often at shows.

"It's a diabolical campaign against me, I tell you! Absolutely disgraceful! They are just jealous of my cats and will do anything to prevent them from getting their rightful recognition."

"That's terrible," I said sympathetically. "I can't believe people would be so vindictive."

Theresa sniffed. "Well, I don't like to point fingers but... Clare Eccleston was exactly the kind of woman who would do something like that!"

"Dame Clare?" I said with polite surprise.

Theresa made a rude noise. "Hah! 'Dame', she calls herself! I knew her when she was plain Clare Rogers! Grew up in this village, she did—same as me and Audrey. Not that we were friends," she added quickly.

"I didn't realise that you were all at school together."

"Well, Audrey and I were in the same class," said Theresa. "Clare was a few years ahead of us. Always thought she was better than us... humph! Audrey might have hero-worshipped her—but I wasn't so easily fooled! I have my pride and my *own* personality. I wouldn't let someone dictate to me like that. I don't know how Audrey put up with it, always pandering to Clare's moods and whims. But then, she never did have any backbone," she said contemptuously. "Audrey was always such a hanger-on, following the bigger girls everywhere in school."

She leaned forwards and scowled at me. "Do you know, last year Clare made the Cotswolds Cat Fancy Club reprint its annual calendar because her cats weren't featured on the first page? And she forced herself onto the committee and had the gall to suggest that she should be elected as Club President! *I* should have been President! I had been on the committee for years and I had far more experience than Clare. She just used her husband's money to buy a few Persians from another breeder and then started calling herself an expert, saying that she was breeding show champions, when really, she didn't know the first thing about cat breeding!'

"So Clare Eccleston stole the President's position from you?" I asked, thinking of "last straws" and motives for murder.

Theresa pursed her lips. "She would have certainly liked to! But in the end, the position went to Jane Banks, another committee member. Jane breeds Ragdolls," she said with a disdainful sniff, as if that said it all. "But I knew that it was just a sop. It was the committee giving in to Clare as usual. She must have told them that if she didn't get the position, I wasn't to get it either! And I'm sure it was Audrey who convinced the committee to submit to Clare's demands. She is always letting Clare walk all over her. This Therapy Cats programme, for instance, was Audrey's idea, but Clare swooped in and claimed all the credit, getting herself interviewed for all the newspapers and TV specials—I told the committee that they should have come to interview *me*! I have been doing therapy work with my cats for years. Not officially, perhaps, but my cats are wonderfully sensitive and they can almost *talk* to you. And there is no friendlier, more outgoing cat than a Siamese. They are ideal for Therapy Pet work!"

"Have you signed up to volunteer?" I asked. "We're taking Muesli for her assessment this evening."

"Oh, well, they haven't asked me yet," Theresa said huffily. "Audrey has taken over again as Leader of the programme, now that Clare is gone, and I'm sure she means to ask me. She has simply been too busy, I expect. All this fuss about Clare's 'murder'," she said irritably. "Really, it's ridiculous how much attention Clare is getting, as usual."

It was on the tip of my tongue to remark dryly that I doubted the dead woman would have arranged her own murder, just to get attention, but I restrained myself. Instead, I said soothingly, "Well, it's understandable that people want to catch a murderer. In fact, I would have thought that the police would be keen to speak to *you*, considering that you were there on the day? You would be an important witness."

Theresa looked a bit embarrassed. "Yes, well... an Inspector from the CID did come to see me yesterday... but I was very busy—very busy—and I didn't have time to answer questions," she said quickly, fiddling with the handle of her mug.

Her fingernails clicked on the china surface of

the mug and I noticed that she was wearing a different colour nail polish today—a sickly shade of orange which made her hands look slightly jaundiced. Theresa Bell certainly didn't have good taste in nail polish!

"That's an unusual colour of nail polish," I commented, indicating her hands.

She spread her fingers and examined her nails. "Yes, I saw this in a sale. I normally prefer purple shades..."

"Oh yeah, you were wearing a lavender-coloured nail polish at the fête, weren't you?" I said. "I remember noticing it on your fingers."

"Oh, that's my lucky bottle," she said, smiling coyly. "I always wear that colour for a show." She rose and went to a cupboard at the side of the room, returning a moment later with a small cosmetics bag. She unzipped it and showed me a collection of little glass bottles inside, most of them in varying shades of purple and violet. She pulled out one bottle and held it up to show me. "This is the one! It's called 'Lilac Karma' and it always brings me luck."

It was exactly the shade of the nails in the photo. I was itching to pull out my phone and show the picture to Theresa, to see her reaction, but I restrained myself with an effort. Instead, I stood up slowly and said, "Thank you for the tea. It's been lovely chatting with you, but I really should go now."

Theresa looked sorry to see me go. I realised suddenly that she was lonely and had enjoyed having the company, particularly having someone she could vent and complain to without fear of comeback.

"Come back anytime," she said. "Particularly if you need any more advice about Cornflake's coat."

"Er... thanks. Oh, can I use your loo before I go?"

Theresa pointed towards the doorway leading into the hallway. "It's the first door down the hall."

I followed her directions and found myself in a spacious bathroom, complete with Siamese-cat-embroidered towels by the sink and a Siamese cat quilted toilet seat cover. It was unusually large for the size of her cottage—I wondered if Theresa had converted an existing bathroom during her house extension or perhaps combined two rooms into one. It was probably just as well that there was so much space because, aside from all the Siamese cat paraphernalia, there were also several litter trays in different corners of the bathroom.

I was washing my hands when I noticed something about the litter trays. Hurriedly drying my hands, I bent to look at them more closely. Yes, my eyes hadn't deceived me. A page of newspaper had been used to line the bottom of the tray—or rather, a page of newspaper supplement. Carefully, I picked up a corner of the plastic tray and gave it a little shake, so that the litter shifted to one side and exposed more of the newspaper below. A headline showed across the top of the page:

"Mix 'n' Match Special for Bedding Plants!"

I stared at the distinctive blue ink of the print, smeared slightly and blurring the letters... the cheap blue ink which stained one's fingers terribly... the same blue ink which was on the anonymous note that Mary had showed me.

I glanced around the bathroom again and noticed a pile of papers stacked on a laundry hamper in the corner. I walked over to look. Yes, it was a stack of garden centre supplements. Surplus printed copies from an old mailing which were now out of date and unwanted by the garden centre. They'd probably offered the surplus copies to anyone who might have a use for them—such as a dog breeder with new puppies or a cat breeder with a lot of litter trays to line...

And if you were planning to send an anonymous note made up of cut-out letters and you had a stack of such newspaper supplements handy, it would make sense to use them...

I stared at the pile of papers, my mind whirling. Was it all just a coincidence? Or had Theresa sent the anonymous note that Dame Clare had received just before she was murdered? And what about the photo showing Theresa reaching towards the cake plate? Surely not another coincidence as well? *Was Theresa Bell the murderer?*

There was only one way to find out.

CHAPTER TWENTY-FIVE

I stepped back into the sitting room and paused on the threshold. Devlin had told me not to question Theresa, not to interfere with the investigation. But Devlin wasn't here. And I had this new knowledge burning in my mind. I couldn't bear the thought of just leaving and waiting again for the police to go through official channels and do something about it.

"Theresa..." I said, advancing on her. "I forgot to ask you—what did you think of that creepy anonymous note that Dame Clare received?"

Her eyes widened. "Anonymous n-note?" she stammered.

"Yes, haven't you heard? I thought it was all around the village. There was an anonymous note discovered amongst Dame Clare's personal papers, with a vicious message on it."

"Oh, well... I try not to listen to any of the gossip going around the village," Theresa said. "It's all horrid lies most of the time. Why, the things they say about me that—"

"This isn't just gossip," I cut in. "The police have been notified and they are treating it very seriously. In fact, I think they believe it's a clue to Dame Clare's murderer."

Theresa had gone slightly pale. "But... but the note was just to scare her a bit. It was nothing to do with the murder!"

"How could you know the note was just to scare her?" I demanded. "Unless... you sent it yourself?"

Theresa took a step back from me. All colour had left her face now.

I stared her in the eye. "It was you, wasn't it? And you cut out the letters from the garden centre supplements. I saw a pile of them in your bathroom. Very handy when you thought of sending this note."

"I... I don't know what you're talking about," Theresa Bell whispered.

"Oh, I think you do," I said grimly. I pulled out my phone and thrust Liam's photo in front of her. "You see this picture? It was taken at the fête last weekend. During the cat show, in fact. Yes, it's a photo of me and my cat, Muesli—but in the background, you can see part of the Ecclestons' table, and in particular, a half-eaten plate of cake

271

which had been left on one side. *Dame Clare's* half-eaten plate of cake." I zoomed in on the picture and pointed. "And there is a hand reaching towards that plate—a hand with pale lavender nail polish, just like your 'Lilac Karma'." I looked at Theresa Bell accusingly. "What were you doing to Clare Eccleston's cake?"

"Nothing!" she cried. "I wasn't doing anything to the cake!"

"Then why were you reaching towards it?"

Theresa squirmed and looked down. Her face was red now. "I... I was just helping myself to a little piece."

"*You were what?*" Of all the things I had thought she would say, it wasn't that.

"I wanted to try some," she said sulkily. "It looked so delicious and Victoria sponge is one of my favourite cakes."

"But you were offered some at the beginning," I said. "I was there. I heard you refuse."

Theresa squirmed again. "Well, I didn't like to accept when Clare was looking at me like that. One does have one's pride, you know," she said, raising her chin.

I stared at her incredulously. "You're telling me you were nicking a piece of Dame Clare's cake?"

Theresa flushed even redder. "Well, she wasn't eating it anymore! I was watching. She had pushed it aside and was busy grooming her cat. It would have just gone to waste—and there was still quite a bit of cake left on the plate. I finished it all off. I... I thought nobody would mind." She gave me an alarmed look. "I didn't poison Clare! *She* was the one who always tried to harm me—and I'm sure she tried to poison my Yum-Yum at the last show! In fact, do you think maybe the poison had been really intended for me? Maybe I was the real victim?"

I sighed and suppressed the urge to roll my eyes. Honestly, the woman had a one-track mind. Then I had an idea.

"You know, that might be true, Theresa, which is why you need to speak to the police and tell them everything," I said earnestly. "Inspector O'Connor tried to see you yesterday—he left you his card, didn't he? You need to ring him as soon as possible and tell him everything that happened. The police have to know all the facts if they are to protect you properly."

Theresa gave a squeak which sounded more delighted than frightened. "Do you think so? Oh, my goodness—I could have been the real victim! Someone might be trying to murder me! I'll ring him now!"

Before I even left the house, Theresa was already on the phone to Oxfordshire police station, hurriedly asking for an interview with Devlin. I let myself out and walked slowly away, mulling over what had just happened. I felt like my head was spinning. I had been so sure that it was Theresa, and now suddenly everything was turned upside down again!

Could she have been telling the truth? Was it really as simple as that? That instead of poisoning Dame Clare, she was actually stealing a piece of her cake? I shook my head. It was ludicrous. So ludicrous, in fact, that I was actually inclined to believe her. I mean, come on—if you were going to think up an excuse, surely you'd come up with a better one than that?

Then I stopped in my tracks. Something else, much more important, just hit me: *if* Theresa Bell was telling the truth and she had eaten the rest of Dame Clare's leftover cake, then that meant that the cake couldn't have been poisoned after all! Because otherwise, Theresa would have been affected too. And I was sure, with her paranoia and tendency to exaggerate, if there had been even a *hint* of discomfort after eating that cake, Theresa would have broadcasted it to the whole of Oxfordshire.

So what did that mean? That the poison which had killed Dame Clare hadn't been in the cake after all? And yet... the post-mortem had showed very clearly that Dame Clare had been poisoned... and it also confirmed that she had only had Victoria sponge cake in her stomach...

The sound of a voice broke into my thoughts. I looked around, puzzled. Where was it coming from? It sounded like a man, speaking in a low crooning tone, like the way one would to a lover or a beloved child. I listened again—the voice was coming from behind a low stone wall on my right. It was the Vicarage, I realised. Someone was speaking in the Vicarage gardens. I wheeled my bike over to the wall and I peered through a gap in the foliage. Was it the vicar? I was sure Audrey had mentioned that her brother wasn't back from his honeymoon until next week. So who could it be?

Then I saw the figure hunched down in the flower bed on the other side of the wall and the answer came to me. Of course. Joseph the gardener. I remembered now: Dame Clare's domineering manner at the cat show when she had practically ordered Audrey to have Joseph re-do the Vicarage gardens. Audrey must have followed her friend's dictate. It seemed that even after death, Clare Eccleston was still managing to exert her influence.

In front of me, the gardener carefully lowered a bulb into a depression in the soil, then gently brushed the surrounding earth into place around the young shoot, his fingers stroking lovingly. I heard that soft, crooning voice again:

"... like it here, you will, my pretty ones... aye, nice, warm sun in the afternoons an' a bit o' shelter from the wind an' rain... s'good home for you... 'course not as nice as the garden at Eccleston but s'all right, no harm will come to you here... and them flowers at Eccleston—am worried about 'em... don't like Mr Edwin... don't think he'll care 'bout the garden... told Miss Mary, he did, that when Dame Clare is dead, they'll be free to do anything they—"

I gasped. Joseph looked up. He saw me and his eyes went hard. He stood up.

"Joseph," I said urgently. "What was that you said? About Edwin and Mary? It was something you overheard, wasn't it?"

He said nothing, just stood there staring at me, his face blank.

I exhaled in frustration. *How could I make him talk?*

Then a fragment of conversation came back to me. That day I had been at the Eccleston House and Mary had come out to find me and Joseph together... she had made that odd comment: *"...he doesn't really speak, unless you talk to his plants."* I thought she had made a mistake—a slip of the tongue—and that she had meant to say: "he doesn't really speak, unless you talk *about* his plants". But now I wondered if *"to"* had been exactly what Mary had meant to say.

In a sudden flash of understanding, it came to me: how to communicate with Joseph. I shifted my gaze from his and dropped it to the row of bulbs at his feet. Should I try it? It was so silly... but what did I have to lose? Only my dignity—and my claim to sanity, if anyone should come past, I thought wryly. Still, surely it was worth a try? I took a deep breath, plastered a smile to my face, and said:

"Uh... um... hello, seedlings... are you comfortably settled in there? Is... uh... the soil nice and soft for you?"

Oh God, this is ridiculous, I thought. I must be crazy, standing here, talking to a bunch of hyacinth bulbs! I stole a glance at Joseph. He was looking at me, an expression of surprise on his face. I squirmed, then took another deep breath and continued:

"It... um... must have been a rough ride from the garden centre but I hope that you've... er... got over the shock of it now. This is a nice spot that Joseph has chosen for you, here in the shelter of the wall. You're probably waiting for a nice drink of water, aren't you? I wonder how you like your water— straight from the tap or warmed up a little in a watering can?"

"Like it cold an' fresh, they do."

I was so shocked to hear Joseph's voice that I nearly fell over the wall. I glanced at him quickly but he was looking determinedly at the bulbs, not meeting my eyes. Still, I was encouraged. I cleared my throat and addressed the bulbs again:

"Yes, you must be very thirsty after your journey from the garden centre. What... um... what about fertiliser? Is there a kind—I mean, a flavour that you really like?"

"Bone meal," said Joseph. "Them's the favourite. Got good phosphorous for the bulbs. Like a feeding o' compost as well when they're just starting out."

He looked down at the bulbs with fatherly pride.

Right. I'm having a conversation about a possible murderer, via some flower bulbs. Talk about surreal.

Still, I wasn't going to waste this opportunity. I continued glibly, "You must be so happy with your new home. The Vicarage has a lovely garden—though not as lovely as Eccleston House, of course..." I glanced at Joseph and hurriedly continued, "Now, those gardens are really old and the flowers there must have seen a lot. I can just imagine what great stories they would have to tell! All the conversations they must have overheard... like... last week when Edwin and Mary were talking... Could the... er... foxgloves hear them?"

There was a long pause and I thought maybe I'd lost him, then Joseph said, "No, foxgloves couldn't hear 'em. Too far away, they were. But the daisies—them's cheeky flowers. They heard 'em. I was deadheading 'em when Mr Edwin an' Miss Mary came past."

"Did they see you?" I blurted out.

Joseph shook his head slowly. "Rosemary was in the way."

"Who? Oh, you mean rosemary the plant." I thought back to the Eccleston House grounds and remembered the tall stand of rosemary hedge which had been planted down the centre of the rear garden, acting as a sort of ornamental screen dividing the two sides. Joseph must have been crouched behind it, working, on one side, whilst

Edwin and Mary had walked past on the other.

"And what were Edwin and Mary talking about? I mean, what did the daisies hear?" I amended hastily.

Joseph frowned. "He was telling her they oughta be married, Mr Edwin was, but Miss Mary was having none o' it. Said her mum—that's Dame Clare—said she wouldn't allow it."

"Yes, and then? What did Mr Edwin say after that?" I prompted, holding my breath.

"He said don't worry. Said when Dame Claree's dead, they'd be free, he reckoned, an' they can do anything they like."

I let out my breath slowly. "Did he say anything else?"

Joseph thought for a moment, then shook his head.

"What about Miss Mary? Did she... did she agree with him?"

"Scared o' everything, she is, Miss Mary. Just like the *Mimosa Pudica*. Touch-Me-Not Plant, it's called. On account o' it closing up its leaves if you touch it. Miss Mary's like that."

"Er... right," I said, slightly lost. "Well, thank you, Joseph. It was nice... er... chatting to you and... er... the hyacinths."

He didn't respond, crouching down next to the bulbs again. I stood for a moment looking down at his bent head and wondering how I was going to explain all this to Devlin. As if it wasn't bad enough that I had disobeyed him and questioned Theresa Bell, now I had to tell him that I had a witness willing to testify against Edwin—except that you had to bring a pot of geraniums to court and ask all the questions through the flowers! I giggled in spite of myself as I started walking again, wheeling my bike away from the Vicarage.

Then I sobered. Hmm. Somehow I didn't think Devlin was going to see the funny side. Still, I couldn't put it off any longer. These revelations were too important. Devlin had to be told. I took out my phone and rang Devlin's mobile. It went straight to answerphone. Frowning, I tried the police station instead and got put through to the CID offices. A familiar cocky young voice came on the line and, for once, I was pleased. Another CID officer might not have been willing to speak to me, but Devlin's sergeant knew me and knew that I'd helped out on investigations before. I asked him where Devlin was.

"The guv'nor? He's out in Oxford, interviewing this bookseller."

"Edwin Perkins?" I said quickly.

"Yeah, that's the one. Said he wanted to have another go at Perkins."

I thought quickly. For Devlin to question Edwin again must have meant that the second-hand bookseller was a strong murder suspect. And what I had just learned from Joseph might be critical in helping Devlin get the truth. I made a split second decision.

"Do you know if Devli—if Inspector O'Connor is likely to be at the store for a while?"

"Yeah, I think so. He only just left the station a couple of minutes ago."

"Okay, listen, I have some important information for him. If he contacts you for any reason, let him know that I'm heading to Edwin Perkins's bookstore and tell him to wait for me."

I hung up and tried Devlin's number again but it went straight to answerphone. I wasted no more time. Jumping on my bike, I pushed off, heading out of Meadowford and back into Oxford.

CHAPTER TWENTY-SIX

I pedalled furiously and arrived puffing and panting outside Edwin's bookstore in central Oxford some thirty minutes later. The door to the store was shut, with a "CLOSED" sign hanging across the pane, but peering through the glass, I could see two people at the back of the store. It was Devlin facing Edwin across his desk. The interview was obviously still in progress.

Testing the handle, I was pleased to discover that the door wasn't locked. Silently, I stepped into the shop. Edwin was speaking, his voice a perfect mixture of impatience and annoyance.

"...I really don't know what is the point of going over this again, Inspector—we went through it all yesterday! I've already told you everything I know. I've explained what I was doing in the cat show pavilion and also why I was asking Dr Foster about the medication. It's ludicrous that you should be treating me as a suspect! For goodness' sake, why would I want to murder Clare Eccleston? She was a long-standing friend and I have a great affection for the whole family—"

"Especially the daughter," I spoke up.

The two men jerked around at the sound of my voice.

"Gemma?" Devlin frowned. "What are you doing he—"

"I've been speaking to Joseph the gardener," I said, advancing towards the desk and keeping my eyes on Edwin. "He told me about a very interesting conversation he overheard while he was working at Eccleston House last week. A conversation between you and Mary Eccleston in the garden."

Edwin stiffened and his eyes flickered nervously, but he said with studied casualness: "Really? Well, there's nothing unusual about that. I'm an old friend of the family and I often chat with Mary—in the gardens or elsewhere. We... we share an interest in a lot of things. And now that dear Clare is gone, I'm sure Mary will appreciate having a friend more than ever."

"Yes, Dame Clare's death was very convenient for you, wasn't it?"

"I...I don't know what you're talking about," Edwin said.

"Gemma." Devlin frowned at me.

I ignored him and carried on recklessly, saying to Edwin, "Not only is there no longer anyone standing in your way, laughing at your feelings and calling you a 'dirty old man'..." I paused as Edwin flushed. "...but it's also left Mary a very rich heiress. Whoever marries her will have a very comfortable life. It would be more than enough reason to murder her mother."

"This is outrageous!" Edwin cried, very red in the face. "How dare you! Clare Eccleston was my dearest friend and I always wished her well. I would never have plotted to kill her!"

"Really?" I raised my eyebrows. "That's interesting, because according to Joseph, you told Mary that when her mother was dead, you and she would be free and able to do anything you liked. That seems a very odd thing for someone to say, doesn't it? Unless they were pretty certain that Dame Clare would die soon because they had already put plans in place to kill her."

"You... you can't believe anything that stupid gardener says!" snarled Edwin. "He probably made it all up. What was he doing anyway, spying on us like that?"

"He wasn't spying on you—he just happened to be working behind the hedge when you and Mary walked past on the other side. But you're right, it is just his word so perhaps I should speak to Mary, ask her what you said that day. I'm sure she would remember that conversation and be happy to repeat it."

I crossed my fingers behind my back, hoping that my bluff would work. If it didn't, I was going to be in *huge* trouble. Devlin already looked like he wanted to throttle me and was restraining himself with an effort. I avoided his eyes and kept my gaze steadfastly on Edwin. I was going on a hunch here: that Edwin's feelings for Mary would make him want to avoid any embarrassment where she was concerned; that he would rather tell the truth than have her dragged into this whole thing.

The bookseller stood staring at me for a moment, his face angry and flushed, then he seemed to deflate in front of my eyes. I breathed a silent sigh of relief. It looked like my bluff had paid off.

"No, don't speak to Mary," said Edwin hastily. "Okay, I... I *may* have said something along those lines... but I was simply referring to a potential future, not a specific one! Clare had a heart condition. It was perfectly natural... er, reasonable to assume that she might not live for very long and for me to talk to Mary about... er... a time when her mother would no longer be around."

"That's a very glib answer, Mr Perkins," Devlin spoke up. "However, with this new piece of information, things are not looking good for you. We have you placed at the scene of the crime, just a short while before the death occurred. We have you asking the victim's doctor about her heart medication and, in particular, questions about their toxicity and lethal potential. And now we find that there is a witness who overheard you talking with anticipation of a time when the victim would be dead. To a jury, that will sound very much like a statement of intent." Devlin leaned forwards. "Intent to murder."

"I didn't murder her!" burst out Edwin. "You have to believe me! I didn't do it!"

"Why were you really in the cat show pavilion?" I demanded. "It wasn't just to say hello to Dame Clare and her daughter. There was something else you were doing in there. That day you overheard my friend discussing her brother's photos in my tearoom, you rushed off suddenly—I think you organised for Liam's camera to be stolen, to prevent his pictures of the fête from falling into the hands of the police. I'm right, aren't I?"

"Uh... what?" Edwin looked like someone caught out with a guilty secret. "No, no... I... No, why would I do that?"

"Because you were afraid that he might have inadvertently photographed you," said Devlin suddenly. "Because the photos might have shown you tampering with Dame Clare's piece of cake, adding poison—"

"No!" cried Edwin. "I never touched her cake or anything else for that matter! In fact, I never went anywhere near the Ecclestons!" He looked at us wildly for a moment, then sank back in his chair and made a defeated gesture with his hands. "All right—you're right. I... I was doing something in the pavilion. But it *wasn't* plotting a murder." He took a deep breath. "I was meeting someone, to show him some... uh... erotic literature."

Devlin gave a humourless laugh. "Erotic literature? You mean you were selling porn."

Edwin bristled with pompous indignation. "These aren't trashy pictures of naked men and women acting like animals! This is very rare, highly valued, vintage erotica depicting hedonists in the pursuit of sensual pleasure."

"You were selling porn," Devlin repeated. "Don't try and dress it up. And that is illegal unless you are doing it in licensed premises, especially if you're selling it to minors—"

"No, no, my client was certainly not a minor!' said Edwin hastily. "He's an experienced collector—I told you, these weren't tattered old copies of *Playboy* magazine or something like that; these were valuable first editions of 18th-century erotica and he wanted to examine them in person before purchasing."

"So why didn't you just meet in your shop after hours or at his house? Why all this skulking around in a public place?" asked Devlin.

"It was my client's idea. He was very cagey about any way to contact him. He suggested the fête as a good place to meet because he was planning to be there already." Edwin hesitated, shooting an uneasy glance at Devlin. "He was the man whose picture was in the papers," he added in a low voice.

"Nate Briggs, the 'Agri-Crime Boss'?" cried Devlin, springing up. "Bloody hell, man, why didn't you say so from the beginning? Can you contact him again?"

Edwin looked shifty. "Er, yes... yes, I suppose so. He was interested in another volume and I promised to contact him when I got hold of it." Then a crafty expression came over his face. "But if I contact him for you, I want police protection and an assurance that you won't be charging me with anything."

"You're not in any position to make bargains, Mr Perkins," Devlin growled. "For one thing, you've lied to the police so I could have you arrested already for obstruction of justice."

"But you can't charge me for the murder of Clare Eccleston," Edwin whined, losing all his bravado in a second. "I tell you, I never went near her! I had nothing to do with her murder!"

Devlin looked at him grimly. "If you are telling the truth about this—and your 'client' can substantiate what you said—then you'll be in the clear. So the best thing for you is to cooperate with the police and help us apprehend this man. His testimony will provide you with an alibi for the murder." He made a gesture of mock invitation. "I think it would be best if you accompany me to the station now to make a new statement. And this time, I suggest you tell the truth—all of it."

CHAPTER TWENTY-SEVEN

I cycled slowly out of Oxford with mixed feelings. Oh, I was delighted that Devlin had finally got a break in his case. But as far as Dame Clare's murder was concerned, we were back to square one. If Edwin was off the hook, who was left now as the key suspect? Could it still be Theresa Bell? Or even Joseph? My mind swung uneasily to Mary, but I pushed the thought away. No, I still couldn't believe it. Not Mary.

The trip into town had taken up more time than I expected and I was now racing to make it back to Devlin's place, pick up Muesli, and get to the Vicarage in time. My mother was a huge stickler for punctuality and I knew that I would never hear the end of it if I was late, particularly after she had called to remind me this morning.

I arrived outside the Vicarage puffing and panting again, with Muesli slightly rattled and very windswept in her carrier in the front basket. I groaned and winced as I dismounted, my thigh muscles aching from all the frantic pedalling I'd done, back and forth to Oxford. *I'm going to die tomorrow*, I thought as I lifted the cat carrier and walked, John Wayne-style, into the Vicarage garden. It didn't have quite the colourful profusion of the Eccleston House gardens—probably because it hadn't had the benefit of Joseph's expertise—but it was pretty in its own way, with a bed of primroses and various types of daisies planted beneath a large dogwood tree, a shady border full of ivy and dainty little white flowers in the shelter of the stone wall and a bank of old-fashioned roses on the far side. I had noticed my mother's car parked outside but was relieved to see that she was standing on the doorstep, just about to ring the bell. *Whew.* I had made it in time.

Audrey answered the door, looking very smart in a black crepe dress and black tights. "It was Clare's funeral today," she explained as she led us into the house.

"Oh, I hadn't realised," said my mother. "Are you sure this is a good time? Perhaps we ought to do this another day—"

"No, no," said Audrey quickly. "It'll be nice to have a distraction. In any case, it was just a small affair in the end. Clare had left some instructions—I think she really wanted quite a grand funeral—but Mary decided that in view of the murder enquiry that is ongoing and the press attention that it's already attracted, it would be better to have a small, quiet affair."

I was surprised to hear of Mary defying her mother's wishes—it seemed that the shy, submissive girl I had originally met was already becoming more of her own person.

"Come into the sitting room," Audrey said, leading the way down the hallway. "I've just prepared the tea and I've baked some scones too. I'm sure they're not as delicious as those in your tearoom, Gemma, but I hope you'll still enjoy them."

I followed my mother as Audrey led us into the Vicarage's cosy, low-beamed sitting room. We sat down and for a while, conversation focused on the wonderful spread of things on the table. There were teacakes and scones, with jam and fresh cream, and little finger sandwiches of cucumber, egg and cress, and Yorkshire ham.

"This is wonderful jam, Audrey," said my mother as she helped herself to another scone and added a generous helping of the strawberry preserve. "Did you get this at the fête?"

"Oh no, that's just from the village shop. We sold out of all the jams donated for the fête, so I didn't get a jar for myself."

"Oh, what a shame. I thought I saw you taking a jar home—in your basket, as you were heading back to your car."

"Really?" Audrey furrowed her brow. "No, you must have been mistaken. I wish I did manage to get a jar, though. They looked so delicious. You know, I'm thinking of extending the Cake and Jam Stall at the fête next year—it was such a hit, I think we could have sold double the number of things and raised so much more money."

"Will you be part of the committee again next year?" I said. "It seems like a lot of work to be taking on."

Audrey smiled. "I enjoy it. It's nice to feel useful, especially as..." She broke off and looked around the house. "Well, now that my brother's married and there will be a new mistress here, I'm not sure how... well, how wanted I'm going to be..."

"Oh, nonsense," said my mother. "I'm sure your brother's very appreciative of the way you've looked after him over the years."

"I never intended to come and live with him, you know, but he got glandular fever several years ago and was very unwell for months. He really needed someone to look after him and, in the end, I was doing so much travelling backwards and forwards, I decided it was easier just to give up the lease on my flat and move in with him. Of course, Jeremy was always such a confirmed bachelor, so dedicated to his work, you know—nobody expected him to marry suddenly at forty-four! So I suppose I was like the spinster sister in novels, looking after the hero."

Audrey gave a self-deprecating laugh. "Jeremy is so much younger than me—there's a thirteen-year age gap between us, you see—so I've always been more like a mother than a sister to him and 'keeping house' for him just sort of came naturally..." A shadow crossed her face. "I suppose that's all going to change now."

"But surely you are planning to go on living here?" said my mother. "I'm sure they'd be more than happy for you to stay on with them. The house is certainly big enough."

"Well, there *is* a self-contained wing on one side, but one doesn't like to impose. And a newlywed couple ought to start their life without someone living with them, I think," said Audrey. "Besides, I'd thought that perhaps..." She flushed slightly. "Well, anyway, that was just wishful thinking."

I wondered if she was thinking of Edwin Perkins and had nursed a hope that he might still return her feelings and ask her to marry him.

"*Meorrw?*" came a little voice at our feet. Muesli had been let out of the carrier and had been amusing herself, scampering about and exploring the house while we had tea. Now she was rubbing herself against our legs, demanding some attention.

"She is so sweet," said Audrey, smiling down at Muesli.

"Appearances can be deceptive," I muttered.

Audrey chuckled. "Yes, your mother was telling me the other day about some of her amusing antics."

"Did she tell you about the time Muesli climbed into a vent and disappeared into our wall cavity?"

"Yes." Audrey laughed. "I once knew a cat who climbed into the exposed roof rafters during a renovation and curled up in a nice, soft bed of insulation... and then got trapped when they boarded things up without realising that he was up there."

"Not your cat, I hope," said my mother, alarmed.

"Oh, no, this was someone in the Cotswolds Cat Fancy Club. Unfortunately, I can't keep a cat here as my brother is extremely allergic. But I enjoy spending time with other people's cats through my duties at the cat club."

"I heard that this Therapy Cats programme was your idea," I said. "It's a fantastic project."

She flushed with pleasure. "Thank you, yes—it's something I'm very proud of. Something that's completely 'mine', in a way, and not just an existing project I'm supporting. Of course, Clare was right— with her superior experience and knowledge of cats, she was a much more appropriate leader for the programme. But now that she is no longer here, the responsibility has reverted to me." She sighed. "Sometimes, I still can't believe that Clare is gone."

There was an awkward silence. Awkward, I think, because neither my mother nor I could think of anything nice to say about the dead woman. Then Audrey roused herself and said briskly:

"Well! Better get on with Muesli's assessment."

"What exactly is she being assessed on?" I asked. "Is it like an exam?"

"Goodness, no, nothing so formal." Audrey gave a little laugh. "Mainly, we just want to see if she is a calm, confident, friendly cat who doesn't mind interacting with strangers."

"Oh, no problems there," I said dryly.

"No, I can see not," said Audrey, smiling as Muesli hopped up onto her lap. The little tabby cat looked at her, then leaned forwards and sniffed Audrey curiously.

"*Meorrw?*" she said, and gave a little sneeze.

"Oh dear, maybe she doesn't like the perfume I'm wearing," said Audrey with a laugh as Muesli jumped off her lap.

"Well, I think it's lovely," said my mother, leaning towards Audrey and sniffing appreciatively. "Where did you purchase it?"

"I made it myself, actually," said Audrey. "From the flowers in my garden. I love the old-fashioned floral fragrances. You don't seem to get those anymore—it's all so exotic now, when you go to the department stores; you know, things like neroli and ylang-ylang and other things I can't pronounce." She gave a self-conscious laugh. "I have to confess, I prefer the Old World fragrances such as lavender and rose... I suppose they would be known as 'grandma' perfumes nowadays."

"Oh, I think the vintage fragrances are lovely," I

said with a smile. "And I'm certainly not 'grandma' age yet! I never realised you could make home-made perfume, though."

"Well, as I say, it's not the complex perfumes you can buy in the department stores, with essential oils and base notes and all that," said Audrey. "It's a very simple, water-based fragrance. But yes, it's not as hard as people think. You just need to soak the flower petals, strain the liquid, and then heat the flower-scented water very gently, until it reduces down. It lasts for a good month, you know, if you keep it in an airtight bottle, in a cool place." She glanced at Muesli and smiled. "Maybe I should try making some catnip perfume. Then Muesli might like me better. Still, I can see that shyness isn't going to be a problem with her. If anything, I think our problem is going to be stopping her scampering off down the hospital corridor in search of new friends!"

"I've trained Muesli to walk on a harness so you can keep hold of her that way. Well, maybe 'walk' is taking it too far," I admitted with a laugh. "But she's happy to wear a harness."

"That's excellent. That was actually one of the questions I needed to ask you. It's a requirement for all cats in the programme to wear a harness in public. For their own safety, really."

Audrey reached down and picked Muesli up again and began running her hands along the little cat's body, touching her everywhere, rolling her over, picking up her paws, waving her hands in front of Muesli's face. The little tabby squirmed slightly, but she accepted the handling without too much fuss, other than an indignant "*Meorrw!*" when Audrey tugged gently on her tail.

"Of course, we wouldn't let people treat her so roughly, but it's hard to know what people might do sometimes, particularly children, or even those who might not have full control of their motor function," Audrey explained. "So it's important that we know the animal is very tolerant and won't react aggressively, and can cope well with unpredictable situations." She smiled and set Muesli back down on the floor. "Well, Muesli has passed with flying colours! I will send you all the official paperwork and then we can start organising some visits for you."

"Splendid," said my mother, beaming as proudly as if Muesli had just graduated from Oxford. "I knew she would do wonderfully. In fact, if the judging hadn't been interrupted, I'm sure Muesli would have won at the cat show last weekend."

"Er, well…" Audrey looked uncomfortable. She glanced at me and I could tell by her expression that she was thinking what I was thinking: that it was probably lucky that the judging had been interrupted by Dame Clare's collapse, otherwise my mother could have suffered a very big disappointment and humiliation. Still, neither of us wanted to ruin her illusions.

"Mother, I think Muesli is much more suited to being a Therapy Cat than a show cat," I said quickly. Then I glanced at the clock on the mantelpiece and rose from the sofa. "I hate to break up the party but I'm meeting some friends for a drink this evening..."

"Oh yes, and I'd better get home to start dinner," said my mother, rising as well. "Thank you for the lovely tea and cakes, Audrey."

As we were standing in the hallway, putting on our coats, my mother glanced at something on the hall table and said, "These are beautiful... I don't believe I have seen these here before."

I followed her gaze. On the hall table were several large pieces of cardboard, with what looked like collages of photos, illustrations, and words cut out from printed material, stuck on them.

"Oh yes, I was having a sort out and I found these," said Audrey with a reminiscent smile. "They were made by Mary when she was in her teens. She loved scrapbooking and used to enjoy cutting out all sorts of things from magazines and newspapers and even gift-wrap paper, and making collages with them. I was planning to take these to show her the next time I went over to Eccleston House."

I stared at the collages, that uneasy feeling rising in me once more. In my mind's eye, I could see the anonymous note again, with its neatly cut-out letters, just like the letters on these collages. I thought back to my interview with Theresa that morning. She had never actually come out and confessed to sending the note, I realised. She had looked guilty and had stammered something—and I had instantly assumed that it was an admission. But what if I had been wrong? What if it was *Mary* who had sent that anonymous note to her mother?

In fact, it actually made more sense for Mary to have written the note—because the note suggested that the murderer was an outsider—which was exactly the kind of thing you would plan if you were the murdered woman's daughter and wanted to divert suspicion from yourself. The anonymous note suggested that the threat came from outside the family.

I swallowed uneasily. Could I have been wrong about Mary Eccleston after all?

CHAPTER TWENTY-EIGHT

I was meeting Cassie and Seth that evening at one of our favourite haunts from student days: the Eagle and Child pub, situated on St Giles Street, that wide boulevard at the north end of Oxford, home to various university colleges, the Theology Faculty, the Oxford Quaker Meeting House, and the 12th-century St Giles' Church. From the outside, the Eagle and Child was a relatively unassuming-looking pub, housed in a small, narrow building that dated from the mid-1600s and was sandwiched amongst a row of mismatched terraced houses that ran along the west side of the boulevard. What made it famous was the fact that it was once the regular meeting place of the Inklings, an Oxford writers' group which included such iconic names as C.S. Lewis and J.R.R. Tolkien. Whenever I'd gone there as a student, I'd always thought it weird to imagine Lewis or Tolkien sitting there, discussing their first drafts and agonising over character development and plot holes, just like any other writer. Of course, like most Oxford students, you get a bit blasé after a while to all the magnificent history around you, and the Eagle and Child—like many other places—becomes just another local pub that you met your friends at.

I stepped through the narrow front door and squeezed past several people queueing at the tiny bar (which did seem to be better built to serve dwarves and elves) and looked around, savouring the atmosphere: the dark wood wainscoting and cosy wooden snugs, the feeling of pleasant claustrophobia that these old English buildings always seemed to give. I was pleased to see that it hadn't changed that much since my student days. Oh, it had been opened up and modernised a bit, but at least it hadn't been turned into a Hollywood shrine with *Lord of the Rings* movie posters on the walls and cheap replica film props on sale behind the bar counter. In fact, with the typical English reserve and tendency towards understatement, you would have hardly been aware of the pub's famous literary connections if you didn't know its history. It was only when you ventured into the back room of the pub that you'd notice an illustration from *The Lord of the Rings* on the wall or the tiny map of Narnia hanging on a door.

I found Cassie and Seth comfortably settled in one of the narrow wooden booths, each nursing a pint of the pub's famous ale.

"At last! We'd given you up for lost," said Cassie as I dropped down beside them.

"Sorry, I didn't think the therapy assessment would take so long and then I had to drop Muesli back at Devlin's place."

"Shall I get you a drink, Gemma?" said Seth, ever the thoughtful gentleman.

I smiled at him, remembering the way he had offered to carry my case up to my college room the very first time we'd met. In many ways, Seth hadn't changed much from that shy, studious boy, even though he was now a Senior Research Fellow at one of Oxford's prestigious colleges.

"Thanks, Seth. A shandy, please."

"So..." Cassie leaned towards me with a conspiratorial grin as soon as Seth was gone. "I've been dying to ask you but never seem to get a chance at the tearoom—and besides, I wasn't sure you'd want the Old Biddies' prying ears—but how's the love nest?"

I hesitated for a fraction of a second before saying, "It's going great," but my best friend knew me too well.

Cassie raised her eyebrows. "But?" she prodded.

I shrugged. "I don't know... It's... well, in a way, it's wonderful living with Devlin. We get to see so much more of each other and, of course, his house is so spacious and comfortable, I'd never be living anywhere as nice on my own... and it's perfectly located for work... and it's great not having my mother breathing down my neck all the time..."

"But...?" said Cassie again.

I hesitated, feeling slightly disloyal to Devlin. "Well, it's just that... there are little things, you know... like we had an argument because Devlin couldn't understand why I dump my clothes on a chair by the bed instead of putting them back in the wardrobe immediately."

Cassie rolled her eyes. "Well, duh! That's just a typical man for you! For one thing, you might want to wear one of the things again, before you put it in the wash... and it might not be really dirty but you wouldn't want to put it back in the cupboard with all the clean clothes... or sometimes you just don't feel like hanging things back up immediately."

"Exactly!" I said. "That's what I told Devlin. I mean, he wasn't using the chair so I didn't see what the problem was. But it really seemed to bother him. Of course, when I pointed out that he leaves his CD collection strewn all over the side table, he didn't seem to think that was a problem!" I scowled. "I don't see why he can't just stack them back on the shelf, instead of leaving them lying about. And then there's the way Devlin is in the mornings: springing out of bed, so full of energy and in such a good mood... ugh..."

Cassie burst out laughing. "So he's a morning

person, huh? Ooh, that's never going to end well with you."

I gave a sheepish smile. "I'm not as bad as that, am I?"

"Gemma, you're *terrible* in the mornings! I often think it's a sign of how much you love your tearoom that you're able to drag yourself in and be so bright and cheerful to the customers in the mornings. I'd hate to see what you're like when you first get out of bed. In fact, I *have* seen what you're like—a bear with a sore head doesn't begin to describe it. I think my sympathies are with Devlin on this one."

"But it's not just me!" I protested. "Devlin isn't perfect either!"

"So what does he do? Snore? Leave the toilet seat up?"

"No, no, he's not uncouth like that. He's a perfect gentleman in that sense. There are just some things he does that really wind me up, especially at the end of the day when I'm tired and irritable. Like... like he has this habit of humming under his breath. I don't think he's aware of it—he does it when he's preoccupied with other stuff, like washing up the dishes, for example. But it's not even a proper song! It's just a sort of tuneless humming. It really starts to grate on your nerves after a while."

Cassie grinned. "It sounds to me like you're just having trouble getting used to sharing a living space with each other."

I sighed and leaned back. "The thing is, I don't

know why these little things are bugging me so much. I mean, Devlin and I used to spend tons of time together at college, staying over in each other's rooms."

"It was different back in college," said Cassie. "I mean, we were all living in these student dorm staircases—all packed in together, sharing a bathroom between sixteen of us and stuff..." She shuddered. "There's no way I could do that now. Besides, I think you get less tolerant as you get older. You want a space of your own."

"I guess..." I was silent for a moment, thinking. "Now that you mention it... maybe that's what it is. I just don't feel like the place is really mine. It's Devlin's house and I'm a sort of guest there, really, even though he's told me to make myself at home." I sighed. "I know I shouldn't complain—I should just count myself lucky that I've got a wonderful boyfriend who's invited me to live in his gorgeous house rent free and he loves Muesli... but..." I sighed again. "I don't know... I guess I'd been dreaming for so long of a place of my own. Not that I'm complaining," I repeated hurriedly.

"No, I can understand that," said Cassie softly. "A place of your own, a place with your own identity, a personal sanctuary that's completely yours."

"Now you're sounding like an advert for some kind of posh spa experience," I said with a laugh.

Seth returned, placing a small glass of shandy—

a beer mixed with lemonade—on the table in front of me. He dropped back into the booth and said brightly, "What did I miss?"

"Nothing much," I said quickly. "Just some girl talk. Did Cassie tell you about the murder at the fête last weekend, by the way?"

"Yeah, she told me all about it. And I read about it in the papers too." Seth shook his head and gave an incredulous laugh. "I can't believe that I don't see you for a week and you've got yourself embroiled in a murder mystery again, Gemma."

Cassie turned eagerly to me. "I heard that the police have arrested Edwin Perkins for the murder. Is it true?"

"No, not arrested. He's just been asked to go down to the station to 'help with enquiries'. I think the village gossips were jumping to conclusions again." Quickly I told them everything, including the scene in Edwin's bookstore earlier that day. "So you see, Edwin couldn't have been the murderer, because he had an alibi for the whole time when the poison might have been given. He was with this Nate Briggs chap."

"Oh." Cassie looked disappointed. "Edwin seemed like the kind of creepy old git who *would* be a murderer."

"That's a bit harsh, Cassie," Seth spoke up in his quiet voice. "Sometimes things aren't what they look like and someone who seems to be in the perfect position to be a murderer is actually completely innocent."

I knew Seth was speaking from experience—only a couple of months back, he had been accused of a violent murder in one of the Oxford colleges. It had been really touch-and-go for a while whether he'd be arrested, and it had been a harrowing time for all of us, racing to solve the case and prove his innocence.

"Oh, Seth... I'm sorry!" said Cassie, immediately contrite. "You're right. I spoke without thinking."

She reached across and gave his hand a quick squeeze. Seth blushed to the roots of his hair. I saw his fingers reach out to clasp Cassie's in return but she had already withdrawn her hand and was turning away to say something to the passing waitress. Seth's eyes filled with frustration and he quickly pulled his hand back again, embarrassment clouding his face.

I felt a familiar prickle of impatience. I knew that Seth had a secret crush on Cassie—in fact, he had fallen head over heels for her from the moment they met as students—but he was shy and hesitant, and too scared to declare his feelings, in case Cassie didn't return them and it ruined their friendship. I could understand that, but still, I wished he would say something. For one thing, I suspected that Cassie did care deeply for him, more than she realised. And for another, if he didn't get a move on, another man would step in—as had often happened in the past. Pretty and vivacious, and with a killer figure to boot, Cassie was never short of male attention. And Seth... I sighed to myself. Watching Seth try to conduct a romance was like watching a tortoise cross the road! At this rate, by the time Seth nerved himself to finally say something, Cassie would probably be married with three kids already!

"Okay, so if it's not Edwin, then who else is left?" said Cassie, turning back to me and returning eagerly to the subject of the murder. "That crazy Siamese cat lady?"

"Theresa Bell? It could still be her, I suppose," I said doubtfully. "She was certainly in the right place at the right time and Liam's photo definitely shows her reaching towards the cake plate. But she's got an answer for that." I repeated my conversation with Theresa Bell that morning.

"She was pinching some of the cake to eat?" said Cassie incredulously. "You're kidding me!"

I shook my head. "Nope, that's her story."

"It's so ridiculous, you almost feel that it must be true," said Seth.

I agreed, "Yeah, that's what I thought. I mean, why think of such a stupid reason unless it's the truth? And also... well... she did really seem to be *embarrassed*—not guilty or scared or desperate, the way you'd expect her to feel if she had been found out as the murderer—but more just genuinely sheepish and embarrassed."

"Anyway, it's not just about the opportunity to tamper with Dame Clare's cake, is it?" said Cassie.

"I mean, in poison cases, you have to think about whether the person could have had access to the toxin as well."

"That's easy in this case," I said. "The poison is a cardiac glycoside; the most commonly known one is digitalis, which you can find in foxgloves. And you know foxgloves grow everywhere, even along the side of country roads!"

"It doesn't even have to be foxgloves," Seth added. "Cardiac glycosides are found in a diverse group of plants of which foxgloves are only one. You can also find them in the oleander, lily of the valley, dogbane, and wallflower. In fact, you can even find them in some butterflies, which feed on the flowers. The ancient Egyptians and Romans knew all about them and used them to treat heart problems." He leaned forwards, his eyes brightening with excitement. "Their mechanism of action is fascinating! The glycoside inhibits the sodium potassium pump in the membrane of cardiac myocytes and so the intracellular sodium concentration increases. Then a second membrane ion exchanger is also affected—"

"Seth!" I gave him an affectionate, exasperated look. "I don't think knowing the molecular action of cardiac glycosides is going to help us find the killer."

"Sorry," said Seth with a sheepish grin. "Anyway, my point was, it doesn't even have to be foxgloves—there's a whole host of other plants that the poison could be derived from."

"Well, I think you should stick with foxgloves. It's the most common and likely—why complicate things?" Cassie said. She looked at me suddenly. "Are there foxgloves at Eccleston House, by the way?"

"Y-yes," I said reluctantly. "Why?"

"Well, we can't forget that Mary Eccleston is one of the suspects too. In fact, I would have thought that she'd be even more of a likely candidate than Theresa Bell—or that weird gardener chap. Mary was on the spot, she could have easily slipped poison into the piece of cake she gave her mother, she had a lot to gain by her mother's death—"

"It's not Mary," I said stubbornly. "I have a gut instinct that it's not her..."

"Gut instincts can be wrong," Cassie said.

"Anyway, there's a bigger problem now," I said. "If Theresa Bell is telling the truth, then that means that she ate all of the cake left on Dame Clare's plate. And yet she was fine. Which suggests that the poison *wasn't* in the cake after all. So how on earth was Clare Eccleston poisoned?"

"Hmm... you've stumped me," said Cassie, frowning.

"She didn't drink anything, did she?" asked Seth.

"Not that I know of—and the autopsy report only mentioned Victoria sponge cake identified in her stomach contents." I shook my head in frustration. "I feel like this is the key to the whole mystery. It's been eluding us from the beginning. First we thought the poison was in a fake angina pill... but that turned out to be legit. Then we thought the poison was in the cake... but it couldn't have been since several of us ate the same cake and were fine. Then we thought that it was only added to Dame Clare's piece of cake, *after* it was cut and given to her... but now it seems that Theresa Bell had some of the same piece as well, and had no symptoms." I spread my hands. "So where *was* the poison? If we could only work that out, I have a feeling we'd crack the case."

CHAPTER TWENTY-NINE

I had a restless night and although I hated proving Cassie right, I was bleary-eyed and grumpy in the tearoom the next morning. I knew that Oxfordshire CID would be a hive of excitement and activity today, with a big operation underway to raid and capture the Agri-Crime gang based on information Devlin had gleaned from Edwin Perkins. The murder enquiry would be relegated to the back burner until that operation had been successfully completed.

I couldn't stop thinking about it, though. As I opened up the tearoom and welcomed the first customers, my mind kept returning to that conundrum: *Where had the poison been placed?* I had a nagging feeling that I was missing something—some vital clue—that I had seen or overheard. I frowned, thinking back over the events of the last few days... was it something my mother had said? Or something the Old Biddies had mentioned? Or even something Seth had said last night...? I had a feeling it was all of those things, and yet I couldn't put a finger on anything specific. It was very frustrating.

The tearoom had barely been open twenty minutes when my phone rang and I was surprised to hear the voice at the other end of the line. It was Jo Ling.

"Oh, hello, Dr Ling—"

"Please, call me Jo," she said and I could hear the smile in her voice. "Lincoln gave me your number—"

"I've been meaning to ring you, actually," I said, feeling slightly embarrassed. "I wanted to thank you for pushing that post-mortem through so quickly and staying late in your own time to do it."

"Oh, no problem," Jo said. "I was just doing my job. In fact, that was the reason I was ringing you— the toxicology reports have come back. I've sent a report over to Dev already but I know he's tied up today and I thought you might like to know first, rather than wait for him to pass them on to you."

"Oh, thanks," I said, pleasantly surprised. "That's really nice of you."

"That's okay. I got the sense that this was really important to you. I'm probably breaking a million police rules sharing this information with a member of the public…" She gave a tinkling laugh, showing how little she cared about following the rules. "But anyway, I trust you, Gemma. Okay, so the results show that the poison which killed Clare Eccleston was convallatoxin."

"Conva-what?"

"Convallatoxin. It's a cardio glycoside, similar to the digitalis compounds, except that it comes from a different plant: *Convallaria majalis*, otherwise known as the lily of the valley."

"Oh, right," I said, suddenly remembering Seth rambling in the pub the night before about other plants which contained cardiac glycosides. "So you mean we've been going down totally the wrong path? We kept thinking that it was digitalis and thinking of foxgloves—"

"Well, not totally wrong. I mean, you find lily of the valley growing in many English gardens too. It's a common native flower—it's very popular for use in bridal bouquets, you know, because the dainty white flowers are so pretty. Of course, most people don't realise how toxic it is—even the water that the cut stalks are put into can be poisonous if drunk."

"Is it as powerful as digitalis?"

"Oh yeah, definitely. It's actually got an even narrower margin of safety than digitalis, which is probably why it was never developed for pharmaceutical use."

"Thanks for telling me all this," I said. "I really appreciate it."

"No probs. I hope it might be useful. Now, I've got a question for *you*," she said, her tone lightening. "You're an old friend of Lincoln's, right?"

"Yes, well, our mothers are best friends and we knew each other as children," I said. "Why?'

"Do you know if he has any phobias? The doctors' mess has got its monthly Social Night coming up and a bunch of us are going to do a comedy sketch. I wanted to do one of Lincoln and I need some fodder." She chuckled.

"Oh... um..." I wracked my brains. "Well, he isn't scared of spiders or snakes or anything like that— from what I remember."

"What about foods? Anything he really can't stand?"

"I don't think he likes custard much," I said. "I remember when we were children and his family came over for lunches and things, he always refused to have custard on his desserts. But that was a long time ago. You know, we were both away from Oxford—we both only came back recently—so I haven't seen him for years. He might have changed since then."

"Hah! I doubt it. Stuff you hate in childhood sticks with you, I think. Ooh... custard... I could do a lot with custard..." Jo gave a wicked laugh.

"Er... well, I hope you guys have a good time."

"Oh we will! Thanks, Gemma, this is brilliant. Cheers!"

I hung up and stared at my phone. But before I

could think about the call further, my phone rang once more. This time, it was my mother.

"Darling, I'm just about to drive out to Eccleston House and I was wondering if you'd like me to stop off at the garden centre and pick up those water lilies for you? They still have that sale on and it's really marvellous value, you know."

"No, thanks, Mother. I told you, I don't want any water lilies. Why are you going over to Eccleston House?" I asked, curious.

"Oh, Mary sent me a note last night, asking me to meet her there this morning. She said she had something she wanted to show me. It sounded quite urgent."

"About the murder?"

"I don't know, darling, the note didn't say. I'm sure I shall find out soon—I'm leaving now. Are you *sure* about the water lilies? Because I think they would make the most fabulous display in the tearoom. In fact, you could even move the water feature to the centre of the room—I don't know why you have it tucked around the side of the counter like that, anyone would think you were ashamed of it!—and then you could fill it with water lilies and maybe even get some goldfish—"

"No, no, Mother! No water lilies or goldfish or anything else," I said desperately. I glanced up to see Cassie signalling from the other side of the dining room, trying to catch my attention. Hurriedly, I said, "Thank you for the thought,

Mother, it's very sweet of you. But honestly, I think the water feature is... uh... fine as it is. I'm sorry— I've got to go now. I'll ring you later, okay?"

I hung up with some relief and looked in the direction that Cassie was pointing. I groaned inwardly as I saw a familiar figure come through the tearoom door: the same balding head, sycophantic smile, and shiny grey suit. It was the salesman with the novelty spoons. I remembered now: we had told him to come back later in the week. I sighed. I might as well see him and get it over with. It was obvious he wasn't going to go away.

He beamed as I went up to him. "Miss Rose? Thank you for making the time to see me. I promise you, you will *love* our products—you will not find the same quality anywhere else and I am sure your customers would appreciate the—"

I held my hand up, stopping him mid-flow. "Why don't we go in the kitchen, Mr... er...?"

"Baxter," he said, taking my hand and pumping it enthusiastically. "Certainly, certainly—and I've brought a selection of spoons to show you." He brandished a small travel case.

I led him into the big, comfortable tearoom kitchen which was filled as usual with the wonderful smell of fresh baking. Trays of freshly baked scones, muffins, and Chelsea buns lay on the side counters and, at the large wooden table in the centre, Dora was up to her elbows in flour as she expertly kneaded a large lump of dough. She looked up as we came in and I was pleased to see that she was wearing a new pair of reading glasses. They suited her, giving her a Mrs Claus sort of look.

"Dora, this is Mr Baxter," I explained. "He's got some items to show us—er, novelty chocolate spoons, is that right?" I turned to the salesman.

"Not just any chocolate spoon!" he exclaimed, his chest swelling importantly. "We pride ourselves on only using the finest quality Belgian couverture chocolate, and premium ingredients which are all minimally processed. You can be assured that there won't be any unpleasant artificial flavourings or preservatives in our products. And all our chocolate spoons are hand-made in our gourmet kitchen. They are practically works of art!"

As he was speaking, he was busily unpacking his case and taking out several chocolate-coated spoons, which he laid out on the wooden table.

"This is our Classic range—beautiful rich dark chocolate, creamy milk chocolate, and lovely vanilla-scented white chocolate... and then there is our Specialty range, with Salted Caramel—this is one of our bestsellers!—and Mini Marshmallows which melt beautifully in your drink... and Mocha, which is a blend of chocolate with pure espresso beans..." He raised his hands with a flourish, like a magician about to begin a conjuring trick. "And now! I will demonstrate..."

Dora and I watched, slightly bemused, as the man took a thermos and mug out of his case and proceeded to pour a cup of hot coffee out of the thermos.

"There, you see? An ordinary cup of coffee... ah... but as you stir in one of our spoons, it will become *extraordinary*!" He demonstrated with one of the chocolate spoons he had brought, stirring it into the hot liquid. "Watch how the chocolate melts off the spoon, to swirl into the coffee and give it a completely new flavour and complexity! Even just the act of stirring the spoon will give pleasure—a moment out of your busy lives—and you don't have to worry about adding anything to your drink. The spoon does it all for you, giving you a delicious—"

"Wait, what did you say?" I burst out.

The salesman paused with his mouth open.

I stared at the mug of coffee in his hand, watching the way the chocolate melted slowly off the wooden spoon and mixed with the hot liquid.

I jabbed my finger frantically at the mug. "That bit you just said—about not having to add anything to the drink... the spoon does it all for you... OH MY GOD!" I gasped. "I know how Dame Clare was poisoned!"

CHAPTER THIRTY

Leaving Dora and Mr Baxter staring open-mouthed after me, I dashed out of the kitchen and ran to the counter, nearly crashing into Cassie.

"Gemma! What's the matter...?"

She stared as I fumbled around under the counter, trying to find my phone. Where had I put it? I dredged my memory, trying to remember: I had been talking to my mother... and then I had seen the salesman come in... and I had put my phone down and gone to greet him... *Ah! Here it is.* I snatched the phone up and dialled the number for Eccleston House.

"It was on the fork," I said in a breathless whisper to Cassie as I waited for the call to be answered. "The poison—it was on the fork! We never thought of that! We kept thinking of the poison being added to the cake—but the murderer was cleverer than that. The fork that Dame Clare used must have been coated with the poison. That's why Theresa Bell ate the same piece of cake and never got sick. Because she used her fingers and the poison was only on the fork. Whereas Clare Eccleston would have put the fork completely in her mouth and probably licked all the jam and cream off as she was eating, unknowingly licking all the poison off as well!"

Cassie looked uncertain. "But... in that case, doesn't that point the finger at Mary? I mean, she was the one who cut up the cakes and served them."

"Yes, but I just remembered something," I said hurriedly. "That day when I drove Mary home from the fête, I helped her carry some stuff from the car to an anteroom, where they kept all their cat show paraphernalia. Mary was rambling a bit—I think she was still in shock—but I distinctly remember her mentioning a bunch of picnic forks lying on a bench." I leaned towards Cassie. "She said she had been looking everywhere for them; she didn't realise until then that she had left them behind by mistake."

"So?"

"So it means that somebody else provided her with the forks for the cakes! We all had a fork to eat with—but Mary hadn't brought any from home—so where had she got them from? I need to ask her..." I frowned as the phone continued to ring in my ear. "Where is she...?"

"Maybe she's not home," Cassie suggested. "Maybe she's at St Cecilia's?"

"It's the weekend—I didn't think... Oh well, I guess it doesn't hurt to try." I hung up and tried the college number. In a minute, I was put through to the college admin offices.

"Oh, hi—Gemma," Mary sounded surprised to hear from me. "Yes, I decided to come into college and do some extra paperwork. The offices aren't usually open on the weekends but I... I didn't really want to stay in the house. It's the first weekend since... since Mummy died..." She cleared her throat. "Anyway, did you want me for anything in particular?"

"Yes, listen, Mary, at the fête last weekend, you cut up and served the Victoria sponge cake, right?"

"Yes." She sounded puzzled.

"Where did you get the forks from? You said you left your own forks at home—so where did you get the ones that we were eating with?"

"Oh..." She was silent for a moment. "I can't really remember... I wasn't paying much attention, to tell you the truth. I think... I think Aunt Audrey was helping me pass the plates around to everyone, so she must have been the one to add the forks. I guess she had some with her in her basket."

I froze, unable to believe my ears. "*Audrey?*"

Suddenly, several things flashed in my mind, like

a camera coming sharply into focus: Jo Ling identifying the poison as convallatoxin, found naturally in the lily of the valley—a popular component of bridal bouquets because of its dainty, bell-shaped white flowers ... me arriving with Muesli for her assessment at the Vicarage and admiring the border of ivy and dark green plants with dainty white flowers... Audrey talking about making home-made perfume, steeping the flowers in water to extract their active ingredients... and Jo Ling's voice again saying: *"...you find lily of the valley growing in many English gardens too. It's a common native flower... Of course, most people don't realise how toxic it is—even the water that the cut stalks are put into can be poisonous if drunk."*

I felt like my head was spinning. *It was Audrey all along.*

Then I remembered something else: yesterday, while we were at the Vicarage for Muesli's assessment, my mother had commented that she saw Audrey taking home a jar of jam from the fête. Audrey had denied it... I thought again of a Victoria sponge cake, slathered in fresh cream and luscious strawberry jam... It would be so easy to dip a fork in some poisoned jam and then add that fork to a plate. Red jam looks much the same wherever it's from. Dame Clare, on picking up the fork and starting to eat the cake, would never guess that the strawberry jam already smeared on the fork was from a different source. And once the fork was licked clean in the course of eating, all traces of poison would disappear. There would be no worry of pieces of cake found afterwards with the incriminating poison.

It was so ingenious. Audrey knew her friend's habits—she knew that Clare normally brought her own cakes to cat shows and that, as a close friend, she would be invited to take part. She simply had to stand by and wait for her opportunity. She had her fork ready—and the jar of poisoned jam, cleverly hidden amongst the other jars in her basket. All she had to do afterwards was keep the poisoned jar aside and quietly take it home at the end of the day... No one would have ever suspected, no one would have known—except for my mother, who had seen her taking that incriminating jar of jam home...

My stomach gave a lurch and I felt a chill come over me.

...no one would have known—except for my mother...

I gasped out loud. "Mary," I said urgently. "Did you send my mother a note last night?"

"A note? No, why?"

"My mother received a note saying you wanted her to go and meet you at Eccleston House this morning."

"I never sent her any message," said Mary, sounding confused. "The last time I spoke to your mother was that day when she and the old ladies from the village came to the house. You were there as well, remember? I had just come back from seeing the solicitors—"

"Who knew you were going to the college this morning? Who knew that nobody would be home at Eccleston House?" I demanded.

"I... Riza knew, I suppose, since I gave her the whole weekend off and I might have mentioned that I was planning to come in. Oh, and Aunt Audrey knew. She rang me last night and asked what I was doing this morning. I think she was worried I might be lonely—"

I heard no more. Cutting her off, I ended the call and immediately called my mother's mobile. I prayed that it wouldn't have been forgotten in her car glove compartment or left on the hall table at home—or dead with a flat battery—all pretty common things that my mother often did. I breathed a sigh of relief as I heard it start to ring... and ring... and ring...

"Come on... pick up... pick up..." I muttered, pacing in a circle.

"Gemma, what's going on?" said Cassie, next to me. "What did Mary say? What's this about your mother?"

I slammed my phone down. "I haven't got time to explain, Cassie, but my mother could be in danger! I'm going straight round to Eccleston House. Can you keep trying her number? If you get through, tell her the murderer is Audrey Simmons! Tell her to stay away from Audrey and, most of all, *don't eat or drink anything* that Audrey offers!"

I was shouting now and I could see the whole tearoom staring goggle-eyed at me, including the Old Biddies, but I didn't care. Turning, I bolted out the door and was on my bike in a flash. Minutes later, I was pedalling frantically towards Eccleston House. My heart pounded furiously in time with my pumping legs.

Faster. Faster. Oh God, I hope I wasn't too late...

The bike careened crazily around the bend of a country lane and shot down the last few hundred yards, until I turned in through the imposing front gates of Eccleston House and started down the long gravel drive. I could see the house up ahead and a car parked by the front door. My mother's red Peugeot. There were two figures standing by the front door.

Are they my mother and Audrey? What are they doing? I pedalled harder, cursing as the bicycle wheels sank in the gravel driveway, churning up pebbles everywhere. I jumped off my bike, threw it aside, and ran the rest of the way. My legs felt like lead and there was a stitch stabbing in my side, but I ignored it, gasping and panting as I hurtled down the last stretch of driveway.

In front of me, the two figures became clearer. One was definitely my mother and she was holding something in her hands. A cardboard box. My eyes widened as I saw her lift something out of the box and raise it to her mouth.

"Mo-ther!" I yelled. "MO-THER! DON'T EAT THAT!"

But even as I shouted, I saw the other figure move suddenly. It was Joseph, I realised, and I watched in surprise as he yanked something out of my mother's hand.

She gave an outraged gasp and stumbled backwards.

Then I was beside them. I heaved myself, wheezing and spluttering, up the front steps. They both turned to look at me, my mother staring in astonishment.

"Gemma, what on earth..."

"Mother!" I was panting so hard I could hardly speak. "Did you... did you eat anything? *Did you eat anything*?" I asked wildly.

"Well, no, darling, I was just about to taste one of these delicious tarts but this man here is abominably rude—he snatched it right out of my hands! Really! When I had offered him one already." She turned to frown at Joseph. "You had your own—you didn't have to snatch mine as well. Has no one taught you any manners?"

I looked down to see that Joseph was holding two jam tarts, one in each hand. The one he had snatched from my mother was clenched in his fist, the pastry shell crumbling slightly and the jam oozing between his fingers. There were more jam tarts in the box that my mother was holding.

"Them's no good," Joseph spoke up suddenly. His voice was hoarse and urgent. "They'll do you harm."

I turned back to my mother and said slowly, not wanting to alarm her, "Mother, give me that box. I don't think you should eat any of those tarts—"

"Why ever not?" said my mother in surprise.

"Here, give them to me..." I took the box gingerly away from her. "Where did you get the box anyway?"

"It was here on the doorstep, with my name on it," my mother explained. "There was a note from Mary attached, saying she had to pop out unexpectedly but that she had baked these tarts this morning and wanted my opinion of them. So I was just about to sample one when I saw the gardener... Joseph, is it?... standing there clipping the hedge. I thought I'd offer him one too—you know, to be polite—although goodness knows why one bothers. Really, it was shockingly bad manners! He had barely helped himself to one, when he reached out and snatched mine as well!"

I glanced at Joseph, then said to my mother, "Actually, Mother, I think you should thank Joseph. I think he saved your life."

"I beg your pardon?" My mother stared.

"Lily of the valley," Joseph said. "Them's pretty flowers. But them's dangerous too." He wrinkled his nose. "Can smell 'em."

The perfume, I realised. I leaned down and

sniffed the tarts. Yes, I recognised the familiar fragrance. Audrey had been wearing it the day we took Muesli to the Vicarage for the assessment. In fact, my little cat had reacted badly to the scent and jumped off Audrey's lap. *I should have listened to Muesli's instincts,* I thought.

And Joseph, I realised, with his expert nose for flowers, must have caught the scent as soon as he raised the tart to his mouth. He might not have realised that the tarts had been deliberately poisoned but he knew enough about the lethal properties of lily of the valley to stop my mother trying to eat hers.

"Oh God, Mother, if you had eaten any—even one bite..." I shuddered. "I think these jam tarts have been poisoned, probably by convallatoxin, a toxin found in lily of the valley—"

"Poisoned?" My mother stared down at the jam tarts in the box, as if suddenly expecting them to turn lime green with skull-and-crossbones signs appearing across their surfaces. "But why on earth would anyone want to poison me?"

I looked out across the treetops into the distance where I could see the church steeple from the village. I thought of a ruthless, calculating woman waiting at the Vicarage. A woman who had concealed her murderous nature beneath a pleasant, helpful exterior.

"Because you knew too much," I said grimly. "And you ruined the perfect murder."

CHAPTER THIRTY-ONE

Everyone in the village gathered solemnly outside the Vicarage and watched as Devlin led Audrey out of the gates. I could see the expressions of disbelief on the people's faces and hear the whispers going around the crowd as we all watched the mousy, middle-aged spinster get into the waiting police car.

"*Audrey Simmons*! Who would have thought?"

"Oh my goodness!"

"But she was such a great help on the church committee... and the charity fundraiser too..."

"Yes, she always seemed so ready to volunteer for things! Always taking on the extra work and never complaining..."

"And that was part of the problem," I said to Cassie as we stood talking in the tearoom one morning a few days later. "Audrey Simmons had an almost pathological desire to be *needed*. I mean, we all like to feel useful and wanted—but with Audrey, it had become like an obsession. It was the only thing that fed her self-esteem and gave her a sense of identity. Volunteering for stuff, taking on all the responsibilities at the various community events—it made her feel important."

"Don't forget her brother," said Cassie. "I always thought that was a bit weird. I mean, everyone used to go on about how nice she was to look after him, but didn't you think it was odd? Living with him and mothering him like that? The guy was in his forties, for heaven's sake!"

"Well, some of that might have been a leftover habit from childhood, because her brother *was* a lot younger than her... but I know what you mean," I agreed. "I think mothering him made Audrey feel good about herself. It's sad, really, because she should have married and had children of her own, so that she could have felt 'needed' that way."

"She would probably have smothered her kids, if she had any," said Cassie darkly. "She's obviously one sandwich short of a picnic."

"Yeah, and when her brother announced that he was getting married, she must have freaked out. Suddenly, he no longer needed her—he had a wife now, who would look after him and be the new mistress at the Vicarage. I think Audrey's world was turned upside down and she began to feel really desperate." I thought of Edwin. "And it didn't help that her own romance was unrequited. She had loved Edwin Perkins so faithfully all those years—I think she never gave up hope that he might still marry her."

"Not with Mary around!" said Cassie.

I nodded. "That must have really eaten away at her—to see the way Edwin only had eyes for Mary, a girl more than half his age. She must have really begun to resent the younger woman."

"Do you think that's what gave her the idea for the whole thing?" asked Cassie. "As a way to get rid of Mary? I mean, if she framed Mary for her mother's murder and the girl was put away in jail, Edwin might then forget his infatuation and notice *her, Audrey,* at last."

I shrugged. "I don't know. Audrey wouldn't talk much when Devlin questioned her. She's gone all sort of distant and withdrawn now. Won't talk much to anybody, not even her lawyer. But from what little she said, Devlin thinks it was a combination of things. The hostility towards Mary was definitely one of the triggers. And then Clare Eccleston herself was another."

"Clare Eccleston? But I thought they were friends?"

I rolled my eyes. "I don't think anyone could have really been friends with Dame Clare. She was too much of a bully. But I think Audrey got used to playing the submissive in that relationship. It was a pattern established from when both were girls at school, I think, and it carried on into their relationship in adulthood."

"So what changed?"

I shrugged again. "Who knows? People just snap, don't they? I don't think you can keep on bullying someone and abusing them forever. Eventually, they just have enough and rebel—and when they do, it's usually in a pretty big way. You can't keep kicking a dog, you know, without it one day turning around to bite you. And I think Audrey had been feeling angry and aggrieved for some time. And then the Therapy Cats programme was the last straw. It had been Audrey's idea, her baby, the first thing that had given her a sense of achievement and identity which was all her own, rather than from propping up others. She was being looked up to, respected, valued... and then Clare Eccleston swooped in and claimed all the credit."

"You know, looking at it like that, you sort of feel sympathetic towards Audrey," said Cassie. "I would have wanted to kill that Eccleston woman myself."

"Yeah," I agreed. "It's a terrible thing to say and murder is always wrong, but I have to admit, you can't help feeling that this was one murder victim who got what she deserved."

"What about the anonymous note?" asked Cassie suddenly. "How does that fit in?"

"Actually, the anonymous note was nothing to do with Audrey. That was a coincidence," I said. "It was from Theresa Bell. It was just a bit of petty nastiness, really. But when Audrey saw it, she instantly recognised another opportunity to frame Mary. She remembered how much Mary had loved scrapbooking as a girl and she knew that she still had a few of Mary's cut-out collages. *That* was why she kept pushing Mary to report the note to the police. I think it was so she could fan the suspicions about Mary later, using the collages in her possession. In fact, she purposefully left them out when she knew my mother and I were coming to the Vicarage. She wanted us to see them and put doubts in our minds about Mary... and I have to admit, it nearly worked with me," I added ruefully.

"What a devious cow," said Cassie, shaking her head. "Winds me up to think that I actually liked her!"

"I liked her too. It was one reason why I never even suspected her. Oh, she played her part really well—like the way she acted so concerned about finding Clare Eccleston's killer and how solicitous she was to Mary. She had us all fooled. And I don't know if anyone would have ever thought of the poisoned fork..."

"You have Mr Baxter to thank for that," said Cassie with a grin.

I laughed. "Oh, I did! I ordered six of each flavour, even though I don't know what I'm going to do with so many chocolate spoons!"

"Still, you know, someone *could* have asked Mary more questions about how the cake was served on the day of the fête and it would have come out that Audrey had provided the forks. She didn't prepare for that," Cassie said.

"No, but it's all a case of 'he says, she says', isn't it? Mary herself said that she wasn't paying that much attention and wasn't sure where the forks had come from—she assumed that Audrey had provided them because the latter was helping her. But Audrey could simply have said that *she* didn't know where the forks had come from either! Or even that when Mary handed her the plates to pass around, the forks were already on them," I pointed out. "You see, there was no reason to suspect Audrey at all, whereas there were plenty of reasons to suspect Mary. Remember, she had the most to gain by her mother's death. So who do you think the police or a jury would have believed more? Audrey's word or Mary's?"

"Clever," said Cassie grudgingly. "And I'll bet she would have played her role for all it was worth, making everyone believe how upset she was about incriminating Mary, when all along she's sticking a knife in the girl's back. I think that's been the scariest thing—how nice Audrey can be to your face when, meanwhile, she's planning to kill you. I mean, look how she was with your mother! Leaving those poisoned tarts for her—and pretending they came from Mary—that was pure evil genius."

I grimaced. "I don't know about genius but it was pretty evil. The police analysed those tarts, you know, and there was enough convallatoxin in the jam to kill a large horse. If Joseph hadn't snatched it out of my mother's hands—if she had taken even one bite..." I shuddered. "I don't even want to think about it."

"I hope you've written him a nice thank you note," said Cassie jokingly.

I smiled. "I'm going to do even better than that— I'm popping over to see him after work today, with a very special present."

***

Later that evening, as the sun began to slip down the horizon, I made my way across Oxford to St Cecilia's College. After asking at the Porter's Lodge, I was directed to a tiny cottage at the rear of the college grounds. There was no doorbell. I rapped on the wooden front door and stood nervously, holding the tall, gift-wrapped box in front of me.

After a few moments, I knocked on the door again.

Still nothing.

I hesitated. I had been sure that Joseph would be home—the college porter had certainly seemed to think so. Then why wasn't he answering the door? I didn't want to leave the gift box on the front doorstep, in case it got nicked or damaged. I looked around and noticed a narrow path leading around the side of the cottage. *Perhaps Joseph's in the garden out back*, I thought suddenly. That would explain why he couldn't hear the door knocking. I hesitated a moment longer, then started following the path around the side of the cottage.

Picking my way past some dense shrubbery, I stepped at last through an old wooden arbour into a tiny cottage garden. It was like a miniature replica of the one at Eccleston House, except far more lovely in a way. The small, compact space here was brimming with flowers and shrubs—romantic climbing roses rambling up the wooden trellis next to me, lavender and rosemary forming a fragrant hedge along the back row, and then crowding all around were blooms of every shape, size, and colour: daffodils, snowdrops, meadowsweet, gentian, foxgloves, hydrangea, columbines, forget-me-nots... and a dozen other flowers I couldn't name. Even though they hadn't all bloomed yet, their sweet perfume mingled and filled the air around me.

And there in the centre—like a magician who had called forth this enchanted garden (and in a way, he had)—was Joseph. He was crouched next to a large clump of delphiniums, carefully staking them. He looked up as I stepped into the garden and rose quickly to his feet, his eyes widening in surprise.

"Uh... hi Joseph..." I gave him a hesitant smile. "I

tried the front door but no one answered, so I came around the back... Um... this is a beautiful garden, like something out of a fairy tale..." I faltered into silence as he continued standing there, saying nothing.

Oh God, I'm not going to have to have a conversation with the pansies or something again, just to speak to him?

Determinedly, I took a step towards Joseph and said, "I came to say thank you, actually."

He looked up, startled, meeting my eyes for the first time.

"For saving my mother's life," I explained. "If you hadn't acted so quickly, I think she would have... well, anyway, thank you."

He said nothing but I saw that his eyes had softened. Encouraged, I lifted the box I had brought and thrust it at him. "For you," I said unnecessarily. "I went to a specialist centre... I was told it's one of the rarest... um... anyway, I hope you like it."

He stared in wonderment at me, then reached out and took the box I offered him, like an orphan receiving his first ever gift on Christmas morning. Slowly, he pulled off the ribbon and unwrapped the coloured paper, then carefully lifted out the container inside. I heard his sharp intake of breath as he saw what was in the container: a small terracotta pot containing a single bulb, from which grew a rich green stalk that ended in a cluster of deep purple, almost black flowers. A rare black hyacinth.

"Midnight Mystic. *Hyacinthus orientalis*," murmured Joseph reverently, his fingers caressing the dainty dark florets. His eyes were shining, his expression rapt. For a moment, it was as if he had forgotten that I was there. Then he looked back at me and, slowly, a broad grin spread across his face.

I blinked. It was like looking at a completely different person. Gone was the creepy, dour gardener—in his place was a stoop-shouldered, middle-aged man with twinkling eyes and a gentle smile.

"Thank you, miss. S'best present anyone's ever given me," he said shyly. "Ta very much."

***

The next morning, I was still feeling warm and fuzzy from my visit to Joseph's cottage (yes, he had even invited me in and offered me some tea!) when a familiar tall handsome figure stepped into the Little Stables Tearoom. Several female eyes widened and heads turned to watch appreciatively as Devlin strode across the room towards me. He was looking very suave and handsome in his work clothes—a charcoal tailored suit with crisp white shirt and Italian silk tie. He paused by the counter and grinned at Cassie, handing her a small package.

"Special delivery... for your brother, Liam."

Cassie's eyes lit up. "You haven't found his camera?"

"Yup. One of our boys found it yesterday as they were sifting through all the stuff we picked up in the raid on the Agri-Crime gang."

"This is brilliant! He's going to be so chuffed," said Cassie. "I'm going to ring him right now!"

She disappeared into the kitchen and Devlin glanced around the tearoom, which was humming with the hubbub of conversation and the cheerful clink of crockery. "I see that life is back to normal," he observed with a smile. "I'm surprised Mabel Cooke and her friends aren't here, actually."

"Oh, I'm sure they will be soon," I assured him. "They're probably in the post office shop at the moment, gossiping with half of Meadowford about the latest news."

"What latest news?"

"Mary Eccleston's decided to sell Eccleston House. She wants a fresh start and she told me she always fancied living in the US for a while, so she's applied to do a graduate degree at one of the colleges there and is going to live in Boston."

Devlin whistled. "She seemed like such a scared little thing—I would never have thought she'd have the guts to go and live in another country."

"I think she's finally coming out of her shell, getting a chance to discover who she really is—or who she wants to be—and I think it's great," I said enthusiastically.

"Good for her," Devlin said with a nod. "Well, I wish her luck. Hey, listen—I'm getting off early today for a change. Fancy going out for a movie tonight?"

I smiled. "Love to—although it'll have to be a later one. I need to pop back to my parents to pick up my mail."

He frowned. "You know, Gemma, why don't you just change all your addresses officially to mine? Saves you having to worry about mail going to your parents' place. Since we're going to be living together now, it makes sense—"

"Actually, Devlin..." I hesitated. "I wanted to speak to you about that.'

He raised his eyebrows at my serious tone. "Yes?"

I took a deep breath. "I... er... I'm not sure if I'm quite ready to... well, to live together. Oh, don't get me wrong," I said hastily. "I've loved staying at your place and it's great being able to spend more time together... and you've been wonderful, letting me and Muesli just barge into your life like that... but... well... I feel like I need to have a place of my own. At least for a little while." I gave him a nervous look. "I... I hope you can understand?"

Devlin looked at me silently for a moment, then he smiled. "Yeah, I can understand."

I felt relief wash over me. "Really? Thank you," I

said gratefully.

"You just want to be able to dump your clothes all over the place with no one telling you off," said Devlin with a teasing grin. "No, but seriously, Gemma, I do understand. And in the meantime, you're still welcome to stay at my place for as long as you need, until you find somewhere to rent."

I felt a rush of love for him. Impulsively, I reached up to hug him but, at that moment, the door to the tearoom burst open and four little old ladies trotted in.

"Inspector O'Connor! Just the man we wanted to see!" came Mabel Cooke's booming voice.

Devlin groaned under his breath. He turned around and squared his shoulders. "Yes, how can I help you, ladies?" he said in his most formal manner.

"It's a hand, Inspector!" said Glenda Bailey excitedly. "A hand in the skip!"

"Perhaps not just a hand," Florence Doyle added.

"I've never liked skips," said Ethel with a shiver.

Devlin looked at them in bewilderment. "What skip? What are you talking about?"

"The skip bin outside No. 14 on Lemon Tree Lane," Mabel said impatiently. "The owners are Londoners—they only keep the cottage for use on odd weekends and they're having some renovations done. There's been a skip bin outside the property for weeks. A real eyesore it is, I tell you! It's no wonder Americans call them 'dumpsters'—much as

I abhor some of the American terms for things, this one seems far more appropriate than the British—"

"Oh, Mabel, never mind what the Americans call it—tell him about the hand!" cried Glenda.

"Ah, yes, that's right—it's a hand, Inspector," said Mabel, as if that explained everything.

Devlin sighed. "Mrs Cooke, I'm afraid I don't follow."

Mabel leaned forwards and said in a loud stage whisper, "The hand might be connected to a body. A murdered body, hidden in the skip."

I suppressed a groan. *Here we go again.*

EPILOGUE

"Thanks for bringing Muesli to meet me, Gemma—she's a darling! We're delighted to have her on the Therapy Cats team." Jane Banks beamed at me from her doorway as she watched me place Muesli's carrier into the front basket on my bike. "And thank you for being so understanding about having to go through an assessment again. I know you'd done it already with Audrey Simmons... *um-ahem...*" She cleared her throat. "But now that I've taken over the programme, it's good for me to meet all the cats again."

"No problem, Mrs Banks," I said with a smile.

"I'll send you the paperwork and, once we've got you in our system, we can get started with scheduling your visits."

I nodded and waved, then pushed off, cycling slowly back towards the centre of Oxford. Jane Banks lived south of Oxford, a few streets down from Folly Bridge, which crossed the River Thames and led into the south end of the university city. It wasn't a particularly pleasant ride this morning— there had been heavy rains in the night and the roads were now wet and slippery, with cars going past spraying me with muddy rainwater as they drove through the puddles.

It only added to my general bad mood. Now that the excitement of the murder investigation was over and life was returning to "normal", I was only too aware of the more mundane problem still facing me: where could I find a place of my own that I could afford? The thought of another day like the last one I'd spent house-hunting with Cassie made me deeply depressed.

I crossed Folly Bridge, then, on a sudden impulse, turned off the road, heading for the towpath that ran alongside the river. I would take a detour, I decided, cycling around the perimeter of the city rather than through the centre. The roads would be quieter and, hopefully, I wouldn't get splashed so much. It seemed like a good plan, until I rolled onto the towpath and found it filled with as many puddles as the main road. An indignant "*Meorrw!*" came from the cat carrier in front of the handlebars as water splashed up.

"Sorry, Muesli!" I said, negotiating my way around two muddy puddles. I was beginning to wonder if I had made a really bad mistake. The ground here was not only wet and slippery but also dotted with potholes. I grimaced as the bike rattled across one, making the cat carrier bounce in the front basket.

"*Meeeorrw!*"

"Sorry, sorry..." I muttered, keeping my eyes on the path ahead. A huge puddle was coming up in front of me, but if I tried to skirt it, it would take me too close to the edge of the towpath. *No thanks, I don't need a dip in the river*, I thought, gritting my teeth. *I'll just have to go through the puddle. Oh well, I can't get much wetter than I am already...*

I pedalled a bit harder, thinking that it might help if I could get through the pool of water quickly. We hit the puddle, and then suddenly the front end of the bike dipped forwards with a scary lurch. *There's a pothole under the puddle!* I realised too late as the front wheel went in and hit the rim of the pothole on the other side. There was a bone-jarring impact that sent me reeling backwards, losing my grip on the handlebars.

"Ooomph!" I tumbled off the bike and onto the towpath. The bicycle swerved sideways and toppled over, its wheels spinning crazily.

"*MEORRW!*" came a wail from the cat carrier as it tipped out of the basket and landed with a crash. The latch on the door sprang open and Muesli rolled out.

"Oh, God, Muesli!" I sat up. "Are you okay?"

She gave me a frightened look, then turned and bolted down the towpath.

"Hey, wait—Muesli!" I struggled to my feet and

limped after her. "Come back!"

Muesli shot down the towpath, farther down the river, and darted towards a line of bushes on the opposite side to the water.

"Muesli! Come back!" I called.

The little grey tabby ignored me. She dived into the nearest bush and disappeared. I arrived, panting, a moment later, and peered over the shrubbery. It seemed to be running along the back of a small residential development. A row of modern cottages sat primly in the centre of a neat semi-circle of landscaped garden, radiating suburban respectability. I bit my lip and scanned the area. Muesli was nowhere to be seen.

Then I caught sight of a striped grey tail. It was flicking around the corner of a small stone building on the far side of the garden, away from the row of cottages. I pushed my way through the gap in the shrubbery and ran across the lawn towards the building. As I approached, I realised that it was also a cottage of sorts—but a very different one to the sleek modern developments on the other side of the manicured lawn. For one thing, it was old, the stone walls faded and worn, and the wooden window frames mottled with age. There were several slate tiles missing from the roof and the entire building looked as if it was leaning slightly to one side.

It was also *tiny*; I doubted if it had more than one bedroom. It looked like it might have once been an outbuilding, perhaps—a little shed or hut that was part of a larger estate—and some effort had been made to convert it into a residence, but it was still very shabby. I was surprised that it had been left here, next to all those slick modern houses, but perhaps it sat on a vestige of land which had not been bought by the property developers.

I walked around it until I came to the front door, which faced the other way, towards the river. To my pleasant surprise, Muesli was sitting on the front step, her tail tucked around her paws.

"*Meorrw!*" she greeted me, her green eyes big and bright.

I approached her cautiously, wondering if I could grab her before she bolted again. Then my attention was caught by something on the door. It was a sign. A sign with a familiar logo—the local real estate agent's logo. I straightened, Muesli temporarily forgotten, as I saw the words next to the logo: "For Lease".

I felt a strange little tingle of excitement. I stepped back and looked up at the cottage again. A voice came suddenly from behind me, making me start.

"You're not thinking of renting that, are you?"

I whirled around to find a middle-aged woman with an old-fashioned nylon shopping buggy standing a few yards behind me. She was peering at me curiously through wire-framed glasses.

"Why?" I asked.

"Oh, only because we'd given it up for lost, really.

TILL DEATH DO US TART

Didn't think anyone would ever want to rent it."

I looked at her in surprise. "What do you mean? It's in a fantastic location—why wouldn't anyone want to rent it?"

She raised her eyebrows. "Didn't you hear the story? That great, big hoo-ha back in June last year? It was in all the local papers."

"I wasn't in England back then," I explained. "What happened?"

"Last owner died in the house. Which isn't unusual in itself—but there were some rumours about her death. Made a lot of people very uncomfortable. I live in the next development myself and I have to say, the whole thing made me nervous, I can tell you. Anyway, there was nothing proven, but since then they've struggled to rent it out again. Doesn't help that it's in a bit of a state."

"Is it in a terrible condition inside?"

She gave the cottage an assessing look. "I think it just needs a good tidy-up really. Hasn't been redecorated for decades, but the bones are pretty solid."

"Do you know what rent they're asking for it?" I asked.

"I can't remember the exact figure—in fact, last I heard, they'd dropped it again. Getting desperate, I shouldn't think. It's been on the market for months now." She shifted her shopping buggy. "Well, I'd better get on. That your cat?" She pointed suddenly.

"Oh... yes, she's mine," I said, looking around at

Muesli.

"Cute wee thing. Acts like she lives there already." The woman chuckled, then turned and walked off, pulling her shopping buggy behind her.

I looked at Muesli thoughtfully, sitting just outside the front door of the cottage. *Yes, she certainly did look like she lived here already.* She stared back at me, her green eyes wide and her little whiskers quivering.

"*Meorrw...?*" she said, tilting her head slightly.

I hesitated. My eyes went back to the sign. Slowly, I pulled my phone out of my pocket, but as I was about to start dialling, I stopped. I shook my head. *I must be mad to even think it!* The rents in this area, so close to the university city and next to the river, must be astronomical. There was no way I could afford a cottage here... I sighed and turned away.

"*Meorrw!*" came an indignant little voice.

I looked down. Muesli hadn't budged from her position by the front door. She was looking up at me, her little face hopeful. I hesitated again. Surely, it didn't hurt to ask? It was a long shot but...

Making a sudden decision, I dialled the number. As the phone rang, I crossed my fingers and smiled at my cat.

"What do you think, Muesli? Have you found our new home...?"

FINIS

THE OXFORD TEAROOM MYSTERIES

A SCONE TO DIE FOR
(OXFORD TEAROOM MYSTERIES 1)

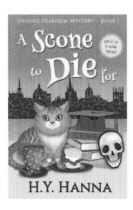

When an American tourist is murdered with a scone in Gemma Rose's quaint Oxfordshire tearoom, she suddenly finds herself apron-deep in a mystery involving long-buried secrets from Oxford's past.

Armed with her insider knowledge of the University and with the help of four nosy old ladies from the village (not to mention a cheeky little tabby cat named Muesli), Gemma sets out to solve the mystery—all while dealing with her matchmaking mother and the return of her old college love, Devlin O'Connor, now a dashing CID detective.

But with the body count rising and her business

going bust, can Gemma find the killer before things turn to custard?

TEA WITH MILK AND MURDER (OXFORD TEAROOM MYSTERIES 2)

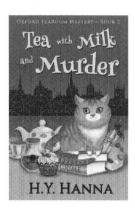

While at an Oxford cocktail party, tearoom owner Gemma Rose overhears a sinister conversation minutes before a University student is fatally poisoned. Could there be a connection? And could her best friend Cassie's new boyfriend have anything to do with the murder?

Gemma decides to start her own investigation, helped by the nosy ladies from her Oxfordshire village and her old college flame, CID detective Devlin O'Connor. But her mother is causing havoc at Gemma's quaint English tearoom and her best friend is furious at her snooping... and this mystery is turning out to have more twists than a chocolate pretzel! Too late, Gemma realises that she could be the next item on the killer's menu. Or will her little tabby cat, Muesli, save the day?

TWO DOWN, BUN TO GO
(OXFORD TEAROOM MYSTERIES 3)

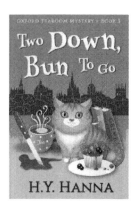

A sinister phone call in the middle of the night throws tearoom owner, Gemma Rose, straight into the heart of a new murder mystery--this time with her friend, Seth, arrested as the key suspect! The grisly killing in the cloisters of an old Oxford college points to a bitter feud within the University--but Gemma finds unexpected clues popping up in her tiny Cotswolds village.

Meanwhile, her love life is in turmoil as Gemma struggles to decide between eminent doctor, Lincoln

Green, and sexy CID detective, Devlin O'Connor... whilst her quaint English tearoom is in hot water as she struggles to find a new baker.

With her exasperating mother and her mischievous little tabby cat, Muesli, driving her nutty as a fruitcake--and the nosy Old Biddies at her heels--Gemma must crack her toughest case yet if she is to save her friend from a life behind bars.

TILL DEATH DO US TART
(OXFORD TEAROOM MYSTERIES 4)

When Oxfordshire tearoom owner, Gemma Rose, enters her little tabby, Muesli, in the cat show at the local village fair, the last thing she expects is to stumble across a murder.

And when her meddling mother and the nosy Old Biddies decide to start their own investigation,

Gemma has no choice but to join in the sleuthing. She soon finds there's something much more sinister sandwiched between the home-made Victoria sponge cakes and luscious jam tarts ...

But murder isn't the only thing on Gemma's mind: there's the desperate house-hunting that's going nowhere, the freaky kitchen explosions at her quaint English tearoom and an offer from her handsome detective boyfriend that she can't refuse!

With things about to reach boiling point, can Gemma solve the mystery before the killer strikes again?

MUFFINS AND MOURNING TEA
(OXFORD TEAROOM MYSTERIES 5)

Cotswolds tearoom owner, Gemma Rose is excited to join the May Day celebrations in Oxford...

until the beautiful spring morning ends in murder. Now, she's embroiled in a deadly mystery —with four nosy old ladies determined to help in the sleuthing! Soon, Gemma finds herself stalking a Russian "princess" while trying to serve delicious cakes and buttery scones in her quaint English tearoom—and keeping up with the Old Biddies in Krav Maga class!

And that's just the start of her worries: there's her little tabby, Muesli, who is causing havoc at the local nursing home... and what should she do with the creepy plants that her mother keeps buying for her new cottage?

But the mystery that's really bothering Gemma is her boyfriend's odd behaviour. Devlin O'Connor has always been enigmatic but recently, the handsome CID detective has been strangely distant and evasive. Could he be lying to her? But why?

ALL-BUTTER SHORTDEAD (OXFORD TEAROOM MYSTERIES PREQUEL)

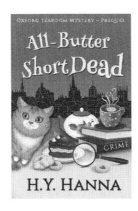

Gemma ditches her high-flying job and returns to Oxford to follow her dream: opening a traditional English tearoom serving warm buttery scones with jam and clotted cream, and fragrant tea in pretty bone china... Only problem is--murder is the first thing on the menu and Gemma is the key suspect! And the only people Gemma can turn to for help are four nosy old ladies from her local Cotswolds village - not to mention a cheeky little tabby cat named Muesli.

Who was the mysterious woman Gemma met on the flight back from Australia and why was she murdered? Now Gemma must find the killer, solve the mystery and clear her name if she's to have her cake--and serve it too.

GLOSSARY OF BRITISH TERMS

(fall into) a shambles – a mess, a chaotic situation

Biscuits – small, hard, baked product, either savoury or sweet *(American: cookies. What is called a "biscuit" in the U.S. is more similar to the English scone)*

Blast! - an exclamation of annoyance

Blighter - a person who is regarded with contempt, irritation, or pity

Bloke – man *(American: guy)*

Bloody – very common adjective used as an intensifier for both positive and negative qualities (e.g. "bloody awful" and "bloody wonderful"), often used to express shock or disbelief ("Bloody Hell!")

Bobby – affectionate slang term for a policeman; derived from the nickname for Sir Robert Peel, the founder of the Metropolitan Police. Often used in the phrase: "village bobby" to refer to the local community police officer who looks after small

English villages.

Bog standard – perfectly ordinary, unexceptional

Bugger! – an exclamation of annoyance

Bum – the behind *(American: butt)*

Cheers – in everyday conversation, a casual way to say "thank you", also often used in farewell

Chuck – throw

Chuffed – very pleased

Clotted cream - a thick cream made by heating full-cream milk using steam or a water bath and then leaving it in shallow pans to cool slowly. Typically eaten with scones and jam for "afternoon tea"

Coconut Shy - a game at a fair where balls are thrown at coconuts to try and knock them off stands

Codswallop – nonsense (an old-fashioned expression expressing contempt / ridicule)

Cow – a derogatory term for a woman who is

unpleasant, stupid or annoying

Cross – angry, annoyed

Cuppa – slang term for "a cup of tea"

Different kettle of fish – a different situation, a different state of affairs

Dogsbody – a junior or unimportant person who does all the running around and menial tasks for others

Fête – a public function, usually held outdoors and in the warmer months of the year, often to raise funds for a charity. It includes entertainment in the form of old-fashioned games and stalls which sell goods and refreshments *(American: fair)*

Git – a despicable person

Gormless – lacking sense, very foolish

Guv'nor – an informal term for one's boss or someone in a position of authority (particularly used in the police force to refer to a higher ranking officer); occasionally still used as a respectful term of address

Have a nosy around – to snoop around, to be curious and sneak in somewhere or look into something, often without permission

Holiday – an extended period of leisure and recreation, especially one spent away from home or in travelling *(American: vacation)*

Hoo-ha – a fuss, a disturbance

Hoopla - a game at a fair where you throw rings from behind a line and try to encircle one of several prizes

Locum - a person who stands in temporarily for someone else of the same profession, especially a cleric or doctor.

Loo – toilet

Moggie – a mix-breed cat

Nappies – a piece of disposable absorbent material wrapped round a baby's bottom and between its legs to absorb waste. *(American: diapers)*

(to) Nick - to steal

Off your trolley – crazy, mad *(American: off your rocker)*

One sandwich short of a picnic – a derogatory term to describe someone who seems simple, stupid or crazy

(to) Pinch - to steal

Plonker – an annoying idiot

Porter – usually a person hired to help carry luggage, however at Oxford, they have a special meaning (see *Special terms used in Oxford University* below)

Pudding – in the U.K., this refers to both "dessert" in general or a specific type of soft, jelly-like dessert, depending on the context.

Queue – an orderly line of people waiting for something *(American: line)*

Ring – call (someone on the phone)

Row – an argument

Skip (Bin) – giant metal container for construction

waste and other big items of rubbish, often used in building & renovation *(American: dumpster)*

Snug - a small, comfortable area in a pub or inn

Sod off – "get lost", go away, stop bothering me; milder version of the phrase using the F-word.

Sort-out – the activity of tidying and organising things, especially sorting them into categories

Sop – something done or given to appease someone who didn't get what they really wanted

Snog / Snogging – kiss / kissing

Ta – slang for "thank you", more often used in the north of England

Takeaway – food that's taken away from the restaurant to be eaten elsewhere *(American: takeout)*

Union Jack - the national flag of the United Kingdom, formed by combining the red and white crosses of St George, St Andrew, and St Patrick and retaining the blue ground of the flag of St Andrew.

Wee – small, tiny

(to) Wind (someone) up – to annoy someone; can also mean to tease someone, depending on context

***

SPECIAL TERMS USED IN OXFORD UNIVERSITY:

College - one of thirty or so institutions that make up the University; all students and academic staff have to be affiliated with a college and most of your life revolves around your own college: studying, dining, socialising. You are, in effect, a member of a College much more than a member of the University. College loyalties can be fierce and there is often friendly rivalry between nearby colleges. The colleges also compete with each other in various University sporting events.

Don / Fellow – a member of the academic staff / governing body of a college *(equivalent to "faculty member" in the U.S.)* – basically refers to a college's tutors. "Don" comes from the Latin, *dominus*— meaning lord, master.

Fresher – a new student who has just started his first term of study; usually referring to First Year undergraduates but can also be used for graduate students.

Porter(s) – a team of college staff who provide a variety of services, including controlling entry to the college, providing security to students and other members of college, sorting mail, and maintenance and repairs to college property.

Porter's Lodge – a room next to the college gates which holds the porters' offices and also the "pigeonholes"—cubby holes where the internal University mail is placed and notes for students can be left by their friends.

Quad – short for quadrangle: a square or rectangular courtyard inside a college; walking on the grass is usually not allowed.

Tutor for Admissions – a member of the college faculty who oversees the intake of new undergraduate students each year

VICTORIA SPONGE CAKE RECIPE

* The most important thing to remember about the ingredients is to have the **same weight of butter, caster sugar and self-raising flour as the eggs**. So it would be best to weigh the eggs first (in their shells) and then to measure out the butter, sugar and flour accordingly. In the recipe below, I have assumed the eggs to be around 50g each but please check your own eggs and adjust accordingly.

The other key is to have all ingredients at **room temperature**, especially the eggs—this will help to prevent the mixture from splitting / curdling

INGREDIENTS:

(U.S. measurements are in brackets but be aware that results may vary since the recipe will not be as accurate as weighing the ingredients.)

- 4 eggs of approx. 50g each, at room temperature (*in the U.S. use "Large Size Eggs"*)
- 200g unsalted butter, softened at room temperature (plus some extra for greasing the cake tins) - (*U.S.: 1 cup*)
- 200g caster sugar (*U.S.: 1 cup & 2 tbsp superfine sugar*)
- 200g self-raising flour (*U.S.: 1-3/4 cup & 2 tbsp, using the spoon and level method*)

- 1 tsp baking powder
- A pinch of salt
- 1 tsp vanilla essence
- 3 tbsp milk (to loosen batter if necessary)

For the filling:
- 250ml double cream or whipping cream (*U.S.: 1 cup*)
- 1 jar of good quality strawberry jam

To finish:
- Fresh strawberries, halved
- Icing (powdered) sugar

INSTRUCTIONS:

1) Preheat the oven to 180C / 160 C fan (350F/gas mark 4)

2) Add the butter and caster sugar to a bowl (or mixer) and combine thoroughly, taking your time. Keep mixing until the mixture is smooth and creamy and you cannot feel any of the sugar granules.

Do not rush this step—even if it takes five minutes—as it is the key to making your sponge cake light and fluffy. The longer you can mix the butter and sugar, the better your cake will be.

3)   Whisk the eggs in a bowl and then add it to your butter & sugar mixture a little bit at a time, making sure to mix thoroughly after each addition before adding more. Again, take the time to cream the mixture as much as possible—the smoother it is, the better the texture of the cake will be.

4)   Finally add in the vanilla extract and mix well.

5)   Sieve the flour into the mixture, together with the baking powder and a pinch of salt, then fold very gently to combine, using a figure of 8 motion. This keeps as much air in the mixture as possible (If using a mixer, keep it on the lowest, gentlest setting) You must not overwork the batter otherwise the cake will come out tough and dense.

6)   Keep mixing gently until the batter is smooth and passes the "dollop test", ie. when you lift some of it up with the spatula, it falls easily off in a dollop. If it sticks to the spatula and is too dry, add a bit of milk to loosen it and mix gently again. Be careful not to add too much milk as you don't want the batter to be runny.

7)   Get two 8-inch round cake tins and lightly grease the insides, then lay a circle of greaseproof paper at the bottom.

8) Divide the batter evenly between the two tins, using the spatula to smooth the tops until they are flat. (Don't worry if they are not perfectly even—they will melt and even out in the oven)

Tip - Weigh the batter as you divide between the cake tins to have equally even cakes.

9) Place in the middle layer of the oven and bake for 20 – 25mins, until the cakes are golden and have risen nicely. To check that they're done, slid a sharp knife or skewer into the centre and it should come out clean. The cake will also spring back when gently pressed and the edges should be shrinking slightly away from the sides of the tin.

10) Take them out and allow to cool for 10 mins in the tin, then remove from the tins, peel off the greaseproof paper and cool on a wire rack, flat side down.

* It is important to allow the cakes to cool completely otherwise it will cause the cream in the filling to melt and will ruin the cake.

11) While the cakes are cooling, prepare the filling by whipping the double cream until it forms soft peaks.

12) Take the "uglier" cake and use that as your base. Spread the top with a generous portion of

strawberry jam, being careful not to go too near the edge. Follow with a layer of fresh whipped cream, using a spatula to carefully spread it over the jam. Finally, place the second cake gently on top to form the "sandwich"

Variation: some people may also like to include fresh sliced strawberries in the filling, between the jam and the cream.

13) Decorate the top of the cake with the strawberry halves and then dust everything with icing sugar.

Enjoy!

ABOUT THE AUTHOR

H.Y. Hanna is an award-winning mystery and suspense writer and the author of the bestselling *Oxford Tearoom Mysteries*. She has also written romantic suspense and sweet romance, as well as a children's middle-grade mystery series. After graduating from Oxford University with a BA in Biological Sciences and a MSt in Social Anthropology, Hsin-Yi tried her hand at a variety of jobs, before returning to her first love: writing.

She worked as a freelance journalist for several years, with articles and short stories published in the UK, Australia and NZ, and has won awards for her novels, poetry, short stories and journalism.

A globe-trotter all her life, Hsin-Yi has lived in a variety of cultures, from Dubai to Auckland, London to New Jersey, but is now happily settled in Perth, Western Australia, with her husband and a rescue kitty named Muesli. You can learn more about her (and the real-life Muesli who inspired the cat character in the story) and her other books at: **www.hyhanna.com**.

Sign up to her newsletter to be notified of new releases, exclusive giveaways and other book news! Go to: **www.hyhanna.com/newsletter**

ACKNOWLEDGMENTS

Thank you once again to my lovely beta readers: Basma Alwesh, Rebecca Wilkinson, and Melanie G. Howe for their tireless enthusiasm and for always finding time to squeeze me into their busy lives. Special thanks also to my proofreaders, Connie Leap and Jenn Roseton, for their eagle eyes in checking the manuscript and helpful suggestions.

I am very grateful to the talented Kim McMahan Davis of _Cinnamon and Sugar... and a Little Bit of Murder_ blog, for acting as my "baking consulant" and helping me test the Victoria sponge cake recipe, and providing the U.S. measurement equivalents. Thank you also to retired West Yorkshire Police Inspector, Kevin Robinson, for helping me check the police procedural details in the story and responding to my endless questions with so much patience.

And as always, to my wonderful husband for his patient encouragement, tireless support, and for always believing in me. I couldn't do it without him.

27443192R00220

Printed in Great Britain
by Amazon